CODE OF HONOR

CODE OF HONOR

a novel by

BETSY BRANNON GREEN

Covenant Communications, Inc.

Cover image: B465RF Portrait of expressionless woman © JUPITERIMAGES/Polka Dot/Alamy

Cover design copyrighted 2009 by Covenant Communications, Inc.

Published by Covenant Communications, Inc.
American Fork, Utah

Printed in Canada
First Printing: June 2009

16 15 14 13 12 11 10 09   10 9 8 7 6 5 4 3 2 1

ISBN 10: 1-59811-804-4
ISBN 13: 978-1-59811-840-7

To my grandchildren—Abbie, Andie, Harrison, and Banx—who have proven that there is something even better than being a mother.

ACKNOWLEDGMENTS

As always I am deeply grateful to my husband, Butch, for his patience, encouragement, and unfailing good humor. I am also thankful for my children and the support they give me. I could not write books without their willingness to make significant sacrifices.

It is an honor and a privilege to work with my editor, Kirk Shaw, and all the talented people at Covenant. They help me to make my books the best they can be, and I will forever be in their debt.

Thanks, too, to all my readers who invest their time and money in the stories I write. And as I complete the final installment in my *Hazardous Duty* series, I want to again express my appreciation to our servicemen and women who sacrifice so much to defend our country and protect freedom and liberty everywhere. May God bless and protect you all!

PROLOGUE

SAVANNAH OPENED HER EYES AND saw a bright light shining above her. Squinting, she tried to determine if she'd died and gone to heaven. Dane leaned into her field of vision, blocking the light. Since she knew Dane wasn't dead, she assumed she wasn't in heaven just yet. But since he was on a plane headed to see Cam's ex-wife, she guessed she must be dreaming. His dark gray eyes were grim, and his soft, full lips were pressed into an angry line. She wanted to reach up and touch his cheek, but her arms felt so heavy.

"Savannah," Dream Dane said, "you're going to be okay."

She smiled and nodded, hoping she didn't wake up anytime soon. "I love you."

Dream Dane reacted exactly the way the real one would have to such a comment. He frowned. "Try not to say too much. You've had a blow to the head, so you're not thinking clearly."

Slowly she became aware of other things. The sounds of traffic passing by. The syncopated flashing of red emergency lights. The smell of warm asphalt.

"I'm awake?" she whispered.

Dane nodded. "Yes."

"But you're on a plane."

He shook his head. "I *was* on a plane. But just as they were about to close the door, I got this overwhelming feeling that I shouldn't go."

Savannah's eyes widened. "I had the same feeling. I wanted to chase after you, but I was afraid I'd get shot."

He gave her a brief smile.

"Caroline is safe?"

"Completely." He checked his watch. "Doc and Steamer should almost have her to the cabin by now."

"How did you find me?"

"Thanks to Corporal Benjamin's phone call, I was waiting at Tulley Gate, prepared to shoot out the tires to stop the car when the door opened and you came flying out." He shuddered. "It was one of the worst moments of my life."

Savannah tried to smile, but her face was too stiff. "And you should know about bad moments."

"I do," he confirmed.

"Did you get Lieutenant Hardy?"

Dane nodded. "The MPs have her."

Savannah tried to concentrate. "Let's go over the sequence of events again. You had a feeling that I was in danger, and therefore you left the plane."

"Yes."

She held her breath. "You chose me over duty."

He had to think about this for a few seconds. "I guess I did."

"Oh, Dane," she whispered. "You do love me. And more than that—you got a warning from God, and you *listened!*"

Dane cringed. "If you don't want to be checked into the psych ward the minute you get to the hospital, you'll take my advice and stop talking!"

She frowned. "I'm going to the hospital?"

"Yes." Dane's voice was almost tender. "You broke your arm, and the paramedics think some of the cuts you got from the gravel may need to be stitched."

"You'll come with me, right?"

He nodded. "I'm never letting you out of my sight again."

She smiled at him and said, "I should have thrown myself out of a moving vehicle weeks ago."

A pair of paramedics from DeWitt Army Hospital joined them at that moment. They insisted that Savannah ride in the ambulance to the emergency room for evaluation, even though she assured them that such extreme measures were unnecessary.

"My injuries are fairly minor, and I'd rather to ride in the car with Dane."

"There's no way to be sure how severe your injuries are," one of the paramedics argued. "You've sustained head trauma, and we have to take precautions."

"It's policy, ma'am," the other paramedic explained as he collapsed a stretcher beside her.

"This is silly," Savannah complained. She turned to Dane. "Tell them I don't need an ambulance."

"Hospital policies are designed to protect their patients, so just do what they ask you to," Dane said. He stood by and watched while she was carefully transferred from the gravel shoulder onto the stretcher.

Although she still felt that the precautions were excessive, her head was starting to pound, and the thick foam pad on the stretcher was much more comfortable than the rocky ground had been. So Savannah discontinued her objections. The paramedics lifted the stretcher and rolled her to the waiting ambulance.

Dane followed them step for step, and once she was settled inside, he climbed up and sat on the stretcher across from hers. "How are you feeling?"

"Numb." Her fingers gingerly explored the lacerations on her face. "Do you think I'll have scars?"

Dane shook his head. "I hope not."

"I wouldn't mind having a few war wounds of my own."

He raised an eyebrow. "I've never heard anyone sound excited by the prospect of a scar."

She smiled. "I'm just trying to fit in with the rest of the team."

"You don't need scars to fit in," he assured her. "Jumping out of a moving vehicle was enough to prove you're as crazy as the rest of us."

Savannah was pleased. "So when are you going to see Cam's ex-wife to tell her about his death?"

"I'm not," Dane surprised her by saying. "I sent Hack."

She couldn't believe she'd heard him correctly. "You sent someone else to do your official duty as commanding officer of the covert operations team?"

He leaned close and whispered, "Taking care of wounded soldiers is an official responsibility too. As commanding officer, I get first pick of the available duties."

"And you chose to stay with me?"

He nodded. "I didn't dare trust your safety to anyone else."

She narrowed her eyes at him. "Admit it. You *wanted* to stay with me."

"I'll admit that." He gave her a wicked smile. "I never did like Cam's ex-wife much."

The ambulance stopped while she was trying to think of an appropriate response. Seconds later, the back doors were flung open, and the paramedics waved for Dane to climb down. They pulled out Savannah's stretcher and rolled her into the hospital's emergency room.

"We're taking her to triage," one of the paramedics told Dane. He pointed to their left. "You can fill out her paperwork at the desk."

"I'll be right back," Dane promised her. Then he was gone.

The paramedics parked Savannah in a tiny cubicle, and a weary-looking nurse gave her a quick examination and started an IV.

"You're going to need an orthopedist to set your broken arm and a plastic surgeon to stitch up the cuts on your face," the nurse said as she worked. "The longer we wait on the stitches, the more chance of scarring, so I'm going to set it up fast."

Savannah decided she really wasn't all that attached to the idea of being a scarred soldier, so she said, "Thank you."

Once the IV fluids were dripping slowly but steadily, the nurse stepped out of the cubicle. She was back a few minutes later with news. "An operating room is being prepared for you now, and the anesthesiologist should be here soon to put you to sleep."

"I'm going to an operating room?" Savannah asked. "Just to set a broken arm and stitch up a few cuts? Is that really necessary?"

"Setting your arm would be very painful if you were awake," the nurse explained. "And the plastic surgeon prefers to work on patients who won't move while he's stitching. It's the best way to handle the situation."

Savannah didn't relish the idea of being put to sleep, or being in an operating room at all, but she kept her uneasiness to herself. "Where's Dane?"

"The major who came in with you?" the nurse clarified.

Savannah nodded, which sent shooting pains through her head. She closed her eyes to block out the light aggravating her headache.

"Try to hold still," the nurse advised unnecessarily. "I think the major is at the admissions desk filling out forms. The anesthesiologist is here, so I can leave you with him and go find your friend."

"Thank you," Savannah whispered, careful not to move her head.

She opened her eyes just enough to see the doctor walk in, swathed in disposable surgical gear. He moved around in the room, opening drawers and reorganizing equipment. He stepped up to the bed and put a new bag on the IV pole.

"This medication will take effect in a matter of minutes," he said, his voice partially muffled by the surgical mask. "You'll fall asleep quickly, and by the time you wake up, it will all be over."

"That's good," she replied with difficulty. Her lips were already slack, and she was starting to feel very drowsy.

The doctor leaned over her. "Don't worry about a thing." He pulled down his mask so she could see his smile.

The last thing Savannah saw before she lost consciousness was the face of Mario Ferrante above her hospital bed.

CHAPTER 1

SAVANNAH WOKE UP GRADUALLY FROM a deep, dreamless sleep. She yawned and tried to stretch, but her left arm refused to cooperate. She looked down and saw a cast that started above her elbow and extended to just past her wrist. Slowly the memories returned. She remembered her escape from Lieutenant Hardy and the injuries she had sustained in the attempt. She remembered that Dane had been there and had ridden with her in the ambulance. With a start, she remembered Mario Ferrante's unexpected presence in her hospital cubicle.

She took a few deep breaths to control her mounting panic and assessed her physical condition. Aside from the cast on her arm, she had a few small cuts on her face. She was able to move her legs but wasn't sure how steady she'd be on her feet.

Next, Savannah studied her surroundings, careful to keep her head still to avoid another terrible headache. Across the room an open door revealed a bathroom. She was in a twin-sized hospital bed pushed against a wall under a small window. In addition to the bed, the room was furnished with an uncomfortable-looking chair, a metal dresser, and a small table. In contrast with the battered, institutional furnishings, there was a large flatscreen television mounted to the wall across from the bed.

The room had the look and smell of a hospital, but the absence of medical equipment confused her. Was she still at DeWitt Medical Center on Fort Belvoir? Was it still the day after Christmas? And where was Dane? She turned her head slightly toward the window. There was no sunlight coming in, so she assumed it was night, but she couldn't be sure. Where was she and why? Panic threatened to overtake her again.

Forcing herself to remain calm, Savannah went over the possibilities. Maybe she had dreamed Ferrante's presence in her hospital room. Or maybe Dane had rescued her from Ferrante and had taken her somewhere safe—

out of Ferrante's reach. Maybe Dane and his merry men were sitting just on the other side of the door, reminiscing about operations past and waiting for her to wake up. There was only one way to find out if this best-case scenario was reality.

She cleared her throat, licked her dry lips, and called, "Dane!" Her voice sounded weak and raspy. "Dane!" she tried again.

Savannah expected the door to open in response to her calls. To her surprise and dismay, the door remained closed and the television screen came to life. Filling the large screen was Mario Ferrante's smiling face.

"Well," he said, "I see that our patient has finally awakened."

"Where am I?" she demanded, hoping to mask her fear with a show of indignation. She knew she'd failed when his smile widened.

"Welcome to Serene Hills." He waved from the screen to encompass her room. "It's a private sanatorium in Pennsylvania, and I think it's safe to say that Major Dane will never look for you here."

Savannah barely managed to control a sob. "How did you get me here?"

"I drugged you and then convinced a couple of underpaid, overworked orderlies that you were dead," Ferrante replied. "So instead of taking you up to the operating room like the nurse had instructed them, they took you to the morgue and put you in a body bag. Then you were transferred to a mortuary van I had commandeered. My plan worked perfectly—executed right under the nose of Major Dane."

She ignored the taunt and asked the more pressing question. "Why?"

"I believe you know the answer to that question," he said.

"To lure Major Dane here?" she asked, dreading his response.

"Of course," Ferrante said impatiently. "He and I have unfinished business. But I don't want to discuss my grievances against the major. Instead let's talk about the excellent care you've received while a guest at Serene Hills. You'll notice that I kindly arranged for a private physician to come here and set your arm and stitch up the cuts on your face."

"The doctors at Fort Belvoir were going to take care of all that before you kidnapped me," Savannah pointed out angrily. "So why would you expect me to thank you?"

"You should," he said. "But no, I didn't really expect gratitude."

"How long have I been here?"

"Two days," was his startling answer. "Poor Major Dane must be frantic with worry by now. I'll call him soon to let him know that I'm providing you with excellent medical care—so far."

Her good hand moved to her throat, where her locket should have been. "Where is my locket?"

He raised an eyebrow in challenge. "Maybe it fell off in the body bag."

Savannah was sure that he knew exactly where her locket was but wouldn't admit it. She tried a different approach. "I want to speak to Wes."

Laughter emanated from the big screen. "You really must decide which dashing major you want," Ferrante's voice chided.

"Wes is the one I want right now," she assured him. "Where is he?"

"Rotting in his grave," Ferrante replied. "He died in that car accident over two years ago."

Savannah flinched at his cruel words. "But you said . . . you led me to believe that maybe . . ."

"I say a lot of things," Ferrante said impatiently. "Wes is dead and of no use to either of us. Now let's talk about how we're going to lure Major Dane into my trap."

Savannah tried to set aside her conflicting feelings for Wes so she could concentrate on the threat to Dane. "Trapping Dane is as unnecessary as kidnapping me. If you wanted to talk to us, all you had to do was ask. We can sit down and discuss our differences and come up with a way to settle your unfinished business in a civilized way."

Ferrante laughed, and it was an ugly, terrifying sound.

Savannah tried again. "It would help if you'd tell me what unfinished business you're talking about."

He laughed again.

Struggling for patience, Savannah decided to cut to the chase. "I have access to considerable assets. I'll pay you whatever you want if you'll forget your grievance against Dane and leave us alone."

Ferrante's magnified expression became serious. "I'm willing to take payment, but it has to be something that means more to Major Dane than money. Like you, for instance."

Desperate now, she went to her last resort. "Dane's very valuable to the Army. If you do anything to hurt him, the government will punish you."

He shrugged. "The government will have to catch me first."

Discouraged and weak, Savannah felt tears pool in her eyes. "Please. I'm asking you as one human being to another . . ."

"That is unquestionably your weakest argument yet. I'm tired of this subject. Instead, let me tell you a little bit about your accommodations. I've explained to the staff that you're delusional, suicidal, and a flight risk. I brought in a private doctor and nurse—so you won't actually see any of the sanatorium's regular personnel. Your door will be locked at all times, and there's a guard just outside—for your own protection, of course."

Savannah smirked at the television. "Of course."

"After I told the hospital staff about you jumping out of a car, I explained how concerned I was about you hurting yourself again. So the hospital kindly agreed to install this two-way monitor. It has several built-in cameras, and it's linked to my computers. So we can watch every move you make. Keep that in mind." The screen went blank.

Discouraged and afraid, Savannah leaned back against the pillow on her hospital bed. As Ferrante had pointed out, this obscure hospital would not be the first place Dane would look for her. But he was an expert at locating and extracting people—the very best the U.S. Army had to offer—so he would find her. She wanted to believe that. She had to believe that. And she didn't want to cry, since she knew that Ferrante would gain satisfaction from her misery. But as the lonely minutes passed, her resolve weakened, and finally she sobbed until she fell back into a restless sleep.

The next time Savannah woke up, she felt stronger, but her arm ached from her shoulder to the tips of her fingers. She was also starving, so she assumed it was near a mealtime. This was confirmed a few minutes later when the door opened and a nurse walked in carrying a tray.

"How are you feeling?" the woman asked pleasantly.

Savannah leaned close to the nurse and whispered, "I've got to get out of here. I've been kidnapped by Mario Ferrante, and other lives are in danger. You have to help me."

The woman smiled tolerantly. "You won't be going anywhere for a while. You need to stay here and rest."

Savannah tried again. "You don't understand. I'm not crazy."

"Of course you're not," the nurse said soothingly. "How did you hurt your arm?"

"I jumped out of a car . . ." Savannah realized her mistake too late. The nurse had tricked her into this self-incriminating admission. "But not because I'm crazy! I had to get away from Lieutenant Hardy. She was trying to kidnap me."

"It sounds like everyone is trying to kidnap you."

Savannah's head started to hurt again, and she pressed a finger to her throbbing temple. "I know it's hard to believe, but it's true. Although actually only Mario Ferrante wanted to kidnap me. Lieutenant Hardy worked for him. That's why I jumped out of the car."

"Of course." The nurse's patient tone was almost insulting as she handed Savannah a little cup of pills. "Now it's time for you to take your pain medication, and then you have chicken noodle soup for lunch."

Savannah wanted to refuse the pills, but she knew that soon the pain would be unbearable. So she held out her hand like a belligerent child. The nurse emptied the cup onto her palm, and Savannah took the pills one at a time. She ate every bite of the soup, knowing that regaining her strength was crucial to any escape plan.

Savannah did have confidence in Dane and the team and their ability to find her. But rather than sit around waiting to be rescued, she wanted to take a more proactive approach. So after the nurse left, Savannah looked around the room searching for a way out.

Knowing she only had a limited amount of time before the pain medicine clouded her ability to think, she first studied the window above her bed. It was small—only about two feet square—and embedded with wire. She doubted she could fit through it even if she could climb up and get it open before the guard outside her door came rushing in.

Next she focused on the door. Ferrante had told her it was locked and guarded, but he had been known to lie. So she swung her legs over the side of the bed and sat up. She was dizzy for a few seconds, and then it passed. She pressed her feet to the floor one at a time and then walked over to the door, holding on to the walls for support. The door was locked. She rested her head against the door for a few minutes and tried not to cry.

Once she had regained a little strength and some composure, she looked around the room again. If she couldn't leave through the window or the door on her own, maybe she could find a weapon and use it to force the nurse to take her out. She walked to the dresser and looked through all the drawers. There was nothing. She looked in the bathroom. Again nothing. Apparently Ferrante's warnings about her suicidal tendencies had made the staff overly vigilant.

Finally she accepted the reality of her situation. She had no money, no transportation, no means of communication. She looked down at the hospital gown she was wearing. She didn't even have clothes. Unless she could get help from the outside, leaving the sanatorium would be impossible. So she would have to work on convincing the nurse when she came in with dinner.

Afraid that she would collapse if she didn't lie back down, Savannah used her last ounce of strength to cover the big screen with a sheet from her bed. As she fell back against the pillows in complete exhaustion, she heard Ferrante's laughter coming from the screen.

"Just because you can't see me doesn't mean I can't see you," he told her. "I have cameras everywhere."

She looked around—trying to identify other camera spots. She found what she thought was a likely possibility and threw her plastic water pitcher at it.

When Ferrante spoke again from the TV screen, he sounded less amused. "If you break anything, I'll have you tied to the bed." Then he was gone. Savannah succumbed to the medicine, thankful for the brief respite from Mario Ferrante and the pain.

The pills made Savannah sleep most of the afternoon. She woke up when the door opened, and she turned, expecting to see the nurse—whom she hoped to enlist in her escape plan. But instead a man walked in with her dinner tray. First he removed the sheet from the television screen. Then he introduced himself as Dr. Lavender. After putting her tray on the small table, he began a quick examination of her arm.

"You will be in this cast for three weeks," he said as he manipulated the fingers of her left hand. "Then we'll take it off, make sure the break is healing correctly, and put a new cast on for an additional three weeks." He moved to her face. "These cuts were glued together rather than stitched. This process reduces scarring and eliminates the need to have stitches removed. The swelling is down and the bruises are fading. In a few days they will barely be noticeable, and you will be back to your lovely self."

"My appearance is the least of my concerns," Savannah muttered.

The doctor ignored her. "We've got you on pain medicine for your arm. We'll gradually reduce the dosage, but let us know if you're uncomfortable."

"I'll be *comfortable* if you let me leave here."

"Yes, my nurse mentioned that you told her a wild story about being kidnapped. Please stop bothering her. As a doctor I want to see you heal properly. But if you continue this nonsense, you'll annoy Mr. Ferrante. Then he will dismiss me and my nurse, and you'll be left without medical care."

Savannah sent a malicious glance toward the television screen and then nodded. Alienating the doctor would probably not be in her best interest. "Okay," she agreed vaguely.

The doctor seemed pleased. "Good. Now take your medicine and eat your dinner."

Savannah swallowed the pills and then spooned the vegetable soup into her mouth while the doctor watched. Finally growing self-conscious, she said, "You don't have to keep me company."

"No, but I do have to take that tray and all the silverware with me when I go. Since you're on suicide watch, I can't leave any potential weapons in your possession."

"You know I'm not suicidal."

He smiled. "I'll have to take the tray just the same."

Savannah finished her soup, ate the Jell-O cubes, and drank a carton of apple juice. Then she pushed the tray toward the doctor. "I'm through."

He made a point of counting the silverware before lifting the tray. "I'll see you tomorrow. Try to get some rest."

Savannah watched the door close behind the doctor and then stared at the television screen. She almost wished Ferrante's hateful face would appear. Even talking to him was better than constantly being alone. And there was always the chance that maybe she could convince him to release her. But the screen remained tauntingly dark. She tried not to think about Dane or Caroline and how much she missed them. But when she closed her eyes, their faces appeared. So she cried herself asleep.

* * *

The next morning Savannah woke up when the nurse walked in with her breakfast.

"The doctor has reduced the dosage on your pain medicine, so you should be able to stay awake more today," the nurse informed her.

Savannah swallowed the pills and looked at the breakfast tray. She was starving.

The nurse followed the direction of her gaze and smiled. "The doctor also gave permission for you to eat solid foods." She lifted the lid to expose scrambled eggs, toast, and an apple.

Savannah ate her breakfast hungrily. When she finished eating, the nurse offered to help her to the bathroom. "Thanks, but I can make it on my own."

"Suit yourself," the nurse replied, "but be careful. You're bound to be weak."

The nurse leaned down to retrieve the tray, and Savannah whispered, "I'm sorry if I got you in trouble by asking for help. I didn't mean to."

The nurse glanced up uncertainly. "It's okay. You didn't really get me in trouble, but I was required to tell the doctor what you said."

"I know all about taking orders," Savannah said casually. "I work for General Steele at Fort Belvoir. Maybe you could call and ask him if I'm crazy." The general's loyalty was in question, so Savannah wasn't sure this would help her even if she could convince the nurse to do it, but she figured it was worth a try.

"Stop harassing the nurse," Ferrante's voice commanded from the television.

Savannah turned to see the face she'd come to loathe watching her with disapproval. "I thought you'd forgotten about me."

"I have more important things to do than to sit here and stare at you," Ferrante said. "But you shouldn't feel neglected. My men watch you constantly, so if you try to end your life, someone will intervene." The screen went blank.

The nurse hurried to leave, and Savannah couldn't blame her. Any doubts she'd had about Savannah's need to be a patient at Serene Hills were certainly assuaged.

Tired of languishing in the bed and determined to get her strength back, Savannah spent the next hour alternately walking around her room and sitting in the uncomfortable chair. By mid-morning she felt noticeably better. The reduced dosage of pain medicine was helping her to think more clearly and remain alert. But even with these improvements, she couldn't come up with a way to get out of the sanatorium unless she could convince the nurse to help.

So when the nurse came in to check her vital signs, Savannah tried to engage the woman in small talk.

"What's your name?" Savannah asked.

The woman kept her eyes on the blood-pressure cuff. "My name is Angie."

Encouraged, Savannah pressed on. "Mine is Savannah McLaughlin. I used to do a lot of public service announcements for local stations in Washington, DC. Maybe you saw me on television?"

Nurse Angie shook her head. "No."

"Do you have any children?"

Angie nodded slightly and said, "I'm not supposed to discuss personal things with patients."

Savannah didn't let this faze her. "I have a six-year-old daughter. Her name is Caroline."

The nurse looked away, but not before Savannah saw the uneasiness in her eyes. Apparently she'd finally found a soft spot. But before Savannah could continue the conversation, Angie picked up the tray and headed for the door.

"The doctor will be in to see you later," Angie said over her shoulder as she hurried into the hallway.

After Nurse Angie left, Savannah paced around the small room and tried to think of ways to manipulate the woman. Maybe she could get Angie to call Dane directly on the pretext of delivering a message. Dane would trace the call and figure out her location. Or maybe she could convince Angie to call the local police and report the suspicious admission of a seemingly healthy patient at Serene Hills. Angie had acted interested when Savannah mentioned Caroline. Maybe she should just talk more about her daughter when the nurse came back with dinner.

Time seemed to crawl by. When she started to get hungry, Savannah assumed it was lunchtime. This was confirmed a few minutes later when the door to her room finally opened and Dr. Lavender walked in with a tray.

Since Savannah had no illusions about her ability to get him to help her, she ate her meal in silence. There was another pain pill in the little cup on her tray. When she finished eating, she took her medication. Then the doctor gave her arm a cursory examination, collected the tray, and left the room.

Discouraged, Savannah sat on the end of the hospital bed and tried not to cry. A whole afternoon alone in the stark hospital room was a daunting prospect. She had just decided to take a nap when the door to her room opened. She looked up, expecting to see the nurse or possibly Dr. Lavender, but instead Rosemary Allen walked into the room. Her long raincoat was dripping wet, her hair hanging in damp clumps against her pale face. Dark rings of exhaustion circled her eyes. She looked almost as pitiful as she had the first night they'd met just outside Tulley Gate at Fort Belvoir.

Savannah was astonished by Rosemary's unexpected arrival. "What are you doing here?"

"When I found out that my father had taken you out of the hospital, I insisted that he let me visit so I could make sure that you were being cared for properly."

The big screen came to life, and Mario Ferrante scowled at them from his remote location. "I was insulted that my own daughter would doubt me."

Rosemary walked over to the bed, leaving a little trail of rainwater behind her. "This is okay, I guess. Nothing fancy, but it looks clean."

"It's a prison cell!" Savannah cried. "Rosemary, you've got to help me get out of here!"

Ferrante laughed from the screen. "Rosemary can't even help herself. What good is she going to be to you?"

Savannah saw Rosemary's expression harden at his comment. She moved closer to the girl and whispered, "I thought you were going into the witness protection program."

Rosemary shrugged as she whispered back, "I was. But I love Chad. I don't want to live without him, and I don't want our baby to grow up without a father. So I decided to stay."

Savannah grasped the girl's hands. "Rosemary, he's a *criminal.*"

Rosemary's gaze dropped to the floor. "I know. He's also my husband." She added in a louder voice, "This is all my fault for involving you and Major Dane in my problems."

"This has nothing to do with you, Rosemary," Ferrante commented from the screen.

Savannah hated to agree with Ferrante on any subject but felt she didn't have a choice. "Your father's problems with Major Dane began a long time ago."

"I still feel responsible, and I want to help but—" Rosemary clutched her stomach and doubled over in pain.

"Rosemary!" Savannah cried. "Are you okay?"

"I think I'm in labor," the girl said as she straightened back up. "The pains started a couple of hours ago, and they weren't bad at first, but now . . ."

"You're in labor?" Ferrante bellowed from the television screen. "And you went to Pennsylvania?"

Rosemary turned to face her father. "The books all say that first babies take forever to be born, so I thought I had time to check on Savannah and then get back."

Ferrante's opinion of his daughter's intelligence was obvious. "So now what?"

"Maybe we could get one of the doctors here to look at her," Savannah suggested.

"There are no obstetricians at the sanatorium!" Ferrante's tone indicated that he thought Savannah was as stupid as Rosemary. "I'll have to find a regular hospital nearby and have them send an ambulance to get you. Then I'll have to drop everything I'm doing and drive to Pennsylvania so I can meet you at the hospital."

"It hurts so bad." Rosemary bent over again.

The guard opened the door. "What's going on?" he demanded.

"Rosemary's in labor," Savannah replied. "Her father is sending an ambulance for her."

"I think I'm going to throw up!" Rosemary wailed, and Savannah rushed the girl toward the bathroom.

The guard's radio began to squawk as Ferrante issued orders.

Savannah tuned out Ferrante's voice and concentrated on getting Rosemary into the bathroom. As soon as they were inside and the door was closed, Rosemary stood up straight, all signs of distress disappearing.

She put a finger to her mouth and whispered, "The sanatorium staff wouldn't allow my father to install any surveillance equipment in here. So as long as we're in the bathroom, my father can't see or hear us."

Savannah nodded. She understood what Rosemary was saying but not the significance.

Rosemary pulled off her coat and let it fall to the floor. She twisted around in the small space. "Help me get my dress unzipped so we can change clothes. You're leaving, and I'm staying here in your place."

Savannah grasped the zipper and pulled it down. "You're not really in labor?"

Rosemary shook her head. "No, I'm helping you escape."

Savannah's heart pounded with hope. "But how?"

"You look enough like me to get past the guard at the door, and the ambulance that will be arriving shortly will be driven by someone you can trust. But we have to move fast before my father has time to get suspicious."

Instead of arguing, Savannah pulled off her hospital gown. Rosemary stepped out of her dress, and the women exchanged clothes. While Rosemary put on the gown, Savannah pulled the damp maternity dress over her head and let it fall into place.

Rosemary grabbed two hospital towels from the rack above the toilet and handed them to Savannah. "Bunch these up and put them under your dress so you'll look pregnant," she said softly. Once the towels were in place, Rosemary zipped the dress for Savannah and then handed her the coat. Savannah pulled it on and was pleased to see that the long sleeves came to her fingertips, completely hiding her cast. Then Rosemary slipped off her shoes and pushed them across the floor with her feet. Savannah leaned down and pulled them on. They were a little tight, but not too bad.

Rosemary turned on the water in the sink and used a wet washcloth to dampen Savannah's hair. She pulled several clumps of hair forward so that they shielded Savannah's face. Rosemary studied the full effect and finally nodded. "That will do. Now you've got to go."

Rosemary was taking a big risk for her, and Savannah was concerned. "Are you going to be okay?"

"Yes," Rosemary replied softly, "my father won't hurt me."

"Thank you," Savannah whispered. She pushed the bathroom door open and peeked out. The guard was by the door, talking into his radio, and the television screen was blank. Remembering that the cameras were still working even when the television was off, Savannah hunched forward and let her hair cover her face. Then she crossed the room and said to the guard, "The ambulance should be here any minute. I've got to get down to the lobby."

He didn't question her identity or her authority. Instead he followed her into the hallway, where a small group of medical personnel had gathered. After locking the door securely behind him, the guard addressed the hospital employees. "I can't leave my position here, so I'm going to need somebody to take her down to the ambulance."

Savannah risked a glance at the people in the hall, and her heart pounded when she saw that one of the onlookers was Dr. Lavender's nurse, Angie. Knowing that if the nurse recognized her, the escape plan was doomed, she quickly averted her face.

"She has to leave in a wheelchair," one of the nurses said. "It's policy."

"It's unnecessary," Savannah insisted. There was an elevator a few feet away, and she moved toward it. "I'm not a patient here. I was just visiting, and now I need to get to the lobby."

"The sanatorium could be liable if something happens to you," the rule-conscious nurse insisted.

Savannah took another step. "I won't sue," she promised.

"I'll walk with her," the security guard offered as Savannah reached the elevator.

Savannah reached out and pushed the DOWN arrow button. Too late she saw that the movement had caused the sleeve of Rosemary's raincoat to slide up and reveal the cast on her left wrist. She stared at the little sliver of white plaster in horror, waiting for the group of sanatorium employees to put the pieces together and end her escape attempt.

But help came from an unexpected source. Dr. Lavender's nurse stepped between Savannah and the others, blocking their view. "You'd better stay at your post," she told the security guard. "I'll walk her out to the ambulance." She took Savannah by the arm and ushered her onto the elevator.

Once inside, the nurse pushed the LOBBY button, and the elevator began its descent. Neither woman spoke.

When they stepped off the elevator, Savannah held her breath while the nurse explained the situation to the security guard at the front entrance. After giving Savannah only a passing glance, he opened the door for them to leave.

Outside the sanatorium, a cold wind billowed Rosemary's coat, and icy droplets of rain hit Savannah's face. She relished the smell of fresh air and freedom for just a second before hurrying down to the ambulance waiting by the curb.

"I presume this ambulance was sent especially for you?" the nurse whispered as they walked.

"I think so," Savannah said, peering through the rain in an effort to identify the ambulance driver. But the windows were tinted, and he was facing away from her. The driver climbed out and rounded the back of the ambulance. He seemed familiar as he opened the double doors, but the brim of the hat he was wearing shadowed his face so she couldn't see him clearly.

"I'd better get back inside," Nurse Angie said. "Good luck."

Savannah smiled at her. "Thanks." The nurse hurried up the hospital stairs, and Savannah turned her attention to the ambulance driver.

"Get in! Quick!" As he leaned forward to grab her good hand, she saw his face and whimpered. "I'm not going anywhere with you! Stay away from me!"

"I'm trying to help you," Chad Allen claimed. "If we don't leave here before the real ambulance arrives, the whole plan will be ruined."

"Why should I trust you?"

"Because you don't have a choice."

There was a lot of truth in his words, but Savannah was still confused. "It doesn't make sense that you would help me escape from your boss and father-in-law."

"It's not the smartest move I've ever made," Chad agreed. "And when Ferrante finds out, he'll probably kill me. Or at least make my life miserable."

Savannah frowned. "Then why are you doing it?"

Chad brought his face close to hers and said, "Because Rosemary wanted me to, and I owe her. Now climb in."

Savannah stared into the sinister-looking bowels of the ambulance with trepidation. She glanced back at Serene Hills Sanatorium, and weighed her options. Given the choice between Chad Allen and Mario Ferrante, she decided to take Chad. She might not be able to trust him, but she knew she couldn't trust Ferrante. So she climbed into the ambulance and sat down on one of the cots.

"Sit still and be quiet," Chad commanded. He slammed the doors closed, plunging Savannah into semidarkness. With her heart pounding, she hoped that for once she had chosen to trust the right person.

CHAPTER 2

As Savannah's eyes adjusted to the limited light inside the ambulance, she looked toward the front of the vehicle. Through a thick glass partition she could see the back of Chad Allen's head. He put the ambulance in gear and hit the gas, causing them to lurch forward.

The sudden movement tossed Savannah against the ambulance wall. She winced in pain as her broken arm hit an IV pole. Righting herself, she held on to the cot for stability while they traveled at an alarming speed for what seemed like a long time. Through the partition and the windshield, Savannah caught distorted glimpses of the road in front of them. By the time Chad Allen pulled the ambulance to a stop on the edge of a gravel road, she had lost all feeling in the fingers of her right hand.

Chad got out of the vehicle, his feet crunching loose rocks as he walked around to the back. The doors swung open with sudden force, allowing rain to pummel Savannah and the rest of the ambulance's interior.

She still wasn't sure she could trust him, but she had committed herself to this course of action, and there was no going back. So when Chad extended his hand to help her out, she accepted it and climbed from the ambulance. He led her over to a battered van with HACKSHAW'S HEATING AND COOLING printed on the side. Opening the back door, he watched while she sat down and put on her seat belt. Once she was settled, he closed the door and climbed in behind the wheel. Then they were careening down back roads again, but Savannah was relieved to at least be out of the ambulance.

"How long will it take Ferrante to discover that a switch has been made?"

Chad shrugged one shoulder. "I'm sure Ferrante already knows about the switch. His challenge will be finding us."

"And how will you prevent that?" She hoped the question sounded more confident that she felt.

"I had some friends leave several false trails, and it will take Ferrante a while to work through all of them," Chad said. "So we should have some time."

Savannah craned her neck to look out the cracked windshield. "Where are you taking me?"

"Home," he replied as the rain hitting the windshield turned to snow. "I should have you there in a couple of hours, assuming the weather doesn't get any worse."

There was nothing she could do except wait and worry. So Savannah leaned her head back against the dirty van seat and closed her eyes. Her most recent dose of pain medication was making her groggy, and eventually it lured her to sleep.

She was awakened later by the sound of Chad Allen's voice. "We're here."

Savannah sat up straight and looked out the window. She expected to see her apartment complex at Fort Belvoir, but instead the van was parked close to the driveway of Dane's cabin.

"I'd take you right up to the door, but I'm afraid Major Dane's men would try to detain me," Chad explained. "So I'm dropping you off here."

Savannah clutched the door handle and pulled. As the door opened, cold, wet air rushed in. "I don't know how I can ever thank—"

"Just leave me and my wife alone. Our lives are complicated enough as it is without your interference."

She nodded and stepped away from the vehicle. She watched until its taillights disappeared into the distance before she turned and started up the drive toward Dane's cabin. As she walked, she thought about Caroline, snuggled under the patchwork quilt in the guest room. Her pace quickened. She thought about Dane, pacing the floor while coming up with plans to locate and free her from Ferrante's grasp. She was sure they'd both be ecstatic when they saw her. She wanted to run but could only manage a slow trot.

When the house came into view, all the windows were dark with only Doc's old Bonneville parked in the yard. Apparently Dane wasn't even home. Savannah was disappointed but not surprised. After he realized that Ferrante had kidnapped her, Dane's first priority would have been to safeguard Caroline, and he wouldn't have considered the cabin a secure location.

If any of Hack's men were guarding the cabin, they weren't doing so openly. She climbed the steps and had just lifted her hand to knock on the door when Doc pulled it open. He was clearly shocked to see her. "Savannah!"

She gave him a tired smile. "It's me."

"But where is Steamer?"

"Steamer?" Savannah repeated stupidly. "Isn't he with you?"

Doc's agitation worsened. "How did you get here?"

Savannah stepped into the warm cabin and closed the door behind her. "Rosemary Allen helped me escape from Ferrante," she told Doc. "Her husband Chad drove me here. He just dropped me off at the end of the driveway."

Doc still looked confused and a little afraid. "That wasn't the plan." His eyes dipped to her bulging stomach, and he seemed even more flustered.

"Don't worry about this." Savannah pushed on the towels, letting them drop to the ground. "Ferrante was holding me prisoner in a sanatorium in Pennsylvania. Rosemary disguised me so I could impersonate her—old habits die hard. She pretended to go into labor, and her husband, Chad, drove the ambulance that came to take her to the hospital."

"I see." Doc was so unexcited about her sudden arrival that Savannah started to worry.

"Where's Caroline?" she asked. "And Dane?"

Doc licked his lips. "Caroline is with Dane's sister. She's safe and perfectly happy. We can call her if you'd like."

Savannah narrowed her gaze at him. "I'd like that very much. But first tell me about—"

"Hack is getting Caroline's security detail in place," Doc continued. "Once he's sure she's secure, he'll come back here."

Savannah sensed his stalling. She clutched Doc's arm and demanded, "Where is Dane?"

"Well," Doc replied with obvious reluctance, "Ferrante said he needed someone with Dane's skills on his staff and offered Dane a job."

"That's ridiculous!" Savannah cried. "Dane would *never* work for Ferrante."

Doc pushed his glasses up securely onto his nose. "Ferrante said if Dane would come to work for him, he'd let you go. So Steamer took Dane to meet Ferrante. The plan was that Dane would stay, and Steamer would bring you back here."

Savannah's heart started to pound. "But I got away."

Doc shook his head. "Dane didn't know that."

CHAPTER 3

SAVANNAH ALLOWED DOC TO LEAD her into the living room, where a small fire was burning. As she sat on the couch, tears stung her eyes. Chad Allen really had brought her home. Just not in time.

"So now Ferrante has Dane?"

"Yes," Doc confirmed. "And he's not likely to let him go."

Savannah felt exhausted and bereft. This homecoming was not at all what she had expected. "I just don't understand how this could have happened."

"We'd been frantically searching for you," Doc explained. "We knew Ferrante had you, but he covered his tracks well, and we couldn't find you. Dane didn't think Ferrante would actually kill you, but he couldn't be sure. So you can imagine his state of mind."

Savannah nodded. She could imagine.

"When the offer from Ferrante came, Dane agreed to the trade. Steamer took him to Ferrante's estate in Maryland a few hours ago. Our instructions were to have Steamer wait in front of the Washington Monument until Ferrante delivered you to him. So I've been waiting for Steamer to bring you here."

"There was never any plan to deliver me at the Washington Monument," Savannah said dully. "If it wasn't for Rosemary and her husband, I'd still be in a sanatorium in Pennsylvania. I can't believe Dane would trust Ferrante!"

"He didn't," Doc said. "But he felt he had to take the chance."

"Surrendering himself to Ferrante was crazy!" Savannah cried. "It's so unlike him to make such a reckless and irrational decision."

Doc nodded. "He's always very sensible—except when it comes to you."

Savannah rubbed her temples and tried to think. "Call Hack, and tell him I'm here. And make sure Steamer is on his way back. We've got to get the team together so we can come up with a plan to rescue Dane. Preferably a plan that doesn't involve putting anyone *else* under Ferrante's control."

Doc was openly skeptical. "I know you're worried and you want to help, but honestly, without Dane, there is no team."

She grabbed a handful of Doc's shirt with her good hand. "If we don't rescue him, who will?"

Doc shrugged. "It's not that we wouldn't want to try. But I'm not sure anyone can rescue him."

"We can't just let Ferrante kill him." Savannah picked up the receiver of Dane's house phone. "Give me the number where I can reach Caroline, and I'll call her while you contact Hack and Steamer. Tell them both to get here quick."

Doc might not have had faith in their ability to free Dane, but he was used to following orders. So he recited a number and then began making his phone calls while Savannah called Dane's sister, Neely. She answered on the third ring and seemed pleasantly surprised to hear from Savannah.

"From the way Dane talked, I thought it was going to be days before you finished up your project and came to get Caroline."

"Our *project* isn't finished," Savannah replied carefully, "but I wanted to check on my daughter."

"Of course," Neely said, "and I'd let you talk to her, but she's taking a nap. Can we call you back after she wakes up?"

Savannah was disappointed. "I'm going to be busy for a while, so I'll call you back later. But when Caroline wakes up, please tell her I called."

"I will," Neely promised.

Savannah said good-bye to Neely, hung up the phone, and turned to Doc. "Are the guys coming?"

Doc nodded. "Steamer's in the driveway now. Hack and Owl will be here in thirty minutes."

Savannah frowned. "Owl?"

"He just got back from Iraq, and Dane asked him to help out since we were a man short."

"Steamer replaced Cam," she reminded him.

Doc nodded. "Owl replaced you."

Savannah's lips trembled with emotion. For so long she'd wanted to be a full member of the team. Ironically, now she'd achieved that status but couldn't enjoy it because Ferrante had Dane. "I'm going to need your pharmaceutical skills, Doc. My arm is killing me."

Doc walked over to the bookcase and opened his medical kit. He took out a bottle of pills and put it into her hand. "Take one of these every four hours."

She thanked him and walked into the kitchen to get a glass of water. Popping a pill into her mouth, she prayed it would work quickly. She picked up the sanatorium towels from the floor and wondered briefly how Rosemary was faring. Then Steamer burst in through the back door.

"You're here!" he cried as he pulled her into a quick hug. "When you weren't waiting at the Washington Monument, I thought we'd surrendered Dane for nothing!"

She disengaged herself from the embrace, feeling cranky and discouraged. "You did surrender Dane for nothing. Ferrante didn't trade me. His daughter helped me escape. If things had been left solely up to Dane and the team, he and I would both be prisoners now!"

Steamer looked chastened, but she couldn't gain any satisfaction from that.

"I'm sorry," she told him. "It wasn't your fault. It was Dane's." She was amazed that she could be so worried about him yet so angry with him at the same time.

"What are we going do?" he asked.

"I'm not sure. I need to be alone for a few minutes. Make us some hot chocolate, and when Hack gets here, we'll have a meeting to decide our next step." She turned and walked into the living room. She sat down in the chair in front of Dane's computer and put her hands on the chair's leather arms. Trying to ignore the pain, Savannah let Dane's essence surround her.

After several minutes without inspiration for a plan, she got discouraged and closed her eyes. If nothing else, she could take a short nap before Hack arrived. Tears seeped out as she pictured Dane the way he had looked when she'd visited him at the prison and had begged him to help her find Caroline. The guarded expression, the sarcastic smile—the man she loved. And suddenly, the beginnings of an idea started to form. She dried her tears, turned on Dane's computer, and got to work.

By the time the rest of the team arrived, she had developed a detailed plan for Dane's rescue and had even taken a few moments to call Caroline. Feeling encouraged, she joined the men in the kitchen, where mugs of hot chocolate were waiting on the table. She hugged Hack and turned to Owl. She judged him to be in his late twenties, and his appearance was very military. He was wearing a crisply starched khaki uniform, not the casual fatigues that had been Cam's preference or the civilian clothes that Dane and the other team members usually wore. His haircut was severely short, and he was regarding her with the same resentful expression she'd received from all of Dane's men initially.

The other team members had all grown to like her over time, but Savannah didn't have that luxury with Owl. She needed his help now and wanted unity within the team, so she held out her hand to him and said, "If you have any hard feelings against me for marrying Wes, you need to let them go. That's in the past, and I've proven myself and my loyalty to the team many times since then. All the others guys love me now. Even Dane loves me. So let's skip the trial period and just be friends."

Owl studied her for a few seconds. He took her hand in his and shook it once firmly. "Friends."

She was pleased that the first skirmish, of what would probably be a long battle to win Owl's affection, had been won easily. Waving to the hot chocolate on the table, she encouraged everyone to grab a mug and a chair. She turned to Hack and added, "If you want coffee, you'll have to make it yourself."

"This is okay." He pointed to the hot chocolate.

The men settled around the table, their mood understandably subdued. They were like a rudderless ship—a team in need of a leader.

Hack took a sip of hot chocolate, winced, and said, "Tell us how you got away from Ferrante."

She leaned against the kitchen counter, clutched her warm mug, and gave him a succinct account of her escape.

When she was finished, Hack nodded. "That Ferrante girl isn't so dumb after all."

"She's very brave," Savannah said. "I'm sure her father won't take her betrayal lightly."

Hack shrugged. "He won't hurt her, and she owed you."

"And now we're even." Savannah raised an eyebrow at Hack. "Why don't you tell me what made Dane think that joining Ferrante's 'staff' was a good idea?"

"We had exhausted all of our leads, and Dane felt we didn't have time to spare," Hack replied. "He hoped Ferrante would let you go if he agreed to the employment contract—but if not, he figured he'd be in a better position to find you from the inside than he could out here."

"It was a foolish thing to do," she stated. "You should have talked him out of it."

"Nobody can ever convince him to see reason where you're concerned," Hack muttered.

Savannah sighed. Apparently she was going to have to take at least partial responsibility for Dane's foolish actions. "Now that we've agreed I'm a bad influence on Dane, let's discuss how we're going to get him back from Ferrante."

The men turned their attention to her, their faces reflecting the same emotions. They were overwhelmed by the seemingly impossible task before them. Someone had to convince them that it could be done. So Savannah walked over to Dane's usual spot at the head of the table and sat down. Then she addressed Hack. "I talked to Caroline. She said she's having fun with Dane's sister."

Hack nodded. "Dane didn't have time to get Wes's parents here, so he figured his sister was the next best thing. She lives in a suburb of Nashville."

"That was a good choice." Savannah was surprised that in spite of her concern for Dane—and her guilt—she was able to concentrate on what needed to be done. She turned to include all the men in her gaze. "Now to discuss the rescue."

"Nobody wants to get Dane more than me," Hack assured her. "But I don't see any way to accomplish it."

"Ferrante is good—maybe as good as Dane," Steamer agreed. "And he has the advantage. We'll never outwit him."

"And Dane wasn't kidnapped," Doc pointed out. "He went to Ferrante on his own. So we can't expect too much help from law enforcement agencies."

"We don't even know where Dane is," Steamer said, adding to the long list of challenges that faced them.

"We don't even know if Dane is *alive*," Hack said bluntly. "Ferrante may have shot him on sight."

"He's alive." Savannah was sure. "I *feel* him."

"We all want to believe he's alive," Steamer said, "but—"

"She felt Caroline too," Doc reminded them. "And she was right about that."

"It doesn't make sense that Ferrante would go to all this trouble to get Dane just to kill him," Owl remarked. "If all he wanted was to kill Dane, he didn't need to kidnap you and coerce Dane into joining his staff. He could have just hired an assassin."

Everyone was quiet for a few seconds. Finally Hack said, "Okay, for the moment we will assume that Dane is alive."

Savannah pressed this minor advantage. "So we have to act quickly."

"Before we can act, we have to have a plan," Hack said.

"I have a plan," Savannah told them. "But in order to implement it, we're going to need help. So I've asked General Steele to come over. He should be here momentarily."

Steamer groaned.

"I know you don't trust the general," Savannah quickly disclaimed. "And involving him is a risk. But he has access to information and resources that we don't. So we're going to have to depend on him to a point."

"I may not trust the general completely, but Dane is a valuable resource, and I know the general doesn't want him dead," Doc said. "I believe he will do what he can to help Dane get away from Ferrante."

Hack spread his hands. "But what can he do?"

"We have no legal recourse," Doc reminded her unnecessarily.

"Which means we can't get a warrant to search Ferrante's estate or even question him," Steamer said.

"Assuming we could *find* Ferrante," Hack added.

Steamer looked more discouraged. "Which nobody ever can."

Hack shook his head, his braids bouncing dejectedly. "The Army is as helpless as we are."

Savannah nodded. "I agree that rescuing Dane is too big a job, even for the Army."

This comment took them off guard, and they all looked up with various degrees of uncertainty.

"That's why I've asked Agent Gray to come too," she continued.

Steamer groaned again. "We trust the FBI even *less* than we do the general."

She smiled. "But we need the FBI as much as we need the Army, and Dane trusts Agent Gray."

Steamer was not impressed. "Look how well that paid off! Agent Gray took Ferrante away from us on the McLaughlins' mountain!"

Savannah couldn't argue this point, but she didn't want her rescue proposal to bog down. "Our options and resources are limited. We have to depend on others."

Hack got a phone call at this point, and the conversation was suspended while they waited for him to conclude his business. Hack listened for a few seconds and then closed his phone. "That was the guards I have posted by the road. General Steele and Agent Gray are both in a vehicle that just turned onto the gravel drive headed our way."

Savannah frowned. "I didn't see any guards when I got here."

"There weren't any," Hack confirmed. "They were all with Steamer at the Washington Monument waiting to protect you when Ferrante turned you over."

Savannah sighed as she pushed her chair back and stood. "I'll go get our visitors, and then we'll continue with our planning session."

She went to the back door and stepped out onto the porch as the general, Agent Gray, and Corporal Benjamin emerged from the general's car. Despite the concerns about General Steele's loyalty to the team, Savannah was happy to see him. She'd been a member of his staff off and on for almost ten years, and he was the closest thing to a father she'd ever known. He'd always been someone she could depend on. She hoped that was still true.

Agent Gray brought back memories of their confrontation with Ferrante at the Brotherly Love Farm, so her reaction to him was negative. She knew he felt bad about stealing Dane's prisoner, and she hoped that his guilt would make him more willing to cooperate with their rescue operation.

Finally her eyes shifted to Corporal Benjamin, who had tried to warn her about Lieutenant Hardy. He induced feelings of both gratitude and regret. His personality was mildly annoying, but his desire to become a part of the team could be used to their advantage. So she wasn't sorry to see him there.

When they joined her on the porch, Savannah gave the general a quick hug and shook hands with the other two men. She thanked them for coming and led them into the kitchen. The other members of the team were less welcoming. No one stood up to greet the visitors, and only Doc acknowledged them at all—and then, only with a little nod.

Savannah invited the general and Agent Gray to sit in the two empty chairs and sent Corporal Benjamin into the living room to get a computer chair for himself. Once everyone was settled, Savannah resumed her position at the head of the table. She didn't sit, though, feeling that the added elevation she gained from standing improved her perceived authority.

"Now that we're all here, I'll explain what I have in mind." She addressed General Steele directly. "I told you that Dane voluntarily joined Ferrante's staff as part of a trade to free me."

The general nodded.

"Although we know that Dane is being held against his will, the 'voluntary' nature of his surrender takes away any possibility of legal action against Ferrante. So we'll have to concentrate on Dane instead."

The general frowned. "Dane?"

"Yes, I want you to arrange for federal charges to be filed against him."

Every face at the table expressed varying degrees of astonishment.

Finally Steamer said, "I didn't see that coming."

"You want me to file charges against Dane?" the general confirmed.

Savannah nodded. "There's bound to be a whole slew of crimes that he committed and was never held accountable for."

"I won't argue with you there," the general said. "But I don't see how prosecuting Dane will help anything."

"I don't want him prosecuted," Savannah clarified. "I just want him *charged*. Then, if Ferrante knowingly harbors a fugitive, charges can be filed against him as well."

"She's right," Doc said softly.

Hack beamed at her. "Way to go, Savannah."

She addressed the general directly. "Will you take care of that for us?"

"Yes," the general agreed. He turned to Corporal Benjamin. "Take notes for me, Corporal."

Corporal Benjamin took the notepad Savannah handed to him and began to write.

"Once the charges are filed, Agent Gray, will you make sure that Ferrante is officially notified and told to release Dane into your custody?"

"I'll do what you ask, but Ferrante won't give in that easily." The agent sounded certain.

"If he refuses, he'll be putting himself in legal jeopardy," Savannah pointed out.

"I doubt that will concern Ferrante much," the general said. "He's got a bevy of lawyers who can keep filing motions, delaying court dates for years. And if it ever looks like jail time is imminent, he'll just leave the country."

"It might concern him if the White House threatens to rescind their earlier deal—absolving him of his many crimes—unless he cooperates by surrendering Dane to the government," Savannah said.

Agent Gray frowned. "I don't know if I can get the White House to go back on their word."

"The White House was willing to let a criminal go free—I'm sure they'll want to help a decorated Army hero," Savannah said grimly. "And if they need convincing, I have plenty of contacts within the national media that I plan to use against Ferrante. But that resource can be directed toward the White House if necessary."

"You don't want to make enemies in high places, Savannah," the general warned her.

"I want to get Dane away from Ferrante," she told him, "no matter how many enemies I make."

The general held up his hands in surrender. "Okay, I'll come up with some charges that we can pin on Dane and file them."

"Then I'll make a formal request that Dane be released to my custody immediately," Gray added.

"I fully expect Ferrante to refuse," Savannah replied. "And when he does—in addition to the formal charges the government will file against him—we'll go to the national media and cause trouble for Ferrante there."

"What kind of trouble?" Doc wanted to know.

"I'll tell the public that Dane has been wrongly accused of a crime, and Ferrante won't release him to the Army so he can clear his name. Then I'll ask them to boycott his businesses until he gives Dane the chance to be tried by his peers."

Steamer whistled. "Talk about making enemies in high places. The White House is bad enough, but if you cross Ferrante, you'll be messing with the mob, baby!"

"Not just the mob," Owl corrected. "The mob's *money*."

Hack nodded. "And there's nothing they take more serious than that."

"That's what I'm counting on," Savannah replied.

"So you think Ferrante will give in to this financial pressure and release Major Dane?" Agent Gray looked doubtful.

"No," Savannah replied. "We hope Ferrante will respond positively to the FBI's request and the barrage of bad press. But I expect that he won't."

"Then what?" Hack asked.

Savannah smiled. "Then we'll move on to Plan B."

"Plan B?" Agent Gray repeated.

Savannah nodded. "Dane might not be here, but we'll run this operation as if he were. We'll have a backup plan in place before the operation begins, and we won't leave anything to chance."

The team members sat a little straighter—much to Savannah's satisfaction. Soon she hoped to have them completely on board.

"So what's our Plan B?" Steamer asked.

"Once we've established that Dane is a fugitive from justice and that Ferrante is harboring him, the government will be within its rights to obtain search warrants for all of Ferrante's known properties. General Steele and Agent Gray will organize teams and present the search warrants in one coordinated sweep."

The general paled. "You want us to carry out a military operation against a U.S. citizen?"

"I want you to serve search warrants in a precise, military way," Savannah restated.

Corporal Benjamin looked concerned as well. "The public gets nervous when government agents wielding guns start searching private property."

"There might be some negative press," Savannah acknowledged, "but nothing you can't handle."

"You hope to find Dane during these searches?"

"That would be ideal," Savannah said. "But if we don't find Dane, I'm sure other questionable things will be found, resulting in the seizure of property and the freezing of assets."

"Oh, boy," Doc whispered.

Hack smiled. "I like it."

"It will be nice to go in shooting for a change," Steamer agreed.

"You're really playing hardball," Owl added.

She shrugged. "There's no other way to play at this point." She turned to address the general. "I was able to identify about twenty-five residence and business properties owned by Ferrante. I'm sure there are more, but that should be sufficient to make our point." She passed a piece of paper to him. "Here are the properties we need search warrants and teams for."

Both the general and Agent Gray seemed stunned. The general glanced over the list. "This seems pretty comprehensive." He glanced over at Agent Gray. "It lists properties in three different states."

Savannah waved his concern aside. "Since the charges against Dane will be federal ones, that shouldn't be a problem."

"This operation has the potential to be very unpopular," General Steele said.

"It might even been illegal," Corporal Benjamin contributed.

Agent Gray leaned forward. "What you're describing would require perfect timing."

"The cooperation of judges in several different jurisdictions," General Steele added.

"Various government agencies would have to be convinced to coordinate their activities," Agent Gray pointed out. "And we'd have to amass a small army of specially trained personnel."

"People we can trust," the general put in.

Corporal Benjamin gave Savannah a sympathetic look. "And we don't trust that many people."

"Nothing is impossible for General Steele," Savannah said confidently.

The general smiled. "You give me too much credit. During my career I've done a lot of things other people might consider difficult, but it was always on a relatively small scale."

"There's no way we can keep this quiet," Corporal Benjamin said.

Savannah shot the corporal a warning look. "When I want your opinion, I'll ask for it, Corporal. Otherwise, just write down what the general needs to remember."

Chastised, the corporal lowered his eyes to the notepad. "Sorry."

"The corporal is right," General Steele said. "An operation this big will receive plenty of public scrutiny."

Agent Gray nodded. "And I think I should mention that if we orchestrate hostile skirmishes between Ferrante's men and law enforcement personnel, there's a good chance that someone will get hurt."

"Or killed," Corporal Benjamin blurted. Hack made a growling noise under his breath, and the corporal slumped back down in his chair.

"Any casualties will obviously make public reaction to the operation worse," General Steele concurred.

"I regret the necessity of risking lives." Savannah looked at General Steele. "But that's part of being a soldier." She looked at Agent Gray. "Or an FBI agent."

"You're also asking us to risk our careers," Agent Gray said.

"I'm asking you to do whatever it takes to help us free Dane, regardless of the personal cost," she said.

There were a few moments of tense silence. Then the men exchanged a look, and finally the general spoke for himself and Agent Gray "We'll do whatever you ask."

Savannah was immensely relieved but tried not to show it. "I don't want this operation to negatively affect either of you, so the armed searches of Ferrante's property are our last resort. We'll wait until every other avenue has been exhausted."

The general nodded, cooperative but no longer friendly. "When will these strikes take place—if they become necessary?"

"We should know by Saturday if Plan A is going to work," Savannah said. "Everything needs to be ready by then."

Agent Gray's eyes widened. "That only gives us two days to organize the whole operation. Wouldn't it be wiser to take our time and plan properly?"

"Ferrante has spies everywhere, so we have to act fast," Savannah said. "If we take our time, he'll know every detail of the plan by the time we try to implement it."

"If we could determine Dane's location, we could limit our seize-and-search operation and the professional fallout that might follow," Doc said. "What about the man the FBI has inside Ferrante's operation? Can he help us with that?"

"We haven't heard from our inside man in quite a while," Agent Gray reported. "That could mean he's being watched and it hasn't been safe to make contact. It could mean he's turned and now works for Ferrante. It could mean he's dead."

Savannah gave the agent a level stare. "I'm sure you have other resources available to you."

Agent Gray returned her gaze steadily. "There's no question that we owe Major Dane. I'll do what I can to locate him. But I can't make you any promises."

"What if Ferrante isn't keeping Dane at a property he owns?" the corporal asked. "Won't that make searching his property a waste of time?"

"Not at all. Once the government has control of all his assets, Ferrante will have to negotiate," Savannah pointed out.

Steamer smiled. "We'll have him in a choke hold."

Owl nodded. "It might work."

Hack looked proud. "Whether it works or not, it's a good plan."

The general interrupted the accolades. He waved the paper Savannah had given him listing Ferrante's major holdings. "I'll arrange for search teams to be waiting near these locations by Saturday at noon. Who will give the go-ahead for the searches?"

"Hack," Savannah said without hesitation, "you'll need to work out a notification system."

Hack nodded.

"Hopefully by the time you're ready, we'll have solid information on Dane's location from the FBI, and we'll only have to search one or two properties," the general continued. "But if necessary, I'll approve a series of simultaneous strikes. We'll use a combination of soldiers, FBI agents, and local police." He glanced at Agent Gray. "The more responsibility we spread around, the better."

Agent Gray added, "I'll arrange the search warrants so that if we have to move, we'll have the legal right to do so."

Savannah knew she was asking a great deal of both men, but Dane deserved that and more. So she just nodded. "You will report to Hack when everything is ready, and he'll give you the go-ahead if the searches become necessary." She turned to Owl. "Will you work with Hack?"

This was a test of her authority with the team's most recently returned member, so Savannah held her breath, waiting for his response.

Slowly Owl nodded. "Yes, sir." Then he looked embarrassed. "I mean yes, ma'am."

Savannah smiled and turned to the two remaining team members. "Doc and Steamer, you'll help me put more pressure on Ferrante by creating a media circus."

"I always love a good circus," Steamer said.

"I'm glad to help however I can," Doc added.

Savannah turned and addressed their guests directly. "Thank you for your time, gentlemen. We'll be anxiously awaiting word that you've completed your assignments."

It was a polite but obvious dismissal, and both the general and Agent Gray stood.

"How will we contact you?" Agent Gray asked.

"Hack will call and give you a number."

The general and Agent Gray walked together out the back door, but Corporal Benjamin remained conspicuously seated in the computer chair by

Dane's kitchen table. Savannah looked over at him and warned, "You're about to miss your ride back to Fort Belvoir."

The corporal cleared his throat. "I'd like to stay and help. I really admire Major Dane, and I'd like to do whatever I can to get him back."

"We need you to work with the general and make sure he doesn't forget anything on his very important to-do list."

The corporal still seemed reluctant, so Savannah leaned closer to the young man and whispered, "Besides, we need a man inside Fort Belvoir. Someone we can trust."

Corporal Benjamin processed this information and then glanced at the back door, where General Steele had just exited. "You can trust me."

She turned to Hack. "I think we can trust him."

Hack nodded. The corporal's eyes shone as he asked, "So I'm a part of the team now?"

"Let's just say you're in the probationary period," Savannah hedged. "If you do a good job for us during this operation, we'll all give good recommendations to Major Dane."

The corporal accepted this. "Okay. Who do I report to?"

"Hack," Savannah said without hesitation, and the big man gave her a look that might strike terror in the heart of someone who didn't know him. "Call him every day."

"I will," the corporal promised. "What number do I call?"

Hack handed him a card. "If I don't answer, leave a message."

"Now hurry before the general leaves you," Savannah encouraged him.

The corporal put Hack's card in his shirt pocket. "I won't let you down," he promised earnestly.

Savannah nodded. "We have confidence in you."

The corporal walked toward the door.

"Pretty soon you're going to have everyone in the Washington, DC, area checking in with me," Hack muttered softly.

She smiled. "He might be of some help to us, but mostly I want him watched. His interest in joining the team seems a little over the top to me, and I want to be sure he's not on Ferrante's payroll."

Hack's eyebrows shot up. "That sounds just like something Dane would say."

"I'm running his team," she pointed out. "I have to do it his way."

Hack shrugged and moved toward the door. "I'll make sure our visitors get away safely."

Savannah knew Hack just wanted to be sure their guests actually exited the premises.

After Hack left, Steamer stood and stretched. "I think I need to take a nap before we start making television appearances. I want to look my best for the cameras."

Owl stood too. "I want to research Ferrante and his businesses a little more to be sure we're really hitting him where it will hurt the most."

Savannah held up a hand to stop them as Hack rejoined the group. "Everyone have a seat. This meeting isn't over."

They settled back into their chairs warily.

"What else do we have to discuss?" Steamer asked.

Savannah took a deep breath before announcing, "Now we have to set up Plan C."

Hack raised an eyebrow. "Plan C?"

"Isn't that the way Dane operates?" she asked rhetorically. "We rally our resources and make a couple of elaborate plans to distract attention. Then we send away the people we don't totally trust and formulate the *real* plan."

They all looked at her. Finally Hack grinned, his gold tooth gleaming in the kitchen's soft light. "Yeah, that's pretty much the way it usually goes."

Steamer said, "Welcome to the team, Savannah baby!"

She smiled briefly.

"So what is Plan C?" Owl wanted to know.

"Trying to figure out exactly where Ferrante has hidden Dane will be like searching for a needle in a haystack," Savannah said. "The odds are against us."

"And Ferrante would kill Dane before he'd hand him over to the Feds."

Savannah did her best to control a shudder. "I asked the FBI and the Army to help us with a huge, complicated operation on purpose," she explained. "Ferrante will hear about it very soon."

"So you want him to know that we're planning a rescue attempt?" Hack asked.

"The Army and the FBI will distract Ferrante while we implement Plan C?" Doc guessed.

Savannah nodded. "Ferrante has successfully used our friends against us several times. I think we need to turn the tables on him."

"I'm not sure Mafia bosses have friends," Doc remarked.

Savannah continued as if Doc hadn't spoken. "Who is the most powerful organized-crime boss in Washington, DC?"

"That's easy," Hack said. "Mario Ferrante."

Savannah waved this aside. "Besides him."

Steamer said, "Raul Giordano."

She smiled. "That's the name I came up with too. He's the one."

"The one for what?" Steamer asked.

"The one I need to set up an appointment with for tomorrow night—after I've had a chance to get the media frenzy started."

The men were simultaneously and completely aghast.

"You want to meet with Raul Giordano?" Steamer nearly whispered.

"Isn't your life dangerous enough with just one Mafia boss involved?" Hack demanded.

"I'm going to convince Giordano to help us," Savannah explained.

"You're not going anywhere near Raul Giordano." Hack was adamant.

"If you need his help, can't you just call him?" Owl asked.

"Or let one of us go meet with him," Doc proposed.

She held up her hand to stop the discussion. "We are talking about Dane's life here. From the start it should be understood that we're not holding anything back. We'll all do anything to save him. That includes me."

Hack shook his head. "Dane wouldn't feel that way. Your life is more important to him than his own. He won't appreciate you risking it—especially to save him."

Savannah leaned closer. "I'm not looking for appreciation here."

Hack didn't retreat. "You'd better consider Dane's feelings if you expect to have a happy reunion with him at some point in the future."

"We'll risk our lives," Steamer joined the conversation. "But you won't."

"We can't leave Caroline an orphan," Doc agreed with the others.

Doc rarely sided against her, but he was a formidable opponent. So Savannah decided to change tactics—partly because she did want to have a happy reunion with Dane at some point in the future and mostly because she didn't want a mutiny on her hands at this critical part of the planning stage of her first operation.

"Okay," she said, pretending to relent, "if you feel so strongly about this, we'll do it your way."

Hack and Steamer both relaxed, but Doc continued to watch her warily.

"When I meet with Giordano, I'll take one of you with me to guarantee my safety."

Hack glowered at her. "That's not my way!"

"You said I couldn't risk my life, and I agreed," she responded. "So I'll take a bodyguard."

Steamer shook his head but didn't argue. Hack was still staring at her, trying to decide whether to give in or continue the fight.

Doc avoided further conflict by saying, "Assuming we can set up this meeting with Giordano, what will you ask him to do?"

"Our only chance of successfully rescuing Dane is to do something Ferrante *won't* expect. And our plan has to take into account the fact that we cannot positively determine the location of either Ferrante or Dane."

"You don't think the FBI can get that information for us?" Owl asked.

She shook her head. "Not information that I'd be willing to risk Dane's life on. So we'll get Ferrante to bring him to us."

The team was quiet following this disclosure, and Savannah slowly felt the mood in the room change. Up to this point they'd been listening out of friendship. Now she saw in their eyes respect and maybe a glimmer of hope.

Hack nodded. "We're listening."

"I'll ask Mr. Giordano to call a meeting of the Mafia bosses in the DC area. His excuse will be the negative press coverage I've created and how they are going to handle it. Ferrante will be aware that the general is planning a rescue attempt and will suspect that we're working on one as well. So when he's invited to the meeting, he won't want to leave Dane behind."

"He'll take Dane with him to the meeting?" Hack asked.

She nodded. "Knowing that the FBI and other government agencies are preparing to move against him, he won't want to leave Dane anywhere for fear they'll find him. So when he goes to the meeting, he'll take Dane with him."

"Maybe he'll just say he can't attend the meeting?"

Savannah shook her head. "I don't think he'll leave himself out of important decisions."

"So Ferrante shows up at the meeting where we have a trap set," Steamer said. "He finds out it's a trap and just gives Dane up without a fight?"

"He won't have a choice," Savannah said. "He'll be outnumbered, and we'll have the element of surprise on our side. And when the FBI shows up, thanks to a tip from us, Ferrante will have more important things than Dane to worry about."

Owl nodded. "It might work if you can get Giordano's cooperation."

"Why would Giordano help you?" Steamer asked. "What's in it for him?"

"Power," Savannah replied. "With Ferrante in prison, Giordano assumes control of all the organized crime in the DC area."

"I understand the why," Doc said. "But *how* are you going to convince him?"

"I'm going to play on his sympathies," she replied.

Owl shook his head. "Mobsters are notoriously uncompassionate."

Savannah shrugged. "Maybe sympathy was the wrong choice of words. I'm going to offer him the chance to take over organized crime in Washington, DC, which should be incentive enough. Helping me free Dane will just be a side effect as far as he's concerned."

"What do we know about Giordano?" Hack wanted to know.

Savannah referred to her notes. "Raul Giordano is fifty-four years old. He's known for straight talk and heartless business practices. He graduated from MIT back in the seventies."

"No dummy," Owl remarked.

"He's very intelligent," Savannah agreed. "He had a rough childhood. His father was abusive, but his mother was a saint."

"You're kidding, right?" Steamer demanded. "She was married to a Mafia boss and raised another one to take his place. That don't qualify her as a saint in *my* book."

"I'm just reading the information I got from the Internet." Savannah gestured toward her notes. "He's been married twice, and both wives were movie-star beautiful. His first wife was killed in a car accident in 1990, and his second died of cancer three years ago. Since then he avoids social situations and concentrates on business. The best part is he's very patriotic. His oldest son was in the Marines, and he regularly contributes to charities that benefit military families."

Steamer smiled. "Oh, baby, he'll be putty in Savannah's hands."

Hack glowered in his direction. "If he's too lonely, and if Savannah appears too appealing, we may have more trouble instead of less."

Savannah saw the alarm on Doc's face and rushed to reassure him. "I'll make it clear from the start that I want to rescue Dane specifically so I can marry him. I'll tell Mr. Giordano about Wes and Russia and . . . afterward."

Some of the group looked surprised after Savannah mentioned this new part of the plan—marrying Dane.

Hack shrugged. "Most of which he'll already know if his intelligence network is what it should be."

"After we talk about everything Dane went through for his country, a patriot like Giordano should be anxious to help."

"I wouldn't count on that too much," Owl warned.

"Then I'll tell him about the charges the government has filed against Dane and that I know things that would incriminate him."

Hack was nodding. "Hence the need for a quick wedding—to prevent you from being forced to testify against Dane."

"Right," she confirmed. "Because his intelligence network should be as good as Ferrante's, we'll need to stick very close to the truth."

"Which means you've got problems from the get-go, because unless I'm mistaken, there were no wedding plans in the works before Dane surrendered himself to Ferrante."

Savannah stood and paced around the kitchen, just the way Dane did when he was trying to solve a problem. "I can tell him that Dane and I have decided to put the past behind us and move on with life by getting married. I'll say we planned the ceremony for this weekend, but then Mario Ferrante kidnapped me and tricked Dane into 'joining his staff.' So now my wedding is in jeopardy again."

"That should keep Mr. Giordano from getting any romantic ideas," Doc said.

"I wouldn't count on it," Hack muttered.

Savannah ignored the remark. "Hopefully his own apparently happy marriages and his appreciation for underappreciated war heroes will encourage him to help us."

Owl shook his head. "It's too far from the truth. If Giordano checks it out—"

"Yeah, we've already established that lying to gangsters can be a bad thing," Steamer contributed.

Savannah frowned. "So we'll tell him that we'd talked about marriage but nothing was arranged before Ferrante kidnapped me. But now that charges have been filed and we know I'll be called on to testify, we've thrown together a wedding for this weekend."

"And then all we'll have to do is throw together a wedding," Doc said thoughtfully.

Savannah felt relieved that the plan was taking shape. "And how hard can that be?"

"It's not as easy as it sounds," Doc said. "In order to get married, or make it look like you're planning to get married, you'll need a marriage license."

Savannah moved over to stand behind Doc. "Will you find out how we could get one fast?"

"And without Dane." Hack was obviously skeptical.

"I'll see what we could do." Doc began typing on his laptop.

Savannah returned to her former position at the head of the table. "Steamer, I'll need something spectacular to wear to my meeting with Mr. Giordano. Can you take care of that for me?"

"It will be a pleasure." Steamer regarded her critically for a few seconds and then said, "Based on Mr. Giordano's age, I'd say your outfit needs to be conservative. But since we're hoping to appeal to his sympathies, it should also be feminine." His eyes dropped to the cast. "And I've got to work around that hunk of synthetic plaster on your arm, so it will have to be long-sleeved."

"Lucky for you, it's also winter and freezing cold," Hack added. "So long sleeves shouldn't be hard to find."

"This isn't an easy assignment," Steamer insisted. "It's very important that I get the right outfit."

"Just get her a nice dress," Hack pleaded. "Why do you have to make such a production out of everything?"

Steamer was undaunted by the criticism. "There's a little boutique on Pennsylvania Avenue that carries a nice selection of dresses for all occasions."

Hack groaned. "No self-respecting soldier would even admit that he knows there are boutiques on Pennsylvania Avenue!"

"I have self-respect," Steamer challenged. "I'm just unique. And my fashion sense comes in handy fairly often."

"That it does," Savannah agreed. "Hack, let Steamer worry about my wardrobe. You set up the meeting with Giordano and all the accompanying security details. And keep in touch with Agent Gray at the FBI. I want to be updated on any information about Dane and Ferrante."

Hack nodded. "Once we have the setup in place, I'll call Giordano. Unless you come to your senses first."

Savannah ignored Hack and took a deep breath before making her assignment to Owl. Although he had passively agreed to her assumption of command, she wasn't sure he would continue to obey her. "Owl, I would appreciate it if you would review my list of Ferrante-owned businesses to make sure that I picked the ones that will hurt him most. Then if you'll monitor Agent Gray at the FBI—I want to know when the charges are filed, what they are, and how Ferrante reacts to the request to surrender Dane to the authorities."

"I can tell you what his response will be right now," Hack predicted. "No."

After the slightest pause, Owl nodded. "I'll review your list and keep tabs on the FBI."

"Thanks." Savannah turned to Doc. "What have you found out about a marriage license?"

Doc looked up from his laptop. "In Washington, DC, there's a five-day waiting period along with blood tests. Since we don't have five days or Dane's blood, that's not going to work."

"What about Virginia?" Savannah asked.

Doc began typing furiously. "Virginia requires both parties to be present when application for the license is made, but there's no waiting period."

Savannah rubbed her temples. "Try Maryland."

Doc entered more commands into the keyboard. "Maryland only requires one party to be present, but there is a waiting period of 48 hours."

"That's a possibility, then," Savannah said. "But I don't want to have to wait 48 hours before I can approach Mr. Giordano. See if there's anything else."

"I've got it!" Doc said triumphantly. "Atlantic City. In New Jersey if you get a court order, which I'm sure the general can arrange, neither party has to be present to apply for a marriage license, and the waiting period is waived."

Savannah was encouraged. "And Atlantic City is a reasonable place to have a quick wedding."

"Almost as good as Vegas," Steamer agreed.

"So you'll take care of that?" Savannah confirmed.

Doc nodded. "I may have to ask for the general's help, but you'll have a marriage license by the end of the day tomorrow."

"And I'll tiptoe into the secure server at a luxurious Atlantic City hotel and make you a reservation for a great suite to honeymoon in," Hack volunteered.

"The Borgata is the best hotel Atlantic City has to offer—almost up to Vegas standards," Steamer said. "But you won't be able to get a reservation for any decent suite this late."

Hack paused from his computer trespassing to give Steamer an incredulous look. "Are you kidding me? I can get a reservation anywhere, anytime."

Steamer grinned. "If you can get a reservation at the Borgata on this late notice, even I'll be impressed."

Hack flexed his large fingers and said, "Watch and learn."

Steamer leaned over Hack's massive shoulder. "I'm watching."

After a few minutes of concentrated effort, Hack pushed away from his laptop and said, "I have you a suite reserved at the Borgata Friday night through the weekend."

Savannah nodded. "That's fine."

Steamer shook his head in amazement. "So nobody will be able to tell that you tampered with their computers?"

"Not a soul," Hack assured him. "And I also found a little wedding chapel down the boardwalk from the hotel. I reserved it for Saturday morning and even made a $500 deposit."

"Don't get carried away," Savannah instructed. "There's not really going to be a wedding. As soon as Dane is released, the charges will be dropped, which eliminates his legal jeopardy. Not that I know anything that would incriminate him anyway."

"In which case we should probably find something," Hack said. "As soon as we know what the general is charging Dane with, we'll come up with some evidence you could reasonably testify about. Like we've already agreed, lying to Giordano would be a very dangerous thing to do."

Savannah nodded. "Yes, you're right."

While still typing into his laptop, Hack said, "Now, back to our wedding plans. Savannah, I've signed you up for the Sweetheart Plan at the wedding chapel. The package includes a nondenominational minister and an organist for the ceremony. For an extra $200 you can add a trumpet player."

Savannah had to smile. "I think we'll forgo the trumpet."

"No trumpet player." He typed a note then asked, "Do you have a flower preference for your bouquet?"

Savannah felt a little tremor of emotion. It was hard to plan a fake wedding when it was something she wanted so much to be real. "Do I have to order a bouquet?"

"It comes with the package," he replied. "If you pay for a bouquet but don't actually order one, it will look like you don't intend to go through with the wedding."

"Roses," Savannah said.

"Color?"

"Red."

"You'll also need a dress," Steamer contributed. "For second weddings the bride traditionally doesn't wear white. I recommend cream or pale yellow. That would look nice with a red bouquet, and it won't clash with your cast."

"Thank goodness you've got Steamer to be your fairy godmother," Hack ridiculed.

Savannah was exasperated, her arm hurt, and she wanted to get things settled. "Can't I just wear a dress I already have?"

Hack didn't even bother to answer. He just raised an eyebrow.

Savannah sighed in defeat. "Then pick one out, Steamer. It doesn't matter to me." This was a lie, and everyone knew it.

Hack turned to Steamer. "Find Savannah a wedding dress online and email me the order information. I'll have it overnighted to this wedding chapel."

Steamer turned on his laptop. "I think I'm going to love this operation. It's giving me a chance to showcase all my talents."

Hack shook his head in despair. "Now for the reception you get a three-tiered wedding cake, and they offer several flavor options."

"Just pick something," Savannah said. "It's all for show."

Hack concentrated on the computer screen. "I think I'll pick the white cake with cheesecake-mousse filling and buttercream icing."

"And he makes fun of *me* for my fashion sense!" Steamer complained. "Hack's acting like he's a professional caterer!"

Hack went on as if Steamer hadn't spoken. "You also get three different kinds of finger sandwiches, punch, nuts, mints, and a cheese ball with crackers."

"All this food talk is making me hungry!" Steamer said.

"I was already starving," Hack agreed. "If I'd have known y'all were making hot chocolate, I'd have stopped for doughnuts."

Savannah checked her watch. "We're almost through here. Then you guys can grab something to eat before you start on your assignments. Doc, tomorrow you'll get the marriage license, and once you have it, let me know. I'll be setting up as many television interviews as I can, and I'll feed the names of the companies we want to boycott to my media contacts."

Doc looked up from his laptop. "Do you think it's safe for you to take your feud with Ferrante public?"

"Maybe not—but it's the best way I can think of to put pressure on him. And if we're lucky, Dane might catch sight of me on TV and realize that Ferrante doesn't have me anymore. That way, if he gets a chance to escape on his own, he can take it."

"That information might be useful to Dane," Doc agreed.

"What are you going to tell the news media?" Owl asked.

"That Dane has been falsely charged and Ferrante won't give him the chance to clear his name."

Hack nodded. "Simple. I like it."

She turned to Hack. "I'll need a picture of Dane," Savannah said, her lips lingering over the name. "Something compelling that will move Giordano to patriotic action."

"Like one from the hospital after his Russian captivity, when he was in traction?" Steamer asked.

She controlled a shudder. "Not that compelling. Just one with him in dress uniform."

"I have a picture," Doc said. "I'll get it for you."

"And I guess we should pass out the disposable phones," Savannah continued in commanding-officer mode. "Everybody discontinue use of your old ones until the end of the operation."

Hack abandoned his wedding planning and walked into the living room. He returned a few minutes later with one of the boxes of disposable phones that Dane kept stashed there. Owl was right behind him.

Savannah watched as Hack handed a phone to each of the men and then was pleasantly surprised when he gave her one as well. Only trusted members of Dane's inner circle received phones during an operation, and she accepted it with near reverence. Possession of the phone made her feel gloriously official. However, her pleasure was tempered by the fact that the extra phone was available for her use only because Dane was being held by Ferrante.

At Hack's request, Owl demonstrated the phone's features. The others had used the phones before, so Savannah knew this was for her benefit. But she wasn't offended. Finally Hack reminded everyone about the importance of secrecy. She knew this was for her benefit as well, and since secrecy was an obvious necessity of any operation, it was harder not to take offense.

"Don't give the numbers of these phones to anyone except the people in this room. And no information will be shared with the general or Agent Gray unless we all agree that it's necessary."

"Understood," Savannah confirmed. "And nothing gets passed on to Corporal Benjamin either."

"At least until he passes his probationary period," Doc amended.

"I have to say that for a first-timer, this plan ain't half bad," Steamer praised. "I think if it's possible to surprise and outwit Ferrante, this is the way to do it."

"Just play your cards close to your chest," Owl advised. "Tell Giordano only as much as you have to, and be prepared for a double cross."

Savannah nodded.

"So what if all our plans fail?" Steamer asked. "A, B, and C? What if Giordano sets up the meeting for us, and Ferrante either doesn't come or doesn't bring Dane with him? Then what?"

Savannah shrugged. "That would be the worst-case scenario."

"Actually that's *not* the worst-case scenario," Hack pointed out. "We can't ignore the possibility that Dane is already dead."

"We're going in after him." Savannah's heart was pounding furiously. "Regardless."

Hack raised an eyebrow. "And if he's dead?"

Savannah struggled to keep her voice level as she answered. "Then at least we'll know."

There was an awkward silence, and finally Steamer said, "And if our plans fail and we can't confirm that Dane is dead?"

Savannah looked each man in the eye and said, "Then we'll have Agent Gray and the general go ahead with the search-and-seizure plan. If we can't get Dane that way, we'll think of something else. We'll keep trying until we get him or we all die trying."

She paused to give them a chance to challenge her. No one did. She looked at Owl. "It would really help if we could determine Dane's location before the meeting. That way we can have him followed and watched—just in case Ferrante outsmarts us."

"Which has been known to happen," Hack muttered.

"I'd like you to help me keep pressure on the FBI," Savannah told Owl. "Even if all our plans fail, if we know where Dane is, we might be able to salvage things in the end."

Owl nodded. "I'll make sure Agent Gray understands that if Ferrante shows up at that meeting without Dane, he'll have to get his location for us—even if it means sacrificing the cover of every agent they have in or near Ferrante's organization."

"Hack, you'll give the order to send in the troops if that becomes necessary?"

Hack nodded. "I know my responsibilities."

"Who will handle that if something happens to Hack?" Doc asked quietly.

This was a contingency Savannah hadn't considered. Hack was invincible. Like Dane. "What could happen?"

"It's standard military policy to assign a backup for crucial parts of an operation. Just in case," Doc explained.

Savannah felt a little ill. "Doc, will you be Hack's backup?"

"I will."

"When and where will Giordano have his meeting?" Owl asked.

Savannah was glad to move to a more pleasant subject. "I'm going to try and get him to call the meeting for this weekend. I'll let him choose the place."

"And hopefully he'll pick somewhere that won't make Ferrante suspicious," Steamer contributed.

Savannah resisted the urge to roll her eyes. "Hopefully."

"What if the general and Agent Gray are successful in gaining Dane's release either through diplomacy or force?" Doc asked.

"Then we'll thank Mr. Giordano for his help and have him cancel the meeting," Savannah said.

"Even if the other plans work, Giordano might still want to have a meeting," Steamer said with a smile, "to announce that he's taking over organized crime in DC while Ferrante rots in prison."

"And while the bosses are conveniently gathered in one place, maybe I'll do the world a favor and take them all out," Hack said without a trace of humor.

Savannah shook her head. "There may not be honor among thieves, but we do have honor. And that definitely matters more to Dane than his life. If we make an arrangement with Giordano, then we'll keep our side of the bargain."

Hack frowned. "But they're criminals! Menaces to society!"

"If we go to Mr. Giordano in good faith and ask for his help, we won't betray him," Savannah insisted. "Punishing the mob bosses for their crimes is not our job. We're just trying to get Dane away from Ferrante."

Owl nodded. "She's right. We can't solve all the world's problems. We need to stick to our main objective."

"I'd still like to shoot them," Hack muttered.

Steamer laughed. "Don't worry about Hack, Savannah. He hates criminals, but he knows how to follow orders, and you're the boss."

Savannah stared at the men seated before her. They were the best team in the U.S. Army, and they were willing to follow her into battle. She hoped she was worthy of their confidence.

Careful to keep her tone brisk and professional, she replied, "The timing of this first phase of the plan is going to be tricky. I'll start making calls this afternoon to set things up, but the real fun starts tomorrow. I hope to have articles about Ferrante and our boycott in all the major morning papers, and I'll do television interviews asking for the public's support throughout the day."

"It could take weeks for the full effect of a boycott to hurt the bottom line for Ferrante and his business associates," Owl pointed out.

Savannah nodded. "That's why we'll have to hope that just the threat of a city-wide boycott will be enough to put some pressure on Ferrante."

"The public loves a good media circus," Hack said. "You'll generate plenty of negative press, which should attract Giordano's attention if nothing else."

"I hope so," Savannah replied. "Now let's get to work."

"Could I say one more thing?" Owl asked.

Savannah watched him warily. "Say whatever you like."

"I think we need to have a final option—to even the odds for Dane in case Plans A, B, and C all fail."

Savannah swallowed hard. "What is the final option?"

"I kill Ferrante," Owl said simply. "Ideally I would do it as he leaves the meeting. If I miss that opportunity, then I'll follow him and take him out as quickly as I can."

All eyes turned to Savannah, waiting for her decision. Finally she nodded. "But that is our absolute last resort."

After a few seconds of awkward silence, Hack stood and asked, "So you want to meet with Giordano tomorrow night?"

"Yes," Savannah confirmed. "Be sure to tell me when you have it arranged."

"And assuming I *can* arrange it," Hack prefaced, "I'll go to the meeting with you."

She shook her head. "You're too intimidating and might make Mr. Giordano less cooperative."

Hack's face settled into a scowl, and Savannah knew that he was about to vigorously object.

She added, "Doc will go with me, and I'm sure you'll pick a meeting place that you can secure."

"Try and find someplace where I can set up my gun and watch from above," Owl suggested. "So if Giordano tries anything, I'll have a clean shot."

Savannah stared at Owl. "You're a sniper?"

"Yes," he confirmed solemnly.

"Why do you think we call him Owl?" Steamer teased.

"He's the best long-distance shooter I've ever seen," Doc said. "You'll be safe with Owl watching over you."

Hack glanced at Owl and then turned to Savannah with a nod. "Okay. Like Steam said—you're the boss."

Savannah didn't know if Hack really had that much confidence in Owl's ability to protect her or if he just wanted to shore up her leadership role, but either way she was grateful to him.

"Since we can't run things through the general, who's paying expenses?" Steamer asked.

Savannah pulled several credit cards from her pocket and passed them out. "I'll cover all the costs of this operation personally."

Hack frowned. "We did a thorough check of your assets, and you don't have the capital to finance a major rescue operation."

"I gave all of Wes's money to the scholarship fund at William and Mary, but until my death, I have access to the accumulated interest, which is a staggering amount."

Steamer raised an eyebrow. "That was clever."

She smiled. "I have my moments."

Hack fidgeted impatiently. "Are you ever going to end this meeting so we can all get busy?"

"Yes." Savannah checked her watch. "This meeting is adjourned. Everybody get something to eat and start on your assignments. I'm going to call the hair salon and see if they can work me in this evening. I can make phone calls to my press contacts while I'm being transformed back into Savannah McLaughlin—former spokeswoman for the Child Advocacy Center. By tomorrow I should be ready to face the cameras."

Steamer looked disappointed. "I was just getting used to you as a brunette."

Dane liked her hair dark too, but there was no time for sentiment. "If I want cooperation from the media, I'll have to give them a face—and hair—that they recognize. So I'll have to become a blond again."

"I need to meet with Agent Gray so we can go over the charges to be filed against Dane and figure out what testimony you will be trying to suppress by the sudden Atlantic City wedding," Hack said. "But I can't allow you to go anywhere without me."

"You're welcome to come on our trip into the city," Savannah invited him. "You can bring a couple of your men along, and they can guard me at the hair salon while you go visit Agent Gray."

"I'll ride along too so I can shop," Steamer proposed.

"That would be perfect," Savannah said. "You know what a big fan Dane is of the buddy system. You can drop me off, and you and Hack can meet with Agent Gray. After you're done, you can shop at the boutiques on Pennsylvania Avenue. And by the time you finish, I should be ready to be picked up at the salon."

Hack shook his head. "I'm not going to be seen going in sissy boutiques—on Pennsylvania Avenue or anywhere else."

Savannah was in no mood for nonsense. "Then you can wait in the car until Steamer finishes his shopping. Now let's get busy."

CHAPTER 4

SAVANNAH WALKED UP TO THE guest room and called the exclusive salon where at one time she'd had a standing weekly appointment. She explained that her appearance was an emergency and convinced the stylists to work late in her behalf. She changed out of Rosemary's maternity dress and into a pair of jeans and a sweater from the limited wardrobe she'd left in the closet. A quick glance in the mirror confirmed that she looked terrible. The stylists at the salon would definitely have their work cut out for them.

She returned to the kitchen and called the team together so they could touch base before she left. Hack was still sulking about having to take Steamer shopping, but she pretended not to notice. Instead she turned to Owl. "Have you finalized the list of Ferrante's companies that we want to ask the public to boycott?"

He extended a computer printout toward her. "Most of the ones you originally picked were good choices, but I've added a few recommendations."

She glanced over the names. "This looks perfect. Thank you."

He nodded his acceptance of her gratitude. "And I just talked to General Steele. The attorney general filed charges against Dane."

Her heart pounded. Even though it was what she'd asked for, the reality of these charges was a little terrifying. "What are the charges?"

"All pretty tame stuff," Owl replied. "Bank fraud, tax evasion, and impersonating a federal officer."

Savannah was relieved. "Has anyone spoken to Ferrante?"

Owl nodded. "The request has already been presented and refused."

This was not unexpected, but Savannah was still disappointed. "It would have been nice if he'd just handed Dane over."

"Agent Gray just called." Hack reluctantly joined the discussion. "He's made tentative assignments for the search-and-seizure groups—based on my approval, of course."

Savannah smiled. "Of course. You can discuss it with him during your meeting. It's good that we're on track with Plan B since it looks like Plan A was a failure." She looked at Doc. "You'll let me know when you've gotten that marriage license?"

He nodded. "I will."

Savannah waved at Hack and Steamer. "If you guys are coming into town with me, we need to go. Returning me to even a shadow of my former self is going to take a minor miracle, so we want to give the salon folks plenty of time." Then she turned and walked out the door, confident that they would follow.

Once they were settled in the Yukon, Savannah showed Owl's list of companies to Hack.

"No surprises there," Hack muttered as he read the names of popular restaurants, hotels, mortgage companies, and banks. "But getting people to boycott them might not be easy."

"I can be very persuasive," Savannah assured him.

Steamer was staring at the list with an uncharacteristically solemn expression. "Accusing these businesses of wrong-doing on television may make you vulnerable to a libel suit, assuming they don't just hire a hit man to kill you."

"I'm going to have to risk it," Savannah said while dialing the cell number for her friend at the *Washington Post*.

Hack growled something under his breath.

"Hunter," she said when her friend Hunter Tomlinson answered her call. "I've got a story for you."

"Savannah!" He sounded surprised yet happy to hear from her. "It's been ages, and I can always use a story. What do you have?"

"Several local businesses are owned by an organized-crime boss named Mario Ferrante."

"That isn't exactly *news*, Savannah," Hunter replied dryly. "Everybody knows that, and we're all civilized enough not to discuss it."

"Well, maybe it's time to end civility and demand justice. I'm calling for a boycott of all the companies owned by or associated with Ferrante."

"I think I'll let somebody else fight for justice in this particular case. I have to have a better story if I'm going to pick a fight with the mob."

Savannah had expected this. "What if I told you that soon there will be a new federal investigation involving Ferrante and his businesses, and anyone caught patronizing his establishments might be arrested as an accessory?"

There was a slight pause, and then Hunter said, "I'd be very surprised but mildly interested. How can I be sure that an investigation is really in the works?"

Since Agent Gray had taken Ferrante from Dane in Colorado, she decided to throw him to the wolves first. "You can talk to an Agent Gray at the FBI. He'll confirm it."

"Okay," Hunter agreed, "but I'll need more. You know it takes a lot to get America's attention."

"Ferrante also has an employee who is a decorated war hero but who has recently been charged with several crimes. Ferrante is refusing to release this employee to the government so he can have a chance to clear his name."

"Who is this employee?"

"Major Christopher Dane." Just saying his name was painful, and Savannah struggled to keep her voice even.

"Isn't he that special-forces guy who rescued your daughter a few months ago?"

"Yes," Savannah confirmed reluctantly.

"And now this Major Dane works for Ferrante?"

"It's a recent thing, and I believe that Major Dane was coerced, but I have no proof. And now Ferrante won't let him answer the charges against him."

"So what do you want me to do?" Hunter sounded wary.

"I just want you to report to the American people that Ferrante is a terrible person who kidnaps children and denies people their constitutional rights," Savannah said. "I want you to ask your readers to boycott the following businesses owned by Ferrante." Savannah quickly read a few from the list. "Supporting criminals is wrong, and it's up to all of us to protect our society's moral conscience."

There was a long silence, and finally Hunter said, "I'll do it under one condition."

Savannah was thrilled. "You name it."

"I want you to tell me about your daughter's kidnapping," Hunter said. "Now *that's* a story—and one that we've been given very few details about!"

The last thing Savannah wanted was to discuss the heart-wrenching experience or to involve Caroline directly in this dangerous operation. "Talk about *old* news." She forced a laugh. "My daughter's kidnapping is ancient history, but there is a new development concerning Major Dane that your readers might find interesting."

"I'm listening," Hunter assured her.

"Major Dane and I have a past." She forced the words from between her lips. "I was romantically involved with him and my deceased husband, Westinghouse McLaughlin, simultaneously."

Hunter laughed. "We print more salacious stories than that in the comic section."

Savannah took a deep breath and told Hunter the whole story. She started with the day she met Dane and Wes in General Steele's office. She described the close friendship that developed and then became an awkward threesome when both men fell in love with her. She told him about proposing to Dane at the practice range and their use of a borrowed engagement ring to spare Wes's pride. Then she told him about Russia—Wes's betrayal and Dane's imprisonment. Finally, she described her unhappy marriage to Wes and Dane's resentment toward her during their efforts to recover Caroline from Mario Ferrante. Conscious of the fact that Steamer and Hack had no choice but to listen to everything she said, Savannah was mildly humiliated and totally exhausted by the time she finished. But Hunter was fully on board with the story.

"Wow, Savannah. This is great!" he enthused. "I presume you're giving me the exclusive."

"I can't give you an exclusive," she told him honestly. "I'm going to tell this story to everyone who will listen in hopes that I can gain sympathy for Dane and ill will toward Ferrante."

"You must be pretty sure Major Dane will be found innocent of the charges if you're so anxious to have him turned over to the authorities."

"I am," Savannah confirmed. "Major Dane and I have settled our differences, and once he gets his legal problems taken care of, we plan to get married."

"But Mario Ferrante stands in your way," Hunter said. "He must not like you very much."

"He's a horrible person," she bit out. "He kidnapped my daughter . . ."

"Allegedly," Hunter corrected. "He was never convicted of that crime."

"Just because he made a deal with the White House."

Hack gave her a warning look in the rearview mirror, but she ignored him. She'd come this far and was determined to get a story in the *Washington Post*.

"Will Agent Gray at the FBI confirm that as well?" Hunter asked.

"No," Savannah told him regretfully. "But you should try to work it in and credit it to an anonymous source. Because I promise it's completely true."

"Okay," he agreed. "I'll run your story. But I want you to promise that when you and Major Dane get married, you'll give me the story and some pictures of the wedding."

Sacrificing a little privacy was well worth the negative publicity for Ferrante. "I promise, Hunter, when Dane is released and a wedding takes place, I'll make sure you get pictures."

"And of course I can quote you as a source."

"You can even add that I'm on General Steele's staff." She knew this might eventually cost her the nice job at Fort Belvoir, but nothing mattered now except getting Dane out safely.

"Look for the article in the morning edition," Hunter said. Then he disconnected the call.

Savannah took a few moments to collect herself before making the next call. When she looked up, she saw Hack watching her.

"I told you I'd do anything to save Dane," she said quietly.

He just nodded and returned his eyes to the road.

Next she called a producer at Channel 1 who owed her several favors and arranged to appear on their morning show the next day. As part of the deal, Channel 1 agreed to do a spot for their evening news on Ferrante and the boycott Savannah was organizing. She even convinced them to film the spot in front of a popular restaurant owned by Ferrante.

Then she called the other channels and told them that unless they wanted to be left out of the loop on this breaking story, they needed to tape sound bites with her as well. By the time they reached the salon, she had a punishing number of interviews scheduled for the next day.

The folks at the salon welcomed her in and commiserated with her over the cuts on her face, the broken arm, and the amateur dye job. Hack positioned several of his men around the salon and left with Steamer for the meeting with Agent Gray and the shopping trip.

Savannah surrendered herself to the skills of the salon professionals. She was resigned to the necessity of looking like the Savannah McLaughlin the public would recognize from her years at the Child Advocacy Center. But when the actual bleaching process began she couldn't help but remember Dane and Steamer in her apartment at Fort Belvoir with the box of Miss Clairol. She remembered the feel of Dane's fingers on her scalp as he turned her into a brunette. She thought about their time in New Orleans and his claim that she looked like a Creole princess. She missed him terribly, and a tear slipped down her cheek.

"Am I hurting you?" the color technician asked.

Savannah wiped away the tear. "No, you're doing fine."

While her hair was processing, the salon staff taught Savannah how to use makeup to cover the bruises and cuts on her face and how to do so with just one good hand. When she was blond again, they gave her a simple cut that didn't require much styling, since for the next few weeks she'd be hampered by the cast on one arm. Finally they gave her hugs of encouragement and made her promise not to wait so long before her next visit.

When she walked into the salon's lobby, she found Steamer looking at one of the hairstyle catalogs and Hack pacing the length of the room, his long legs taking in the space with just a few strides. "Finally!" he bellowed when he saw her.

Steamer whistled. "Wow, you look great."

She touched the blunt edges of her new hair. "Thanks."

He held up the catalog and pointed at a picture. "How do you think this style would look on me?"

She studied the photograph of a very pale young man with very white, spiky hair. "Since Dane wants you to be inconspicuous, you might want to go with something more conservative."

"You might want to try going to a regular barbershop like a real man," Hack suggested.

This was a strange comment from a man with a multitude of braids that hung to his shoulders. But neither Savannah nor Steamer dared point that out.

As they climbed into the Yukon, Hack complained about the time he felt they had wasted.

Savannah smiled. "Just be grateful that I'm wearing a cast and couldn't take advantage of the mud bath and steam room."

Hack muttered under his breath, and she didn't even try to hear what he said. Instead she turned to the dress bag hanging in the back. "So Steamer, did you find me just the right outfit?"

"Actually," he said, "I found you three perfect outfits."

"Three?" she repeated.

"I couldn't choose," he explained. "They were all beautiful. So I figured I'd let you make the decision of which one to wear. Then you can return the ones you don't use, or you can keep them," he added with a sly smile.

"I've neglected my wardrobe lately," she remarked, "so I probably won't return any of them."

"Please keep them all," Hack begged. "I can't go back to that place. Shopping with Steamer is horrible. He has to find shoes and purses and jewelry to match everything."

"You got shoes and accessories to match each dress?"

Steamer nodded. "And a long, black cashmere coat that looks great with all three."

"Don't ask him how much the stuff cost," Hack warned.

Savannah settled back into the seat with a smile on her face. "I don't even care."

* * *

When they got back to the cabin, Doc had a simple dinner of vegetable soup and cheese toast ready. Hack sat down at the table and began devouring the food. Steamer ate too, with less enthusiasm. Doc encouraged Savannah to have some soup, but she wanted to try on her new clothes first. She gave the team a quick fashion show and then put it to a vote. The men unanimously chose a suit made of soft, sage-green wool as their favorite.

"It complements your blond hair," Doc said.

"It reminds me of guacamole," Hack said between spoonfuls of soup.

"Everything has a food association with you," Steamer accused.

Hack shrugged. "So I like to eat."

Savannah stepped in before a fight could develop. "I'll wear the green suit tomorrow. I think the color will show up well on television. And I'll keep the others in reserve in case something else comes up."

"It's always wise to have a wardrobe reserve," Steamer concurred.

"Can we talk about something besides clothes?" Hack begged.

"We need to go over plans for tomorrow," Doc reminded them.

"As soon as I change, we can go over everything," Savannah said, "so we'll be ready for whatever happens."

Doc pointed at the soup. "If you don't eat, you won't have the strength to complete the operation."

Savannah nodded. "I'll eat."

On the way up the stairs, she started unbuttoning the suit jacket. Once inside Dane's guest room, she pulled it off and spread it out neatly on the rocking chair. She caught a glimpse her reflection in the mirror above the dresser and paused to study herself closely. The salon had done a good job of hiding her cuts and bruises, although she regretted having to change her hair from the dark color Dane preferred. She didn't look like a Creole princess anymore, but she was no longer the old Savannah either. The woman in the mirror looked confident and tough. Savannah hoped that in this case looks weren't deceiving. She would need to be both in order to successfully complete the rescue mission.

She called Dane's sister and talked to Caroline for a few minutes. By the time she hung up the phone, she felt encouraged. When she got downstairs, she accepted a bowl of soup from Doc. Then she sat at the table and asked everyone to report on their assignments.

"I got your marriage license," Doc told her. He held out the official document for her review.

Savannah glanced over it. "Thanks, Doc." She turned to Hack and Steamer. "So what did Agent Gray have to say?"

Hack passed her a sheet of paper. "This is the incriminating testimony that we are supposedly trying to prevent by rushing you and Dane into marriage. Study it, then destroy it."

Savannah's eyes skimmed the document. "Has he been able to locate Dane?"

"No," Steamer reported.

Savannah was disappointed but not surprised. "I presume he's still working on that."

Hack shrugged. "So he says. In my experience, the FBI rarely comes up with anything useful."

She took a bite of cheese toast. "How about search warrants?"

"He's got most of them," Steamer said. "I think we'll be ready to implement Plan B by Saturday if necessary."

Savannah nodded. "That's good." Turning to Doc, she said, "What about the general? How are the search teams coming?"

"He says he'll have them ready," Doc replied.

"The general would like a little more specific time frame for Saturday," Owl told her.

"Wouldn't we all," Hack muttered.

"He'll know as soon as we do," Savannah promised. "First we've got to try to implement Plan C."

"Unless you can get Giordano to help you, Plan C is dead in the water," Steamer pointed out.

Savannah waved her toast at Hack. "Do I have an appointment yet?"

Hack shook his head. "Giordano has agreed to meet with you, but so far we haven't been able to agree on a location. We need a place that's neutral and public yet easy to secure."

"I can see why it would be difficult to find a place that meets all the criteria," Savannah remarked. "But I know you'll come up with something."

Hack nodded. "And I'll let you know as soon as I do."

Doc stood and started clearing dishes. "Well, that's enough for tonight. Savannah has to get to bed."

She didn't argue. The events of the day had taken a toll on her, and she knew she'd need all her strength and wits for the challenges ahead. Doc gave her another pain pill, and she trudged upstairs. She walked into Dane's room and took a pillow from his bed. Then she went into the guest room and changed into her pajamas.

As the pain pill began to take effect, she curled up on Caroline's bed by the window and clutched Dane's pillow to her face. She fell into a deep, blissfully dreamless sleep.

* * *

The next morning Savannah woke up before dawn and took a shower. She styled her hair almost as well as the stylists at the salon had done. Makeup was more difficult, but she finally managed to cover the bruising on her face. She put on the guacamole-green suit along with the matching faux-alligator purse and pumps. Then she draped the long, black cashmere coat over her arm and walked downstairs.

She found the team gathered in the kitchen. Doc was standing by the stove, scrambling eggs. A platter piled high with crisp bacon was in the middle of the well-worn wooden table. Steamer was mixing up hot chocolate. Hack was removing doughnuts from a bag. Owl was watching the proceedings with an unreadable expression.

"Just in time for breakfast!" Steamer greeted her.

Doc pulled out Dane's chair and took the coat from her. "It's almost ready."

Savannah sat down and took a sip from the mug of hot chocolate Steamer put in her hands. She wasn't hungry but knew it would be futile to argue with her self-appointed caregivers, so she allowed the guys to load her plate.

After she'd eaten a few bites, Doc gave her half of a pain pill. "That will only take the edge off the pain," he warned, "but we can't risk you looking doped-up on TV."

"Yes," she agreed. "I need to be credible when I start hurling accusations at Mario Ferrante."

When they were finished eating, Hack led her to the door. The other guys followed.

Doc patted her good arm awkwardly. "I hope everything goes well for you today."

She smiled. "Thanks."

"You'll be fine," Steamer encouraged.

"We'll take care of things here," Owl promised.

Savannah thanked them and hurried outside before they could see the fear in her eyes.

The Yukon was parked by the back porch. Two escort cars containing an assortment of Hack's men were waiting as well. Hack opened the front passenger door of the Yukon for her and got in behind the wheel. He gave his men a signal and followed the lead car down the gravel drive to the road.

For Savannah, the morning was a blur of cameras and questions. But this was familiar territory, and after the first few hours, she had her story down pat and could have recited it in her sleep. They finished up the midday interviews around two, and Hack insisted that they go to a steakhouse for lunch.

"I'm not hungry," she complained as he led her inside.

"You don't have to eat much," he told her, "but you have to eat something." He chose a booth near the back and skimmed the menus he'd picked up when they passed the hostess station. "How about a nice salad?"

She nodded without much interest. Her arm hurt, and she was tired. All she wanted was to finish the interviews, convince Giordano to help them, and get back to the cabin where she could cuddle up with Dane's pillow in Caroline's bed and sleep.

Hack ordered a huge steak with all the trimmings and extra bread. Savannah ordered a garden salad. While waiting for their food to arrive, Savannah called Doc and learned that her campaign against Ferrante was more successful than she had dared to dream.

"We're following blog comments and monitoring emails posted on the websites of all the newspapers and television stations in the DC area," Doc told her. "The public is apparently appalled by Ferrante's refusal to allow Dane to answer the charges against him and the possibility that through White House intervention, Ferrante has managed to avoid prosecution for Caroline's kidnapping. So in addition to the voluntary boycott that you're asking for, people are organizing picket lines at Ferrante's businesses and even planning to pass out fliers."

Savannah was stunned. "Wow."

"And that's before your appearances on the more widely watched evening news programs," Doc reminded her. "I predict that by tonight you'll have attracted national attention."

Savannah relayed the news to Hack and then said, "I didn't expect our little campaign to be this successful this fast."

Hack grinned. "You're better than you thought you were."

"Just keep it up," Doc encouraged through the phone. "And after you eat that salad, Hack will give you another half a pill so your arm will stop hurting. But not until you eat."

Savannah looked over at Hack. He was holding the partial pill between his forefinger and thumb. She made a face at him. "That's blackmail."

"Eat your salad," Doc said. Then he disconnected the call.

Savannah closed the phone as the waitress delivered their food. She ate her salad quickly and then held out her hand for the pill. Hack checked her plate for longer than necessary. Then with a grin, he dropped the partial pill into her upturned palm.

After swallowing the medicine, she asked, "Were you able to arrange the meeting with Giordano?"

He nodded. "You're to be at the Reptile Discovery Center at the National Zoo precisely at eight tonight."

Savannah raised an eyebrow. "We're meeting at the zoo?"

Hack shrugged. "Giordano suggested it. Apparently he goes to the reptile house often, after hours when it's quiet. Honestly, it didn't surprise me to find out that the guy is a big fan of snakes."

Savannah controlled a shudder. She hated snakes.

"It's a good location for a meeting between two parties who don't trust each other," Hack continued. "I've already got men there checking things out and finding positions for tonight."

"Positions?" Savannah repeated.

"For armed observers and snipers—just in case Giordano decides to turn this friendly little meeting into something else."

Savannah swallowed hard. "Owl will be there?"

Hack nodded. "I told Owl to make sure he has the best vantage point."

Savannah was comforted by the knowledge that Owl would be watching over her. She knew Hack would do everything possible to safeguard her. And it was ridiculous to have second thoughts, since the whole thing had been her idea. But she was still afraid—both of approaching a Mafia boss and of failing to gain his cooperation. A mistake on her part could cost Dane his life. And while Dane didn't value his existence much, his life was precious to her.

Anxious to get the interviews over with so she could concentrate on Raul Giordano, she slid out of the booth. "We'd better get busy. We have a lot of damage to do before our meeting at the zoo."

Their afternoon schedule was more grueling than the morning had been, and by the time Savannah left the Channel 1 studios after doing a live spot on their six o'clock news, she was exhausted. Hack had a smoothie for her and insisted that she drink it all. "It has protein and vitamins and fructose for energy," he said.

She sipped it during the drive to the zoo. It didn't taste terrible, and she did feel somewhat refreshed after drinking the last cold, fruity swallow. Savannah repaired her makeup and ran a brush through her new haircut. When she was satisfied that she had done all she could to improve her appearance, she leaned back against the cool leather seat and closed her eyes.

"Are you ready for this?" Hack asked.

"I am," she replied with more confidence than she felt.

"You're scared." There was no accusation in his tone. He was just stating a fact.

She opened her eyes, squared her shoulders, and said, "I can do anything for Dane."

Their eyes met briefly. Finally Hack said softly, "Yes, I believe you can."

They were quiet as they drove through the bustling streets of downtown Washington, DC. When they passed the offices that had once housed the Child Advocacy Center, Savannah studied the dark, vacant windows. It was hard to believe that not too far in the past she had spent many hours every week there with Doug and Lacie, helping defenseless children receive the representation they deserved. She wondered who was looking out for the children of Washington, DC, now.

When they reached the zoo, Hack turned off of Connecticut Avenue and circled around to the far side of the complex. He parked in a loading zone near an entrance. One escort car parked in front of them and one behind. Hack watched while his men climbed out and stationed themselves in strategic positions along the zoo's exterior wall. Then he opened his door and got out.

"I thought we agreed that you weren't coming in with me," Savannah reminded him.

"I'm only going as far as the entrance." Hack pointed to the escort car in front of them as Doc climbed out. The medic looked small and uncertain and not much of a threat to anyone.

"You'll be right here, though," Savannah confirmed.

"Yes. And I've got men everywhere." He waved to include the entire area.

"Owl?" she whispered, and he nodded.

"I won't let anything happen to you," Hack promised. "If I did, Dane would kill me the minute you set him free."

She took a deep breath, pasted a brave smile on her face, and climbed out of the Yukon.

Doc joined her on the sidewalk and led the way to a metal gate separating the zoo from the outside world. A zoo employee with a nametag that identified him as Delor Odum was waiting to admit them. He unlocked the gate and said that he would be their escort. If he thought it unusual that they were meeting Mr. Giordano in the snake house after normal business hours, he didn't say so.

As she watched Mr. Odum lock the door behind them, Savannah looked out at Hack. She didn't like being separated from him by the heavy metal. He gave her a brief nod of encouragement. She tried to smile back but knew she failed. She turned and hurried to catch up with Doc and Mr. Odum.

"It's awfully quiet," she said as she glanced around at the empty sidewalks illuminated with stark, artificial light.

"That's because the zoo closed at six o'clock," Mr. Odum informed them. "The only folks left here are employees and the cleaning service."

They followed the sidewalk until they reached the entrance to the Reptile Discovery Center. Under the archway that showcased the entrance were several grim-faced men. Based on their tense postures and stern expressions, she assumed they comprised at least a portion of Raul Giordano's security staff.

One of them stepped up and said, "Mr. G wants to meet with her alone." He spoke directly to Doc and hooked a thumb toward Savannah. "You can look inside and satisfy yourself that she won't be in any danger. Then you're to wait out here with me."

This was more than a request—it was a command.

"A search of the reptile building won't be necessary," Doc said quietly. "We'll comply with your terms, but if anything happens to Mrs. McLaughlin while she's inside, no one will leave the building alive—including Mr. Giordano." Somehow the words coming from the mild-mannered medic were more chilling than if Hack had spoken them.

The other man nodded. "Understood."

Doc leaned close and whispered to Savannah, "Hack's men checked the place out just before the zoo closed, and everything looked okay. But if anything suspicious happens . . ."

She put a hand on his arm to reassure him. "I'll be fine."

Then she walked through the glass doors and into the warm, dark confines of the reptile house. She paused in a small lobby area to let her eyes adjust to the dim lighting before she moved forward. The sound of her heels hitting the stone floor echoed ominously in the empty space. As she turned the corner, she saw a man standing in the shadows beside an enclosure that housed a black snake with yellow rings. The man and the snake were equally terrifying, and Savannah had to force herself to keep walking until she was just a couple of feet from both.

The man remained in the shadows but held out his hand. "My name is Raul Giordano."

She accepted the handshake. "I'm Savannah McLaughlin."

"You need no introduction," he assured her. "Every time I glanced at a television today, I saw your face."

She was pleased but didn't want to gloat, so she just said, "Thank you for agreeing to meet with me."

He nodded in acknowledgment of her appreciation and asked, "Do you like reptiles?"

"Not particularly," she said.

His lips turned up at the corners. "Perhaps a tour of the center will change your mind."

"I doubt it."

He stepped out of the shadows and pointed to the enclosure beside them. "This is a Mangrove snake. It's from southeast Asia and is only mildly venomous."

She was comforted more by the thick glass barrier than his claim that the snake was nearly harmless. Forcing her eyes away from the snake, she studied Raul Giordano. In person he looked much less intimidating than he had in the Internet photos. He was an average-size man with gray hair and sad brown eyes. He was no stranger to grief, and her first reaction was sympathy. But she knew she couldn't let compassion make her underestimate him. He was a dangerous criminal.

He started walking down the corridor, and she had no choice but to follow. He paused beside the section that housed a black mamba. Savannah stared in morbid fascination at the huge snake. It stared back with soulless eyes.

In direct violation of the posted instructions, Mr. Giordano tapped the glass barrier. The snake drew up and struck with enough force to make the glass vibrate. Savannah jumped back instinctively and couldn't control a little whimper.

"You must be careful about the enemies you choose, Mrs. McLaughlin," Giordano said as the snake retreated to the far side of its living quarters.

"I didn't choose Ferrante as an enemy," Savannah replied. "He chose me."

Giordano's eyes dropped to the edge of her cast, visible along the end of her sleeve. "How did you break your arm?"

"I threw myself out of a moving vehicle in a futile attempt to avoid being kidnapped by Ferrante. He took me to a sanatorium in Pennsylvania, and I'd still be there if his daughter hadn't helped me to escape."

Giordano looked skeptical. "Why would Mario want to kidnap you?"

She shrugged. "He was using me to get to Major Christopher Dane of the United States Army." She pulled the picture of Dane from her purse and handed it to Giordano. "And his plan worked. Major Dane surrendered himself to Ferrante in exchange for my freedom."

Mr. Giordano studied the photograph for a few seconds. "I called Mario after I saw you on the morning news, and he confirmed that Major Dane recently joined his staff. However, he claims that the major is free to leave at any time."

"That is a lie," Savannah stated flatly. "The U.S. government has demanded that Ferrante release Dane so he can stand trial for the federal charges against him, but Ferrante won't allow him to clear his name."

"Perhaps Mario is trying to protect Major Dane," Giordano proposed. "If he goes to trial, it's possible that the major will be convicted."

Savannah shook her head. "That's impossible. The only witness they have against him is me, and I'm going to be sure I'm ineligible to testify."

Giordano frowned. "And how do you propose to do that?"

"I'm going to marry him. I've got a wedding chapel reserved for Saturday morning in Atlantic City. If I can get Dane away from Ferrante, we'll hurry and get married, and then he'll surrender himself to the authorities."

"Without your testimony, the charges will be dropped, and you and Major Dane can dissolve your marriage?"

She shook her head. "We love each other and have wanted to marry for many years. Once the ceremony takes place—even under these unusual circumstances—I believe we can try to form a family."

Giordano considered this for a few seconds. Then he nodded. "I read an article in the newspaper this morning about your long and misfortune-ridden romance with Major Dane," Giordano said. "Mario claims that Major Dane has no desire to marry you. In fact, he says that you have proposed to the major several times, and he has repeatedly refused."

Savannah was grateful for the dim lighting that hid her embarrassment. "It's true. I haven't had any success in convincing Dane that we can be happy together. But since we have to marry to keep him out of jail, I'm hoping that he'll choose to remain married even after his legal problems are eliminated."

"Mario says Major Dane will have the marriage annulled."

She looked away. "It's possible, I suppose."

"So you planned the wedding without his knowledge?"

She nodded. "I planned it as soon as I heard about the charges against him and knew that I would be called as a witness for the government. Now all I need is a groom, but Mario Ferrante is refusing to cooperate."

"I can see why a man with Major Dane's skills would be very useful to Mario, but I'm surprised that he's willing to risk a contempt-of-court citation."

"Mario Ferrante has some kind of grievance against Dane," Savannah admitted. "It may be something related to my deceased husband, Wes. Honestly I'm not sure why he's so determined to disrupt our lives. But I do know he'll stop at almost nothing to make us miserable. He's kidnapped my daughter and me, and now he's taken Dane prisoner." Her fingers strayed up to her neck, where her locket should have been. "He even stole a locket that Dane gave me years ago—just out of meanness."

Giordano tapped Dane's picture. "Tell me about him."

Savannah glanced at the picture and then looked away so she could maintain her composure. "If you saw my television interviews and read the articles in the paper, you know all about him."

"I want to know the things you *didn't* say on television."

She took a deep breath and said, "Dane is a war hero many times over. His chest is covered by a network of scars earned in the service of his country. One leg is shorter than the other thanks to a break that the Russians refused to set. He was deserted by his best friend, forgotten by his country, and temporarily abandoned by me." She paused when her trembling lips made it impossible for her to continue.

Giordano considered her words for a few minutes. Then he moved down and stopped before the display of a Gaboon viper.

Savannah reluctantly joined him. "Dane has been through so much," she said. "He deserves some happiness, but Mario Ferrante won't allow it."

Mr. Giordano frowned and stared at the snake. "Is Major Dane guilty of the crimes he's accused of?"

Savannah shook her head. "He was fulfilling his duties as a soldier. He shouldn't be held accountable."

Giordano was silent for several more awkward minutes. Finally he said, "I don't understand why you're involving me in your problems."

"All I need from you is an opportunity."

He looked at her reflection in the glass. "Why me?"

She shrugged. "Because you have a reptutaion for succeeding where others have failed."

He gave her a small smile. "I don't give up easily." He left the viper and led the way down the row to the next display. "Thanks to this massive media campaign you've been mounting against Mario, you should soon have him in financial ruin—if not behind bars. And the rest of us may not be far behind him."

"I don't want to ruin any business or have anyone arrested. I just want Ferrante to release Dane. As soon as that happens, everything else will go away."

Giordano nodded. "And if no amount of pressure—financial or legal—can force Mario to cooperate with the government and release Major Dane?"

"Then the Army will seize and search several of his major properties in a simultaneous, coordinated military operation. They are sure to find things that will incriminate Ferrante and possibly others. That will give them an excuse to impound his property until he releases Dane."

"And what if these actions by the government cause him, or others, to lose their businesses?"

Savannah shrugged heartlessly. "Then he should have given Dane up sooner. And his friends should have encouraged him to do so."

"Again, if that is the case, why do you need me?"

"Because Ferrante has money and property all over the world," she replied. "He could take Dane and leave the country, and I'd never see him again."

Apparently Giordano felt that this was a reasonable possibility, because he nodded and asked, "So what is this opportunity you want from me?"

"The major problem we face with any rescue attempt is that we don't know where Ferrante is keeping Dane. But if you were to become concerned about all this negative press coverage and decided to call a meeting of your . . ." She faltered, unable to come up with an appropriate yet inoffensive word.

"My business associates," he provided.

"Yes, if you called a meeting of your business associates, Mr. Ferrante would come."

He nodded. "I think I can guarantee that. He is the source of our problems, and the only way for him to defend himself is to come in person."

Savannah wanted to smile. She wanted to celebrate this small victory. But she knew she had to remain focused. "Since Mr. Ferrante has employees everywhere, he's sure to know that the Army and FBI are working together to attempt a rescue for Dane. So I feel confident that to keep his prisoner from being removed while he's gone to your meeting, he'll take Major Dane with him."

"I think I can guarantee that as well," Mr. Giordano said. "Since I've already expressed an interest in Major Dane, Mario won't find it odd if I ask to meet him."

Savannah tried to ignore the wild beating of her heart. This was more than she had dared to hope. "That would be perfect."

"So once Mario arrives with Major Dane, how will you separate them?"

"We'll tip off the FBI. They'll come and arrest Mr. Ferrante, thereby freeing Dane."

"If I allow the FBI to arrest Mario while he is at a meeting I have arranged, our working relationship will be seriously damaged."

"If Mr. Ferrante is in jail, the quality of your relationship with him will be unimportant," Savannah stated flatly. "And when he's out of the picture, someone else will have to assume his role as leader of your . . . people."

"You think I'd be interested in replacing Mario?"

She nodded. "Yes, but that's your business. All I care about is getting

Major Dane away from Ferrante."

"So that you can get married this weekend and prevent any attempt on the government's part to make you testify against him?"

She couldn't tell if he was challenging her story or confirming it. But because she really did very much want to marry Dane, a blush rose convincingly in her cheeks. "Yes."

He turned the corner past the Cuban crocodile and entered the back part of the building. She didn't like being so far from the center's entrance, where Doc was waiting, but she forced herself to follow him.

When she caught up with Raul Giordano, he asked, "And after you're married to your major, you'll expect my continued protection?"

She shook her head. "Once Dane is free, he'll be responsible for his own safety—and mine."

Mr. Giordano considered this for several minutes, and Savannah tried not to fidget. Finally he nodded. "I will call an emergency meeting for tomorrow evening to discuss the negative press coverage you've created and how it will affect our various businesses. Since your wedding is set to take place in Atlantic City, we can have the meeting there. You will accompany me, and once you're reunited with Major Dane, the wedding can proceed as planned."

Savannah tried to hide her alarm. She hadn't expected to be present at the meeting, and she knew how Dane's men would feel about the invitation. But even though the plan wasn't working out exactly as she'd hoped, this was the best chance they were likely to get at freeing Dane, and she could not let the opportunity pass her by. The most important thing to her at the moment was gaining Giordano's cooperation, so she pushed her troubled thoughts to the back of her mind. She couldn't trust Raul Giordano, and yet she had to.

"I will go with you to the meeting."

"I've been patient with Mr. Buchanan and his army of oversized security guards tonight, but there can be no sign of Major Dane's men at the meeting tomorrow," Mr. Giordano warned her.

It took Savannah a few seconds to realize that the "Mr. Buchanan" he referred to was Hack. Then she smiled. "I don't think Dane's men will allow me to go anywhere without them."

The corners of his mouth lifted again. "Smart men."

"The best in the world," she agreed.

"But somehow you will convince them to stay back." Mr. Giordano was firm. "If Mario senses danger, he won't come, and then all your efforts will have been for nothing. So you will have to depend on me to provide security."

"I think I can convince them."

Giordano nodded. "I'm sure you can."

She leaned forward and extended her hand to him. "I will need your word of honor that I will be safe and that you will deliver Dane to us at the meeting tomorrow."

Mr. Giordano stared at her hand. Finally he clasped it in his. "It's a rare thing for someone to assume that I have honor—let alone ask for my word on it."

She gave his hand one firm shake. "So?"

He nodded. "You will be safe with me, and I will get Major Dane out of Mario's grasp for you."

"Thank you." She was careful to hide her lingering doubts about his trustworthiness.

He continued down the corridor past a boa constrictor and a king cobra. Savannah walked along beside him and kept her eyes averted from the caged reptiles.

"I have a private jet housed at a small airport near Poplar Springs," he informed her. "Meet me there tomorrow at noon. If you can't convince your security detail to stay at home, at least instruct them to remain discreetly out of sight while in Atlantic City."

"I'll make sure that Ferrante doesn't see them," she promised.

His eyes moved back to a display case where a black cottonmouth slithered through clumps of transplanted sagebrush. "So have I turned you into a snake lover?"

She shook her head. "Not really."

"It's an acquired taste," he acknowledged. "But there is much to be learned about human nature in a place like this."

Savannah wasn't sure she wanted to know all the qualities humans had in common with snakes. And since their business was concluded to her satisfaction, she was more than ready to leave the eerie reptile center. But before she made her escape, she felt obligated to express her appreciation again.

"Thank you for your help," she told him. "Dane deserves it."

"I have no doubt." Mr. Giordano's expression warmed as his eyes moved from her newly styled blond hair to the faux-alligator shoes. "He's a lucky man."

More anxious than ever to put some distance between them, Savannah took a step backward. "I'll see you tomorrow at the airport."

There was amusement in his eyes, and she knew he sensed her fear. "Don't be late."

She nodded and then turned and hurried around the final curve of the corridor. She kept her eyes facing straight ahead but felt the center's inmates watching as she passed. The urge to run was almost uncontrollable, but she forced herself to maintain a steady, dignified walk.

When she reached the entrance, she put her hand on the push plate and pressed, half expecting to find she was locked inside the terrible place with Raul Giordano. But the door swung open, and she rushed outside. Doc was hovering nearby, and she hurled herself into his arms.

"Are you okay?" he asked as he patted her back awkwardly.

"I'm fine," she whispered and collected herself. "But I *hate* snakes."

Doc took her by the arm and guided her gently but firmly toward the zoo's exit. "Let's get out of here."

Mr. Odum was standing by the gate and let them out with a canned invitation to come back and visit again soon.

Hack was waiting for them just on the other side of the substantial metal fence. The relief he felt when he saw them was obvious. The fact that Savannah had made it out alive seemed enough for the moment, and he didn't press her for details as he ushered her to the Yukon and opened the front passenger door. Doc climbed into the backseat as Hack was pulling away from the curb.

Savannah wasn't able to completely relax until they were anonymously mixed in with the DC commuter traffic, headed south toward Dane's cabin. She leaned her head against the back of her seat and closed her eyes. It had been a long, stressful day.

"So what did Giordano say?" Hack demanded.

"He agreed to call a meeting for tomorrow night in Atlantic City," Savannah said without opening her eyes. "He's going to tell Ferrante that he wants to meet Dane, thereby assuring that Ferrante will bring Dane along. The only catch is that Giordano wants me to go with him to the meeting—alone."

The Yukon swerved, and Savannah's eyes flew open. She clutched the dashboard for balance.

"No way!" Hack bellowed.

"I'm going," Savannah said calmly. "He's guaranteeing my safety."

"You're willing to risk your life on the word of a criminal?" Hack pressed.

She nodded. "I have no choice." She turned her head and met Hack's gaze. "And even though it makes no sense, I do trust him. We're to meet him at the airport near Poplar Springs tomorrow at noon."

Before Hack could argue further, Doc joined the conversation. "Why does Giordano want you to come to the meeting?"

"So that Dane and I can be married as scheduled," Savannah said. "I think he might be testing me—I can't be sure. But since that's my excuse for wanting him to help us free Dane, I can't very well refuse to go."

"She has a point," Doc said.

"You know Dane would never agree to this," Hack muttered.

"Dane's not here," Savannah reminded him unnecessarily, "so the decision is mine." This wasn't precisely true, since if the men refused to cooperate, she would have no operation.

"I'm not happy about this," Hack said.

"I know," Savannah acknowledged, "and I'm sorry."

Doc inserted his opinion. "If Savannah is determined to go with Giordano, it's pointless to argue. Instead we should be coming up with a plan to guarantee her safety."

Hack looked at Doc in the rearview mirror. "What kind of plan do you have in mind?"

"We'll need some kind of insurance to keep Giordano honest," Doc replied.

"I guess we can kidnap his kids and hold them hostage until he returns you safely," Hack said.

She would have laughed if she'd had the energy. "We're not going to kidnap anyone."

"Not yet anyway," Doc agreed. "But you should determine the whereabouts of Giordano's family just in case desperate measures are called for."

The smile disappeared from her face. They were serious.

Hack pulled his cell phone from his pocket. "I'm on it."

Too exhausted by the long day and her encounter with Giordano to argue, Savannah clutched the picture of Dane to her chest and closed her eyes. She thought about his face: his dark, fathomless eyes; his now military-short hair; and his rare smile. "Dane." She didn't realize she had said the word aloud until Doc spoke from the backseat.

"We'll get him back."

She nodded. Anything else was unbearable.

Hack closed his phone. "I've got men locating all three of Raul Giordano's children, and once they find them, they'll follow them. If Giordano breaks our trust, he'll be sorry."

"I can't condone kidnapping," Savannah felt obligated to say.

"I'm not asking for permission," Hack informed her. "There's something you need to understand. These guys may look like Wall Street executives, but they aren't. They don't respect any boundaries—legal, ethical, or moral. If you deal with them, you have to be willing to go as far as they go."

"But if we sink to their level, are we any better than them?" she whispered.

Hack nodded. "Yes, because they started it."

"Maybe it won't be necessary to pick up Giordano's children," Doc added. "And if we take them, it will be more like an arrest or protective custody than a kidnapping. We'll make sure nothing happens to them."

"And they are adults," Hack pointed out. "Not a six-year-old little girl."

The reference to Caroline's kidnapping put things into perspective, and reluctantly Savannah nodded. They had agreed they would do anything for Dane.

When they arrived at the cabin, they went inside and gathered around the kitchen table. While Savannah filled Steamer and Owl in on her meeting with Giordano, Hack typed furiously on his laptop.

Finally he looked up and said, "Giordano just made a reservation for a suite at the Trump Marina Hotel in Atlantic City. He's scheduled to arrive tomorrow afternoon. He requested the use of their largest conference room as well."

"So we know where they'll be meeting," Steamer thought out loud. "Now we just need to figure out how to secure the area."

"None of you can be visible," Savannah warned. "Mr. Giordano was very specific about that."

"If Ferrante sees any of us, it will scare him off," Owl concurred.

Hack nodded. "So we'll make sure he doesn't recognize our people when he sees them. I figure I can put several of my men around the Trump Marina Hotel pretending to be tourists. And I'll see if I can get a couple on staff at the restaurants and shops along the boardwalk."

Savannah laughed.

"What?" Hack demanded.

"I'm just trying to imagine one of your men standing around inconspicuously," she explained.

Steamer nodded. "Yeah, your guys don't exactly blend in."

"We could ask General Steele to loan us a few people who are less obvious," Owl suggested.

"We're going to tell the general about Plan C?" Doc was alarmed.

"No," Savannah assured him, "if we need more manpower, we'll have to find it elsewhere."

"We could still ask the general but make up another excuse," Owl suggested.

Savannah shook her head. "Until we're sure which side he's on, we can't take any chances."

"Not all my employees are the size of NFL linebackers," Hack said. "I have a few that can blend into a crowd. We'll use Dane and Savannah's suite at the Borgata as our command center. My guys can gather there, and I'll need someone to manage them. Owl, I've got to stay with Savannah. So will you go over to Atlantic City and scope out the situation and then give assignments to my people?"

Owl nodded. "I can handle that."

"General Steele is expecting to mobilize the search-and-seizure teams on Saturday," Savannah said. "We need to tell him that the timetable has been moved up. His teams will need to be prepared to search Ferrante's various properties tomorrow night if we're unable to get Dane at the meeting. On your order, Hack."

"The general isn't going to be happy about that change," Hack said.

She nodded. "I'm sure you're right. But the sooner he knows that his time is even more limited than he previously thought, the better. So call him please."

Hack stood. "You're the boss."

While Hack was in the living room talking to General Steele, Owl suggested that Savannah be fitted with a tracking device of some kind. "Just in case we lose you."

Savannah shook her head. "I understand that you're trying to protect me, but I can't do anything that Mr. Giordano might consider a breach of our agreement. He'll expect us to have a discreet security detail there, but a tracking device is going too far."

Doc didn't look happy when he said, "I agree. We'll try to keep a visual of Savannah as much as possible so at least we'll know her general location. But we can't track her. Giordano would know immediately, and that would undermine the cooperation we're trying to gain."

"And they are meeting in a public hotel, not some fortified private estate," Steamer pointed out.

Hack returned to the room and said, "Things are all set. Twenty of my less-obvious employees are headed to Atlantic City. I talked to the general, and he said most of the teams are already in place. They'll all be ready by tomorrow night."

Savannah was pleased. "Doc, will you call Agent Gray and tell him to have a team of agents in Trump Marina Hotel in Atlantic City tomorrow night, prepared to arrest Ferrante? You can decide whether you'll give them the go-ahead or if you want Hack to do that too."

Hack scowled at her. "Hey, how much do you think I can do at once?"

Doc nodded. "I'll work that out."

Savannah pushed away from the table and stood. "Well, everyone has their assignments, so we're done for now." She checked her watch. "I was planning to call Caroline, but it's too late. So I guess that will have to wait until tomorrow."

"What you need to do now is get some sleep," Doc advised.

She didn't argue. "I am exhausted."

"In the morning I'll help you pack so we can be sure you have the right accessories with the right outfits," Steamer offered.

She smiled. "Thank you."

Savannah climbed up the stairs and changed into her pajamas, collapsing on Caroline's bed by the window. Then she burrowed her head into Dane's pillow. If all went well, in just a few hours she would see Dane again. She fell asleep with a smile on her face.

CHAPTER 5

SAVANNAH SLEPT SOUNDLY FOR ALMOST eight hours. When she woke, her arm was throbbing, but she felt rested and refreshed. The prospect of having to face Raul Giordano again didn't seem so bad—especially since she would also be seeing Dane.

While sitting in Caroline's bed, watching the sun rise over the creek, Savannah called Dane's sister, Neely. They talked for a few minutes, and after Savannah was assured that all was well, she asked to speak to Caroline.

"Hello, Mama!" Caroline's cheerful voice bridged the distance. "Yesterday I got to ride a pony, and today we're going to look at a museum. Then we'll get Happy Meals for lunch."

Savannah blinked back tears. She was glad that Caroline was so happy but jealous that someone else was getting to share all the pleasant experiences with Caroline while she dealt with dangerous crime bosses. "That sounds like so much fun."

"It is," Caroline agreed. "When are you and Major Dane coming to get me?"

Savannah's tears dried up, and her resolve solidified. Caroline was safe and happy. Dane was in danger. She had her priorities straight. "Very soon. You mind Neely."

Caroline laughed. "I always do."

Savannah smiled at the phone. "Good. I love you."

"I love you too, Mama!"

After she ended the call, Savannah put on a pair of jeans and a sweater. She pulled her hair single-handedly into a ponytail and secured it with one of Caroline's Barbie bows. Then she went downstairs and found Hack, Steamer, and Doc gathered around the kitchen table, eating doughnuts and drinking hot chocolate.

Savannah helped herself to a cream-filled doughnut and picked up the unclaimed mug.

"I trust that you're not planning to go to the Mafia meeting dressed like that!" Steamer begged as his eyes moved from her sloppy ponytail to her bare feet.

She smiled. "I thought I'd wear the gray suit today. It's beautiful but seems to say, 'You'd better take me seriously.'"

Hack groaned. "I can't be involved in another fashion conversation—especially one where the clothes actually talk."

Savannah laughed. "Okay, no more clothing discussions." Then she took a bite of doughnut, and, with her mouth full, she asked, "So did Owl make it to Atlantic City?"

Hack nodded. "Owl is there, and we just got word that Ferrante's pilot has filed flight plans for Atlantic City later today."

Savannah felt relieved and terrified at the same time. "Now we just need confirmation that Dane will be going with him."

"I'll let you know as soon as I have that," Hack promised. "Owl and I are working to maximize our manpower. He's getting our people situated in strategic positions along the boardwalk and inside the hotel. They all have cameras that I can monitor from my laptop, so by the time you arrive, no matter where you go you'll be under my watchful eye."

She took a sip of hot chocolate. "That's very comforting. Now that Hack's told me about Owl and the setup in Atlantic City, everybody else needs to give me a report on their assignments."

"As I predicted yesterday, your boycott of all things Ferrante has gone national," Doc said. "We may not be able to stop it even if we want to after Dane is released."

"I don't see how a boycott of Ferrante's businesses can be a bad thing," Savannah said. "But once Dane is released, our involvement with it will be over."

"I recommend that we turn the boycott and everything related to it over to Corporal Benjamin," Hack advised. "Sometimes those things can get out of hand, and that boy needs something else to do. He's driving me crazy."

Savannah smiled. "Sounds like a plan to me. Doc, will you talk to Corporal Benjamin today and pass everything on over to him?"

Doc nodded.

"I talked to the general again this morning just to be sure all his teams are in place," Hack said. "He says they are ready and awaiting my order."

Savannah was pleased. "Good. I want Ferrante to be distracted as much as possible so he won't suspect Giordano's motives for the meeting."

"And Agent Gray says he'll have a location on Dane and Ferrante by tonight, even if he has to sacrifice the covers of every agent they have in or near Ferrante's operation," Steamer said. "So if Owl's final 'kill Ferrante' contingency plan becomes necessary, we should have the information we need to implement it. But we won't be able to reach you, so you're going to have to trust us to make the decision of whether or not to go there."

Savannah nodded. "I do trust you." And secretly she was glad she wouldn't have to make the decision herself.

Hack took a deep breath, causing his massive shoulders to heave. "After we drop you off at the airport near Poplar Springs, the rest of us will fly to Atlantic City on a charter jet. I hope we beat you there, but I'll have Owl at the airport in case you arrive first. If everything is fine up to that point, keep your coat buttoned. If you want Owl to interfere, your coat should be open. That will be our signal."

Savannah thought it sounded simple enough. "Okay."

"After it's all over, do we come back here?" Doc asked.

"Once Dane is free, he'll decide what our next move is," Savannah replied. She was more than anxious to return control of the team to the rightful owner. "So let's plan to meet in the command-center room at the Borgata."

Hack said, "It will take us over an hour to get to the airport, so we'd better leave soon."

Steamer inspected Savannah's appearance again and shook his head. "You've got a long way to go before you'll be ready."

Savannah stood. "Then I guess this meeting is over."

Steamer held up a hand to stop them from dispersing. "I have something to say to Savannah," he said. "From all of us."

Doc returned to his seat and regarded Steamer with an expectant expression.

Hack frowned and said, "If I've got something to say, I'll say it myself."

Steamer addressed Savannah. "I just want to say that however this turns out, you've come up with a great plan. You've shown a lot of courage, and I'm proud to be working with you. And more than that—I know Dane will be proud when he sees all you've accomplished."

Savannah blinked back tears. "I can't thank all of you enough for your help. The whole thing would be impossible without your cooperation."

Hack nodded and sent his braids dancing. "That's true."

Steamer frowned. "You know you're proud of her!"

"I'll agree that I'm proud of the way you've handled yourself," Hack conceded, "but I'm not going to give an opinion about the wisdom of this plan until we see how it turns out." He pointed toward the kitchen door. "Now I suggest you go get ready."

Anxious to escape before Hack and Steamer found anything else to argue about, she hurried up the stairs and into the guest room.

Once Savannah was dressed, she packed an overnight case. She pulled on the beautiful coat Steamer had purchased and returned to the kitchen. All the men stood when she walked in.

Hack's eyes did a quick inventory, ending with the buttons of her coat, which were tightly secured. Then he headed for the door. "Let's go."

Doc stepped forward to halt her progress. He extended an official-looking document toward her. "Put this in your bag, just in case Giordano demands proof that a marriage is actually scheduled."

Savannah looked at the names on the license, hers and Dane's. Her hand trembled slightly as she took the license and stowed it in her overnight bag.

Hack used the drive into Washington, DC, to review safety and security procedures with Savannah. By the time they arrived at the small airport at Poplar Springs, he seemed resigned to the situation if not completely satisfied with their preparations. They all insisted on accompanying her out to Giordano's jet. While this show of force might prove to be unwise, Savannah recognized that it was necessary for their peace of mind. So she didn't object.

They were met by one of Giordano's men at the airport entrance and were led around to a private landing strip on the north end of the airport. When Savannah saw the sleek Learjet parked on the tarmac, her heart started to pound. During the planning stages, putting herself at Giordano's mercy had seemed essential and reasonably sensible. Now that she was faced with the reality of getting on a jet with a stranger, a known criminal, and leaving behind the men who would protect her with their lives, her courage failed. She stopped in her tracks and stared at the jet.

"We'll never be far away," Doc encouraged her.

"Giordano would have to be crazy to cross us, baby!" Steamer contributed.

"You can do anything for Dane," Hack whispered.

Savannah took a deep breath and squared her shoulders. Then she started walking again.

When they reached the plane, Giordano himself walked down the metal stairway to greet them. "Good afternoon."

"Good afternoon," she replied.

He turned his attention to her escorts. "I thought I made it clear that Mrs. McLaughlin would be traveling alone."

Hack nodded. "I got that message and came to deliver one of my own."

Giordano raised an eyebrow. "Which is?"

"That if anything happens to Savannah, I'll come after you personally."

Giordano smiled. "That would be suicide."

"If something happens to Savannah, I won't have any reason to live," Hack said. "Except to kill you."

Savannah held her breath, but Giordano didn't seem offended.

"Mrs. McLaughlin will be perfectly safe in my company." He turned to Savannah. "Our scheduled takeoff time is in thirty minutes, and before we can board, you will have to be searched for weapons and tracking and listening devices."

"I'm not carrying weapons or wearing any devices," Savannah told him.

Giordano was watching Hack warily. "You'll forgive me if I insist on having you searched just the same."

Savannah glanced at Hack, who nodded.

"Of course," she said.

"Your luggage, too." He pointed to her overnight bag.

Savannah surrendered the bag and was led into the hangar, where a woman was waiting to search her. After this thorough and humiliating process, she was scanned with the magnetic device intended to disable any devices that weren't located during the search. Finally the woman took Savannah back outside and declared her clean.

Giordano appeared satisfied and led her up the metal stairs. Just before she ducked into the luxurious plane, Savannah looked back down at Dane's men. Doc waved. Hack nodded. Steamer gave her a little salute. She moved inside.

Giordano returned her overnight bag. "You packed awfully light for a wedding."

"My dress was mailed directly to the wedding chapel, and we can only stay for the weekend, so I didn't need much."

He accepted this with a nod. "Follow me." Giordano led Savannah to a recliner seat in the next compartment. "Please sit down and get strapped in. I have some business to take care of during takeoff, but once we're airborne, I'll come back. We'll have lunch and a nice visit."

The interior of the plane was warm, so Savannah removed her coat and draped it on the empty chair beside hers. Then she tried to hide her dread at the prospect of making small talk with Giordano as she sat down and put on her seat belt. She waited anxiously as the pilot went through his preflight routine, unable to enjoy her brief solitude.

Once the plane was in the air, her host returned as promised. He took the seat across from her and asked what she'd like for lunch.

"You have a choice of trout almandine or filet mignon," he told her. "Both prepared fresh in the plane's galley kitchen by my private chef."

"I think I'll try the steak."

"Then I'll have the fish." He pressed an intercom button and placed their order.

Seconds later a waiter walked in and set up a small table in the space between her seat and Giordano's. Then he put two salads on the table and asked what they wanted to drink. Savannah chose water. Giordano chose white wine.

"So tell me about yourself," he requested when they were alone again.

While idly toying with a piece of lettuce, Savannah said, "There's really not that much to tell. I never knew my father. He left us before I was born. My mother was a stressed-out single parent, always struggling to make ends meet. She took no pleasure in life—or me."

He frowned. "I'm sure you're wrong about her feelings for you."

Savannah shrugged. "We were two people trapped in the same life—nothing more."

"And how did you meet Major Dane?"

"I was hired for a civilian position on General Nolan Steele's staff right after I graduated from college," she told him. "I met Major Dane and my deceased husband, Wes, on that first day in the general's office."

"You said Major Dane and your husband were friends?"

"Best friends. They co-commanded a very successful covert extraction team for the Army."

"Until you came along, and they both fell in love with you."

She nodded. "I chose Dane, and Wes seemed to take it well. They were leaving for a big mission in Russia, and I wanted to us to get married before they left. But Dane wanted to wait. During the operation, Dane was injured."

"And your husband left his wounded friend to die in Russia so he could marry you."

It was still a painful subject, even after all this time. "Yes," she whispered. "I thought Dane was dead, and Wes was always there, sharing my grief and trying to comfort me. And I did love him—just not the way I love Dane. So finally I agreed to marry him. I was pregnant with our daughter when we got word that Dane had been found and rescued."

"Did he report your husband's dishonorable actions to the Army?"

She shook her head. "No, that's not the way the team handles things. They just ostracized Wes—which was worse than a court martial. My husband got involved with Mario Ferrante somehow, and that ultimately resulted in his death. When Ferrante kidnapped my daughter, I went to Dane for help. In the process of finding her, Dane and I reconnected."

"And now Major Dane has set aside his resentments?"

In an effort to avoid an obvious lie, Savannah hedged the question. "We have reestablished a romantic relationship, but he has shown reluctance to marry me because he thinks he poses a danger to me—both physical and emotional."

"What kind of danger?"

"He has nightmares, and he's afraid he'll choke me in my sleep."

Giordano's eyebrows rose. "That's a legitimate concern."

"It's one we can deal with," Savannah said. "He also thinks that he draws dangerous people like Ferrante to me and my daughter."

"That, too, seems reasonable."

"Dane and the team can protect us, and I refuse to allow Mario Ferrante to ruin our chance to be a family."

Giordano mulled this while the waiter cleared their salad plates and put the main course in front of them. "Now tell me about your daughter's kidnapping."

"It's hard to talk about," Savannah told him honestly. She gave him only the barest details.

When she finished, he nodded. "I want you to enjoy your meal, so I'll stop asking painful questions."

She was relieved. "Thank you."

As they ate, he said, "You obviously have good reason to hate Mario."

"I do have plenty of reasons," she agreed. "But oddly I don't hate him. I just want him to leave my family alone."

"Family is most important," he agreed. "And I'm surprised by Mario's tenacity. Whatever problem he has with your deceased husband and Major Dane should be handled without involving women and children. It's the unspoken code."

Savannah decided she had shared enough about herself and turned the tables on him. "Do you have children?" she asked as if she didn't know that he had three and that Hack was currently having all of them followed.

"I have one son and two daughters," Giordano told her, and he couldn't keep the pride from his voice. "They are all grown now and choose to keep their distance from my businesses, but not from me. I see them all regularly."

During the rest of the meal, Savannah asked questions about his family, and Giordano was happy to provide her with answers. When they were finished, the waiter cleared away their dishes and returned with a small piece of chocolate roulade for each of them.

Savannah took a bite, savoring it as it melted in her mouth. "This is incredible."

Giordano nodded. "My chef is the best."

They finished dessert just as the pilot announced that they were approaching the Atlantic City International Airport. The waiter reappeared. He quickly disposed of the dessert dishes and removed the table. Giordano stayed in the large seat just across from Savannah during the landing.

As they prepared to leave the plane, Savannah buttoned her coat up to signal anyone watching their arrival that all was well. Then she followed

Raul Giordano down the portable staircase that had been pushed up against his private plane and through a small parking area. Savannah searched the periphery, looking for Owl or some of Hack's men. If any were present, they were well disguised.

Giordano led her toward a beautiful black sedan. A chauffeur jumped out and opened the door to the backseat for her. Mr. Giordano waited until she was settled comfortably and then walked around to sit in the front seat with the driver. He pulled his phone out and was soon engaged in a muffled conversation.

Savannah was glad for the respite from awkward conversation. The temperature inside the car was perfect, and the classical music was soothing. Savannah sat back and commanded herself to relax as they drove onto an elevated expressway. From the passenger window she had an impressive view of Atlantic City and a glimpse of the marina in the distance, with a cluster of luxury hotels jutting up into the sky. The Borgata was dazzling gold against the nautical backdrop, and Savannah's heart pounded painfully.

The driver exited the expressway and drove on a street that ran along the water's edge. Now Savannah had to crane her neck to see the signs that identified the hotels and casinos. When they passed the Trump Marina Hotel and proceeded on to the harbor, Savannah glanced over at Raul Giordano, who was just closing his cell phone.

"I assumed you'd hold your meeting in one of the hotels here," she commented as casually as possible.

"That was my original intention," Giordano agreed. "But as we discussed at the zoo, you have to pick your enemies carefully, and I decided that I didn't want one as powerful and well-connected as Mario Ferrante."

Her heart was pounding again, and she felt all the blood leave her face. "You promised."

"I did give you my word of honor," he agreed. "I offered you my protection and said I'd give you and Major Dane a chance to marry. But I decided I could accomplish that without alienating a friend and business associate. So I called Mario and explained it all to him."

"You what?!" she demanded. "Ferrante *knows* I'm coming?"

Giordano nodded. "I told him how important it is that the two of you get married before the authorities find a way to arrest Major Dane. And I have to tell you that Mario strongly doubts this. He claims that the charges against Major Dane were trumped up and that your incriminating testimony against him was fabricated as well. In fact, he predicts that when the moment comes, Major Dane will refuse to marry you—regardless of the stakes—since he's steadfastly refused you in the past."

Savannah felt ill. Giordano had double-crossed her just as Owl had warned. But could the operation still be salvaged? "That shows how much

Mario Ferrante knows," Savannah claimed bravely. "Dane loves me and will marry me, especially once he understands the legal implications of my testifying against him. But when that's all over with, I'll give him the option to either remain married or have our marriage annulled. I'm trying to help him—not trap him."

Giordano considered this for a few seconds and then nodded. "Either way, this evening promises to be very interesting."

"So where are we going?"

"I'm taking you to my yacht docked here in the harbor," Giordano told her. "Mario and Major Dane are already there."

"So you're going to have the meeting with your business associates on your yacht?" Savannah asked.

"There is no meeting," Giordano told her. "Involving others was unnecessary. And once you and the major are married, I'm sure you'll keep your part of the bargain and make the boycott and all that unpleasant press coverage go away."

Savannah smirked at him. "In the same way you're keeping your part of our bargain?"

His eyes narrowed. "I'm keeping my word. You and the major will be married on my yacht to protect him from any testimony that the government might try to make you give against him. You will then have access to a luxurious and very private stateroom for a brief honeymoon—if you both desire to make use of it. When the weekend is over, Major Dane will go back to his duties with Mario's businesses."

"What about the federal charges against him?"

"Mario has promised to have his legal team handle that," Giordano said. "And without your testimony, that should be an easy task."

Savannah felt desperate. Was it possible that she was going to manage to marry Dane but not free him? "I want Dane to come home and be with me and my daughter," she tried. "You know he doesn't want to work for Ferrante."

"Mario says the major is handling a project for him that will take a few more weeks. During that time you will clear up the boycott misunderstanding. Once our names are cleared with the public and Mario's project is finished, Major Dane will be returned to you."

"That's a lie," she said. "Ferrante will never give Dane back."

"He promised that he will," Giordano pointed out.

"But people often lie," she said bitterly. "Especially to me."

Giordano smiled. "Let's not dwell on your sad past," he encouraged. "Today you will be a bride. That is cause for much happiness. And I'm sure you understand that I had to look out for my own interests."

She did understand. Everyone had to look out for themselves. She hadn't helped Dane at all, and once again she'd trusted the wrong person. She'd been so looking forward to seeing Dane. Now she almost dreaded it.

"I presume that the FBI will not be arresting Ferrante tonight?"

Giordano smiled. "It would be foolish to allow such a thing after I've gone to so much trouble trying to appease Mario. And it's only fair that I inform you too that Mario used his influence with the White House and General Steele to have Major Dane's men recalled to Fort Belvoir to face charges of being absent without leave. They were escorted away by armed guard shortly before we arrived here."

Savannah kept from crying aloud by sheer force of will. She was cut off from Dane's men. And if the general had agreed to arrest them, it was unlikely that any Army search-and-seizure teams would be sent in to confiscate Ferrante's property. Even the plan of last resort was no longer an option. Owl couldn't shoot Ferrante if he was in jail at Fort Belvoir. Why had she ever thought she was a match for the mob?

"But that was your incentive to help us," she said. "Why would you throw this opportunity away when it was welcoming you with open arms?"

"I will eventually take the reins of leadership from Mario—but not tonight, not under circumstances that might cause my other business associates to distrust me."

The sedan pulled to a stop beside a yacht that looked more like a three-story building than a boat. "Isn't she lovely?" Giordano asked. "I named her the *Arabella,* after my second wife. She's a 247-foot floating marvel."

Savannah was in no mood to appreciate the yacht's opulent beauty, so she merely nodded. The driver opened the door for her, and as she climbed from the car, she slowly unbuttoned her coat, just in case any of Dane's men had evaded capture and were still watching her.

Giordano met her as she stepped onto the dock. His eyes took in her open coat, and he smiled. "It's kind of chilly to leave your coat open."

"I'm comfortable," she claimed.

Giordano took her arm and assisted her more than necessary across a ramp onto the lower deck of the yacht. She gave the shore one last, wistful look, hoping to see a familiar face. Then Giordano rushed her through a door and quickly inside. The interior was even more incredible than the exterior, with armed guards tucked tastefully in every corner. To the left was a spectacular wooden staircase. To her right, she saw a formal dining room set up buffet style. In the center of the head table was a three-tiered wedding cake.

"I presume it has cream-cheese filing?" she said.

Giordano nodded. "Just like you ordered. I sent a few guys over to that tacky little wedding chapel where you were planning to have the ceremony."

He gave her a reproachful look. "Marriage should be more dignified than that. So I told them to bring the cake and the flowers and your dress here, where we can do it right."

She could fairly argue that a wedding on a multimillion-dollar yacht with armed criminals was less than tasteful, but she let it go. "Where's Dane?"

Giordano shook a finger at her. "It's bad luck for the groom to see the bride before the ceremony."

Savannah stared at him. "Goodness knows we don't want to invite any bad luck."

Giordano had the good grace to smile. "The upper floor is divided into two sleeping sections and a large lounge. There are six guest suites above the bow and a large master suite at the helm. I'm giving up my room to you and Major Dane after the ceremony."

Savannah couldn't bear to thank him.

"You'll have all your meals served privately, and my chef and his staff are second to none," he added. "And it goes without saying that I will keep Mario occupied so he won't bother you." Giordano looked very pleased with himself. "This will be a honeymoon to remember."

"Instead of all this," Savannah waved to encompass their elegant surroundings, "I wish you'd just done what I asked you to. We want to be away from Ferrante—permanently."

"Sometimes we have to be satisfied with what we are offered," he said softly.

She looked into his eyes. He was a stranger, and she had no reason to trust him, but he was her only hope. So rather than fight Giordano, she decided to remind him of his obligations.

"You gave me your word of honor," she whispered back. "I'll accept the revision of my plan since I have no choice, but I'll expect your help in having Dane freed from Ferrante once I end the boycott."

"The boycott must end," Giordano agreed, but he made no promises about Dane.

Savannah felt a slight shifting under her feet and realized that the yacht was moving. "Are we actually leaving the harbor?"

Giordano nodded. "We'll be out at sea in a matter of moments."

Savannah tried to hide her despair as the last glimmer of hope for her best-laid plans died. Even if Agent Gray was still loyal to them, he wouldn't be able to find Ferrante to arrest him if they were gone.

Giordano smiled, and she had the feeling that he knew the details of all her plans—A through C. Maybe he even knew about Owl's desperate contingency plan. Then he turned to the foot of the staircase where the man who had driven them to the yacht was standing. "Escort Mrs. McLaughlin up to my stateroom and wait outside the door until she's ready to come back down."

The insult of putting her under armed guard did not escape her as she climbed the stairs. The driver led her through a sitting area lined with windows to maximize the incredible views of the ocean and into a small hallway dominated by a double door. He unlocked the door, handed her the overnight bag, and said, "Just knock when you're ready to go back downstairs."

She walked into the beautiful suite that spanned the entire width of the boat. This room, too, had a plentiful supply of windows. Through them she could see Atlantic City disappearing on the horizon. There was a huge bathroom to her left and a media area to her right. Straight ahead was the bedroom, and spread out on the king-size bed was the wedding dress Steamer had ordered for her. Made of pale yellow silk, it was exquisite—delicate and feminine without being frilly. The matching shoes, a slip, and a pair of hose were arranged neatly beside the dress.

Since she wasn't sure how much time she'd be allotted, Savannah removed her coat and placed it on the bed by her dress. Then she took off her suit and put it in the overnight bag. The wedding license was missing, so she assumed one of Giordano's goons had taken it out. With her mind searching for a way to salvage this disastrous rescue mission, she changed into her wedding garb. It came as no surprise that the dress fit perfectly. Steamer was a marvel.

Once she was dressed, she studied her reflection in the large mirror hanging on the wall. She was pale, her hair a little windblown, marring the overall effect of her bridal ensemble. But considering all she'd been through over the past few days, she didn't look too bad. And under the circumstances, her appearance was not her major concern. So she turned away from the mirror and said a quick prayer for courage. She picked up her coat and overnight bag before knocking on the door. When her jailer opened it, she told him that she was ready to return downstairs.

Giordano was standing at the bottom of the staircase and watched her descent with approval.

"You look lovely," he said when she reached him. He took her coat and overnight bag and deposited both on a chair by the door. "Although you could have left these up in your room."

"Thank you," she replied while trying to see into the dining room.

"And I have a little gift for you. Something to make your wedding day extra special."

She tensed. "A gift?"

He smiled. "Actually I'm just returning something that was taken from you earlier." He opened her hand and dropped her locket onto the waiting palm.

Her fingers closed protectively around the little necklace. "So Ferrante did have it!"

He nodded. "Let me help you put it on."

His fingers seemed to linger on her neck, and Savannah tried hard not to shudder. Once the locket was in place, she pressed it against her heart and asked, "How did you get it back from him?"

"I told him it was missing and asked him to have the sanatorium where you stayed searched. Miraculously he found it."

"Miraculously," Savannah agreed.

"Then I asked him to bring it as a wedding gift. Although he still maintains that no wedding will take place."

Savannah shrugged. "There is only one way to tell." She craved the sight of Dane and was desperate to know that he was okay. She was equally anxious to get away from Giordano. So she squared her shoulders and said, "I'm ready."

Giordano led her into the dining room, which was set up very nicely. Under other circumstances, she would have been pleased. With everything that had happened—that was going to happen—she could barely breathe. A nervous-looking man wearing an ill-fitting dark suit was standing on the far side of the room.

Giordano took Savannah by the arm and guided her toward the man. "Let's go meet the minister who will be performing the ceremony."

The man watched them approach with obvious anxiety. "Are you Mr. Giordano?" he wanted to know. "Some men insisted that I come here, but I have two other weddings scheduled tonight, and I really must get back to my chapel."

Giordano gave the man a soothing smile. "Don't worry, Mr. Mixon was it?"

The man's head bobbed in a brief nod. "Yes. Alistair Mixon."

Giordano turned to Savannah. "Mr. Mixon is not only the owner of his own wedding chapel—a unique little establishment called Wedded Bliss— but he's also an ordained Presbyterian minister. Of course you probably already know this since I'm sure you researched the various wedding chapels carefully before deciding to have your ceremony at Wedded Bliss."

"Of course," Savannah replied.

"Mr. Mixon has looked over the marriage license and determined that everything is in order."

Savannah glanced at the license that had been taken from her bag, which was now on a nearby table.

Giordano turned to address the minister directly. "Your other weddings are being handled by someone else, and you will be well compensated for your services this weekend."

"This weekend?" Mr. Mixon seemed near panic. "I'll be away from Wedded Bliss all weekend?"

Giordano nodded. "We're out to sea and won't be headed back in until Sunday evening. But as I said, your business is being taken care of, so enjoy your stay on one of the nicest yachts ever built. Think of it as an all-expense-paid vacation."

Mr. Mixon ran his fingers through his thinning hair. "Oh, I don't know . . ."

Giordano motioned for a waiter standing near the galley door to come over. "Will you take Mr. Mixon to the galley and get him some refreshment please? Maybe a nice glass of wine?"

The minister looked even more distressed. "I don't drink alcohol."

"Oh, but exceptions can be made for special occasions," Giordano replied. Then he spoke to the waiter. "I'll let you know when we're ready for him."

The waiter nodded and led Mr. Mixon away.

Savannah's eyes strayed to the door. She was anxious to get the moment of truth over with. And she longed to see Dane. Giordano noticed the direction of her gaze and said, "It's only a matter of seconds now."

She stared at the door, her heart pounding so hard she was sure Giordano and probably the guards at the door could hear it. Finally a shadow fell across the threshold, and for a second her heart stopped completely. Then Mario Ferrante stepped into the room. She had time to see the smug smile on his face before Dane moved through the door. Then she had eyes for only him.

He was wearing his blue dress uniform, and the multitude of medals across his chest glittered in the light cast by the yacht's chandeliers. Their eyes met, and she didn't even try to hide her feelings from him. Love, fear, a plea for forgiveness.

His only visible reaction to her unexpected presence was the tightening of his jaw. He gave her a little nod, which she interpreted as a signal of confidence. Even though he didn't know exactly why she was there, they were on the same team and would work together. He would let her lead him along until he understood his role.

She was grateful to see him looking healthy. She appreciated his cooperation and began to feel a little encouraged. With Dane back in the mix, all things were possible. Even doomed operations could be resurrected.

Peripherally aware that both Giordano and Ferrante were watching them with avid interest, Savannah took a couple of steps toward Dane. He did the same. Soon they were only inches apart.

"Mario, Major Dane, I believe you've both met my guest, Mrs. McLaughlin," Giordano said from behind her.

"Unfortunately I have," Ferrante sneered.

Dane managed only, "Savannah." After a quick visual examination to make sure she was okay, his arms went around her, and he held her tightly for a few seconds.

Giordano interrupted their reunion by saying, "Major Dane, Mrs. McLaughlin came to see me yesterday. She explained the legal jeopardy you find yourself in with the federal charges that have just been filed. She was particularly concerned about the risk she poses to you personally, since she is the only witness against you. With the help of your team, she determined that the best way to prevent you from spending time in prison is to marry you."

Dane was too good a soldier to react openly, but she felt him stiffen. Whether he was reacting to the thought of marriage or her visit to Giordano, she couldn't tell.

"But since you're working for Mario now, and he says he can't spare you, we had to come up with a compromise that would satisfy all the parties involved. As incentive, Mrs. McLaughlin has put some media pressure on Mario, which we expect will trickle down to his business associates, like myself, rather soon. I was anxious to avoid that, and," Giordano paused to smile at Savannah, "I never could say no to a pretty face, so I told her I would work things out."

Ferrante smirked at Savannah. "Major Dane has no intention of becoming your husband. I think he's made that quite clear on the several occasions when you've begged him to marry you."

Savannah focused on Dane. "This isn't a typical proposal," she said. "I've arranged a marriage so that I won't be able to testify against him during his trial. But Major Dane is under no long-term obligations. Once his legal problems are over, he will have the option to annul the marriage if that's what he wants to do."

"Oh, that's what he'll do, all right," Ferrante predicted.

The words stung, but Savannah forced herself to remain calm. "You don't know anything about our relationship."

Dane was quiet, and Savannah knew he was analyzing each word—trying to figure out exactly what was going on.

"I know that the charges against Dane and the subsequent demands for me to surrender him to the authorities for prosecution were both transparent and amateurish attempts to make me release him," Ferrante said. "The whole marriage thing is just another silly component of a ridiculous plan. But I'm playing along because I figure the one who suffers most in this is Major Dane." Ferrante leaned closer to her. "Since no matter what happens here tonight, we both know he doesn't want to marry you."

"Don't go too far, Mario," Giordano warned with a frown. "Mrs. McLaughlin is my guest, and I won't allow you to treat her with disrespect."

Ferrante ignored him and turned to Dane. "Will you swear on your honor as a soldier that you want to marry her?"

Dane didn't even hesitate. "I will."

Ferrante scowled.

"Any man would be honored to marry Mrs. McLaughlin," Giordano said and gave her a warm look.

Dane raised an eyebrow, and Savannah shivered—more anxious than ever to get away from Giordano and his yacht.

"I'm telling you there's more going on here than meets the eye!" Ferrante snarled. "If he'd wanted to marry her, he had plenty of chances, but he's refused them all." He cocked his head to one side as if an idea had just occurred to him. "Maybe he sees this as an opportunity to get the little girl—the child of his dead best friend."

Savannah winced, and Dane tightened his hold on her.

Giordano dismissed Ferrante's accusation as ridiculous. Then he gestured toward the man guarding the door. "Bring the minister back in please."

"We're getting married now?" Dane asked as the minister joined them. "Here?"

"Yes," Giordano confirmed. "The ceremony scheduled for tomorrow at Wedded Bliss was going to be . . . inconvenient. So we brought the wedding chapel to you—so to speak."

"But what about Caroline and the members of my team?" Dane asked. "They'll want to be present for the ceremony."

This sounded ominously like an attempt to stall, and Ferrante gave Savannah a sly grin.

She turned away as Giordano pointed at the cake on the table and the bouquet of blood-red roses beside it. Savannah shuddered, regretting her color choice among other things.

"Your team members were here, but they have been recalled to Fort Belvoir," Giordano informed Dane. "Apparently they left the post without permission and are now facing a court martial. Hopefully it can all be worked out—but not in time for them to attend your wedding, I'm afraid. And it was rude of me not to locate Mrs. McLaughlin's daughter and bring her here so that she could witness the ceremony. Please forgive me."

Savannah's heart pounded as she realized that the situation could be much worse. At least Caroline was a safe distance away from Giordano and Ferrante.

The guard returned with Mr. Mixon, who now had a wineglass in his hand and seemed more at peace with his temporary fate.

Savannah gave Giordano a disapproving look. "He said he didn't drink."

Giordano shrugged. "We convinced him to make an exception. Mr. Mixon, we are now ready to proceed with the wedding."

"This is not a real wedding," Ferrante scoffed. "It's a farce."

This got the minister's attention. "Not a real wedding?" he repeated.

"They've got a marriage license," Giordano pointed out.

"Obtained by court order," Ferrante said, divulging his specific knowledge of their plan.

"It's still legal," Giordano said. "I checked."

Savannah sighed. Apparently everyone knew all the details. "I reserved a chapel and ordered a cake." Savannah ran her hand along the silk fabric on her arm. "I even bought a wedding dress."

Dane squeezed her fingers gently in a gesture of support. "And you've got a groom."

Giordano smiled. "That sounds like a wedding to me. Now, Mr. Mixon, let's get this wedding underway. Our young couple is anxious to be married."

Mr. Mixon put his wineglass down beside the cake and smoothed his hair with his hands. "I'll need to see some identification."

Savannah and Dane both produced driver's licenses. Mr. Mixon scrutinized the licenses and returned them to their rightful owners. Then he looked around the room. "Where are we going to hold the ceremony?" he asked.

Giordano took as step back. "Right here is fine. Mario and I will be the witnesses."

Mr. Mixon frowned. "It doesn't seem quite right . . ."

Giordano handed him his wineglass. "Have another sip, and then you'll be ready."

The minister obeyed, and Savannah watched him with a frown. Mr. Mixon cleared his throat and began. "Dearly beloved . . ."

Savannah clutched Dane's hand as many emotions assailed her at once. Mr. Mixon's delivery of the marriage vows was almost laughable, and the circumstances were anything but romantic. Savannah glimpsed Mario Ferrante, scowling from his position behind them, and noted the guards at the door. It was not the wedding of anyone's dream. But she was marrying Dane. So with an effort, she ignored everything else and concentrated all her attention on him.

Finally Mr. Mixon reached the end of his bumbling, alcohol-marred wedding presentation, and Savannah sighed with relief. But just before he pronounced them man and wife, Ferrante interrupted.

"I'm sure they have vows to say to each other," he challenged. "This would be a nice time for them to exchange them."

Savannah shot Dane a nervous glance as Giordano nodded. "I think that is an excellent idea." He turned to Savannah. "Ladies first."

She cleared her throat and looked at Dane. "I've loved you since the moment we met, and for years I've dreamed of being your wife. In the past our lives have been full of struggle and pain. I'm sure there will be difficulties in our future as well, but together I know we can find happiness."

Giordano nodded his approval. "Excellent." Then he turned to Dane. "Now it's your turn, Major."

Dane pulled her a little closer. "You deserve someone much better than me, and I can't promise you happily ever after, but I will promise to try my best to be a good husband to you and a father to Caroline." Dane brought her fingers to his lips and kissed them.

Giordano nodded. "Very nice." Then he turned to Mr. Mixon. "I think it's time for you to pronounce them husband and wife."

The minister and owner of Wedded Bliss blinked his bloodshot eyes and nodded. "I hereby pronounce you husband and wife."

Giordano held up a hand. "Wait just a second before you kiss the bride!" He motioned to the guard by the door, and the guard quickly opened it to admit a man carrying a camera. "I've arranged for a photographer to take wedding pictures!"

A look of annoyance crossed Dane's features, but he didn't refuse.

Once the photographer was in place beside them, Giordano said, "All right, Major Dane, *now* you may kiss your bride."

Savannah leaned toward him, expecting a quick, official peck. But Dane put his hands behind her head, lacing his fingers through her hair, and pulled her face close to his. Then he pressed his lips to hers in a deep, passionate kiss that suffused her entire body with longing. She was vaguely aware of Giordano's deep chuckle and the whirring of the camera as the photographer documented the kiss for posterity.

Finally Dane pulled away, and she swiped at the tears that leaked from her eyes. He seemed shaken too. The minister signed the marriage certificate and then pointed out the places for the other necessary signatures. He handed the completed document to Dane, who folded it and stuck it in his coat pocket.

The photographer insisted they pose with the minister and with Giordano and even Ferrante. After these awkward group shots, Giordano led them to the cake and watched with amusement as they cut it and fed each other.

Sensing Dane's reluctant participation, Giordano said, "You may think this is silly now, but when you're old and gray, you'll be glad you have pictures of this day to look at and remember."

Dane wiped some buttercream frosting from his face. "I doubt I'll ever forget anything about this day."

"Well then, in the future when you look at these pictures, maybe you'll want to thank me," Giordano proposed.

Dane didn't seem convinced. "Maybe."

Ferrante walked over, looking bored and annoyed. "Surely this is enough, even for a romantic like you, Raul."

Giordano sighed. "Yes, I guess the wedding must now come to an end." He dismissed the photographer and sent Mr. Mixon with one of the guards. "Take him to his room and keep him there with plenty to eat and drink."

Once the others were gone, Ferrante cut a wedge of cake from the large layer at the base. "I believe I'll have a piece of this cake," he said. "No point in letting it to go to waste."

Savannah watched him—wishing she'd thought to poison the cake.

Giordano smiled at Ferrante and addressed Dane. "Your wife's plan was to for me to call a meeting of my business associates to discuss the boycott she started through her friends in the press. She had elaborate schemes in place involving both the Army and the FBI—not to mention all of your team, including someone called Owl, who has recently returned from Iraq."

Savannah was embarrassed, but Dane was listening intently.

"She thought Mario was going to bring you to a meeting at the Trump Marina Hotel, where the FBI would arrest him, and you would be free to go. However my romantic streak only extends so far. I helped the two of you to get married so she can legally refuse to testify against you. But I cannot betray my friend Mario, so there will be no FBI. Your honeymoon begins now, and I promise to keep Mario occupied until we return to port on Sunday evening. But at that point, you will go back to your duties until Mario's project is finished."

Ferrante shot Savannah a smug smile. "Maybe you've learned a lesson about your limitations."

Savannah felt humiliated. Dane squeezed her hand again—whether to indicate comfort or forgiveness, she couldn't tell. But she did feel a little better. He didn't seem angry with her for the failure of her plan or even anxious about the fact that they were now married.

"There is a lesson to be learned here," Giordano agreed with a stern look at Savannah.

She nodded. "I trust too easily. I've been warned against that many times, but I can't seem to stop myself."

Giordano shook his head. "The issue isn't trust. It is, as we discussed before, the importance of choosing your friends and your enemies wisely."

"I disagree," Ferrante amended. "The real lesson you should learn from this experience is don't mess with me. Major Dane is almost a challenge, but you can't even come close."

Giordano ignored this and said pleasantly, "I should mention that the pictures of your wedding will be on the front page of the *Washington Post* tomorrow."

Savannah stared at him, confused. "You're putting the pictures of this," she waved to encompass the room, "in the paper?"

He nodded. "The accompanying article will be written by a virtually unknown freelance writer who will have the exclusive rights to the story and the pictures. When your friends in the press see that you passed over them with this installment of your love story with Major Dane, they'll be less than cooperative the next time you want to start a negative media campaign on any subject. And your boycott should die a quick, natural death."

Savannah sighed. Giordano had outmaneuvered her on every level.

Ferrante took a big bite of cake and waved his fork at them. "You really should have some of this. It's delicious."

The door opened, and a man walked quickly into the room. He approached Giordano and leaned down to deliver a whispered message. All good humor left Giordano's face.

After sending Ferrante an annoyed glance, he turned to Savannah and Dane. "We have uninvited company. Won't you all join me on the deck to receive them?"

CHAPTER 6

SAVANNAH LOOKED AT DANE, BUT his eyes were on the door. They followed Ferrante and Giordano into the yacht's grand entryway. Giordano paused to hand Savannah her coat and then led them out onto the lower deck. In the distance, Savannah could see several boats approaching at extreme speeds. The deck of the lead boat was dominated by a commanding presence.

Controlling a gasp, she leaned toward Dane and whispered, "That can't be anyone but Hack."

He nodded briefly in response.

Savannah squinted at the incoming boats. UNITED STATES COAST GUARD was emblazoned on the sides, and standing on the deck beside Hack was a smaller, more official figure. "Agent Gray?" she asked.

This time Dane spoke. "Yes."

The boats drew close as they watched. Several formed a circle to surround the *Arabella* while the boat carrying Hack and Agent Gray came alongside the yacht.

"Aren't we going to fight?" Ferrante demanded as he pulled a gun from a shoulder holster.

Giordano gave him a look of exasperation. "Put your gun away, Mario. We're outnumbered here, and I don't want to start a war with the U.S. government. We will concede the battle and win the war through legal means. It's always the best way."

Ferrante didn't look convinced, but he didn't argue as uniformed men from the Coast Guard boat threw a line over and secured it to the *Arabella*. They positioned a small plank bridge, and several armed men boarded the yacht. They demanded that all weapons be surrendered, and slowly Ferrante, Giordano, and their men complied.

Giordano waited until Hack and Agent Gray crossed the bridge and stood on the deck beside him before he expressed his outrage. "This is an illegal action, and I warn you that I will file a protest in the strongest terms!"

Agent Gray removed a document and extended it toward Giordano. "I have a warrant for the arrest of Major Christopher Dane." The agent turned to Dane. "If you'll go with Captain Perry." Agent Gray motioned toward the Coast Guard captain standing next to Hack.

Dane put a hand on Savannah's elbow, and they walked over to join Hack.

"I'll also take Mr. Ferrante," Agent Gray continued.

"Me?" Ferrante seemed shocked.

The agent nodded. "Yes, sir. I also have a warrant for your arrest."

Ferrante's face turned red with fury. "For what?"

"Harboring a fugitive," Agent Gray replied. "You knew that Major Dane was wanted on federal charges and refused to surrender him to us."

"This is ridiculous!" Ferrante objected. "You know those are trumped-up charges! Because you trumped them up yourself!"

Agent Gray shrugged. "You and Major Dane are both entitled to your day in court. It's the American way."

"You'll be sorry about this," Ferrante hissed at Agent Gray. "Men have lost their jobs and much more for much less."

"I'm not afraid of you," Agent Gray told him. "Now turn around so I can put on these handcuffs."

"I really must object." Giordano tried belatedly to help his friend and business associate. "You are harassing a guest of mine over charges we all know are false."

"You're welcome to take it up with the judge who arraigns Ferrante," Agent Gray invited. "But he's coming with me. And if you continue to interfere with this arrest, I'll have to take you in as well."

Giordano shot Ferrante an apologetic look and stepped back. "Sorry, Mario, but there's no point in all of us getting arrested."

Savannah watched as the agent handcuffed Ferrante. The fact that Dane was not being restrained did not miss the crime boss's attention.

"Why isn't Dane being handcuffed?" Ferrante demanded.

Agent Gray glanced over his shoulder at Dane and then shrugged. "Major Dane is under the Coast Guard's jurisdiction. They have their procedures when making an arrest, and I have mine."

Another Coast Guard boat pulled up beside the *Arabella,* and Agent Gray led the unwilling Ferrante over onto it. As he was taken away, Ferrante sent Dane one last malevolent look that promised retribution.

Dane ignored him.

They all watched as the boat with Ferrante and Agent Gray on board disappeared toward Atlantic City. Savannah let go of Dane's hand and hugged Hack.

"You saved the operation," she whispered. "How can I ever thank you?"

"Learn to make coffee," he suggested. Then he smiled at Dane. "Good to see you in one piece, boss."

Dane nodded. "It's good to see you too, Hack."

"I hear that congratulations are in order." Hack turned to Savannah. "Although considering what I know about your groom, maybe condolences are more appropriate."

"How did you know we're married?" Savannah asked.

"That Mixon guy is employed by me," Hack explained. "I put a video transmitter in the decoration on top of the cake and in his tie tack. So I saw the whole ceremony from two different, equally terrible angles. I'm thinking about submitting it to one of those reality shows where you can win money for the world's worst wedding video."

"You won't be submitting a tape of that ceremony anywhere," Dane assured him.

Savannah frowned. "So if Mr. Mixon is working for you, that means he isn't a real minister. So Dane and I aren't really married?"

"Oh, Mixon is for real," Hack assured her. "He's only been my employee since this morning when we saw Giordano's men stop by his place and leave with your wedding dress. We went in behind them and found out that the wedding was being moved. We were prepared for an all-out war but wanted to avoid one. So we hired Mr. Mixon to help us keep track of where you were and what was going on."

"Then you're not in trouble with the Army?" Savannah asked.

Hack glowered at Giordano. "No. General Steele didn't bow to the pressure. He stood strong even against the White House."

Savannah felt warm all over. She was really married to Dane, and the general had proven his loyalty to them.

"The general pretended to comply with Giordano's request, and we went through the farce of a military arrest. But as soon as Giordano's men stopped watching, we turned around and headed back here. With Agent Gray's help, we enlisted the aid of the Coast Guard, and I guess you could say things turned out pretty well." He turned to Dane. "And even when we were temporarily arrested, I had men in place. Savannah was never left unprotected."

Savannah gave him another hug. "Things turned out great."

Hack grinned. "Now let's get out of here." He started toward the bridge that temporarily connected the Coast Guard's boat with the *Arabella*.

Savannah moved back to Dane's side, expecting him to follow Hack. But his eyes were focused on Giordano, who was standing passively by the yacht's railing.

"I can't help but think that you weren't trying very hard to keep Ferrante from being arrested," Dane said to Giordano.

Giordano frowned. "What do you mean?"

"The Coast Guard was able to sneak up on your boat in broad daylight, and your men stopped watching my team before they even made it back to Fort Belvoir," Dane replied. "What are the odds that you'd have two huge security lapses within a few hours of each other?"

"We all make mistakes," was Giordano's excuse.

Dane glanced down at Savannah. Then he turned back to Giordano and said softly, "Thank you."

Savannah was so astonished that she could only look from one man to the other for several seconds. Finally she managed to ask, "Mr. Giordano *did* help us?"

Dane nodded solemnly.

"Your wife asked for my word of honor," Giordano explained. "That's not something I give often or lightly." He turned to Savannah. "But I was very serious about the importance of choosing good friends. Obviously you've been fortunate in your choices there."

Savannah smiled at Dane and Hack. "Yes."

"But it is at least as important to avoid making powerful enemies," Giordano continued. "You could use a little improvement there."

Savannah nodded. "I'll remember that."

Dane pulled Savannah toward the waiting Coast Guard boat. "Let's go before he changes his mind."

Giordano laughed softly as he moved close to them. "It was my pleasure to help you get your married life off to a good start. But I must warn you that, to use a sports analogy, we play for different teams. So if we were to meet at some point in the future, you must not count on me to be your ally."

Savannah nodded, accepting this. Then she said, "You have fulfilled your word of honor. We won't ask for help again."

"Then I'll leave you in your husband's care." With a little wave, Giordano walked back inside his yacht.

Hack crossed over first. Once he was on the Coast Guard boat, Dane helped Savannah onto the temporary bridge and climbed up behind her. The golden fabric of her dress whipped around their legs as they walked. When they reached the other boat, Hack was waiting to help her down. She put her hands on his shoulders and allowed him to lift her onto the deck.

From her vantage point, she could see countless little beads of moisture and sea salt trapped in Hack's long braids. She was overcome with tenderness and gratitude for her friend and gave him another quick hug as Dane jumped down beside them.

"Enough of that," he said while the Coast Guard crew removed the bridge that connected the two boats. Savannah watched the luxury yacht disappear with mixed emotions as they headed away from the *Arabella*. She was glad to leave it, but the time she had spent there would forever be etched in her memory.

"Let's get you out of this cold wind," Dane suggested.

"And out of firing range in case Giordano has a change of heart," Hack muttered.

A member of the Coast Guard crew led them into the boat's tiny cabin. There were two benches. Hack took one while Dane and Savannah shared the other. The small size of the bench necessitated Savannah sitting close to Dane. To make the most of the limited space, Dane put his arm around her.

She savored the contact as Dane said, "So who's going to explain this rescue plan to me?"

"It was my fault," Savannah said.

"It worked." Hack diverted Dane's attention back to him. "And I take the responsibility. Savannah didn't make us help her—we chose to."

"What made you even consider a plan that put Savannah at so much risk?" Dane asked. His body had stiffened, and Savannah could tell he was angry.

Hack didn't seem concerned. "I told you she was never left unprotected."

"You couldn't be sure that it would work out that way," Dane countered.

"There's risk involved in every operation," Hack replied. "We had a man down and had to go in after him. Savannah's part of the team, so she took her share of the risk. Or maybe you don't consider her a full team member."

"You should have just shot Ferrante," Dane said.

Hack nodded. "That was the plan I favored, but I was outvoted."

"Things didn't work out the way I'd planned," Savannah said. "But fortunately Hack anticipated that and had some additional backup ready." She tried to keep the disappointment from her voice. "And as usual, he didn't fill me in."

"One of your plans might have worked," Hack told her. "I didn't think it was right to overrule you. But I had to be prepared, just in case."

She nodded. "I understand."

Hack grinned. "Good. So how was the cake?"

"The cake?" Dane repeated.

Hack gave him an incredulous look. "The *wedding* cake. Was it good?"

"Hack picked it out," Savannah explained. Then she answered the original question. "The cake itself was good, but the cheesecake filling was delicious."

Hack smiled. "I knew that was going to be a good combination."

Dane was looking at them like they'd gone crazy.

"Sorry about the whole wedding thing," Savannah said. "But the need to protect you from my eyewitness testimony was the only compelling excuse we could come up with for our presentation to Giordano."

"Everybody pitched in to help plan it," Hack said. "Doc got the marriage license. I reserved the wedding chapel and ordered the cake."

"And Steamer picked out my dress." She fingered the fabric, now stained by sea salt and boat grime. She took a deep breath and said bravely, "I won't hold you to it. It shouldn't take much to have it annulled."

Dane nuzzled her temple with his lips. "I thought you wanted to marry me."

She blinked at him in surprise. "I never meant to force you."

His lips turned up in a small smile. "Nobody could *force* me to marry anyone—even to save my life."

She was stunned by this near declaration—especially in front of Hack. "Are you saying we're really married, and we're going to stay that way?"

He nodded. "I'm not going to have the marriage annulled," he said. "So we're really married, unless the marriage license was a fake."

"Doc got the license, so I'm sure it's legit," Hack contributed.

Dane relaxed against the wall behind them. "Then we're married."

She snuggled closer to him. "So now we just live happily ever after?"

"I still don't believe in fairy tales, but I'm willing to admit that being married has a lot of practical advantages," Dane conceded. "If we're living together, I can protect you better. Caroline will have a father, and if anything happens to me, you'll have my assets and death benefits to supplement your income. We'll even get a tax break for being married."

"A tax break!" Savannah repeated.

He nodded. "I don't know why I resisted the idea for so long. It really makes perfect sense."

She leaned close and whispered, "Those were not the advantages I had hoped you'd be looking forward to. What about love and romance and . . ."

He smiled. "Now you're talking fairy tales again."

His words evoked a mixture of feelings for Savannah. She was disappointed and uncertain and a little afraid. She settled back against the wall, and even though her arm was still touching Dane's, she felt emotionally removed from him.

The Coast Guard captain stuck his head in the door. "We'll get you back to shore as quick as possible," he promised. "But we're operating with a reduced crew." He hooked a thumb toward Hack. "The big guy there insisted on coming with us, and he takes the same space as two of my men."

"One Army man is worth two Coast Guard guys any day," Hack replied.

The captain laughed. "I may not agree with you, but I'm certainly not going to argue with you."

The captain left, and Dane leaned forward to talk to Hack. It was too much of an effort to try and hear what was being said over the roar of the engine, so Savannah just rested her head on the vibrating cabin wall and tried to calm her nerves. She'd gone from a very dangerous situation to a very confusing one in a short period of time. She didn't know where she stood with Dane and was anxious to get some time alone with him so they could settle things.

When they arrived at the dock, the Coast Guard crew secured the boat and allowed the passengers to disembark. After expressing gratitude to the captain, Dane took Savannah by the hand and led her away from the water. As he walked, he asked for her cell phone. She surrendered it reluctantly, knowing she'd probably never have possession of it again.

"I presume you've got guys watching Giordano?" Dane asked.

Hack nodded. "The Coast Guard is officially monitoring Giordano and the *Arabella* until they dock on Sunday night. And I've got a team following Ferrante and the FBI—just in case."

Some of the tension seemed to leave Dane's shoulders. "Ferrante's not too much of a concern at the moment since he's in FBI custody. Giordano either for that matter. But we need to figure out our next move and get on with it," he told Hack. "What's the plan?"

"As part of the wedding plans, I reserved a suite at the Borgata," Hack told him. "We've been using it as our command post."

"Have all the guys meet us there," Dane told him. "What about transportation?"

Hack pulled a set of keys from his pocket. "You and Savannah take that black F-150 truck to your right. I've got another vehicle parked a few blocks down that I can use to round up the guys."

Dane opened the passenger door for Savannah. Once she was settled, he walked around the truck and climbed in behind the wheel. "So how did you manage to get away from Ferrante?" Dane asked her as he backed out of the parking space.

"Rosemary rescued me." Savannah gave him the basic details of her escape from Serene Hills Sanatorium. "Does that surprise you?"

"It's more suspicious than surprising," Dane replied. "It makes me wonder if Ferrante let you go on purpose, and his daughter just helped him do it."

"Why can't you accept the possibility that Rosemary felt she owed me and wanted to help?"

"We've been over this before," he replied. "People can rarely be trusted."

Savannah had no defense for this. She'd trusted unwisely again, and they were fortunate that Dane was free and his men weren't doing time in military prison. She didn't want to believe that Rosemary's daring rescue had really been part of a plan instigated by Mario Ferrante, but she didn't want to fight with Dane either. So she asked, "Is there any way for us to check and be sure that Rosemary is all right?"

He nodded. "When we get to the hotel, I'll have one of the guys call around and find out where she is and if she's okay."

She accepted this. "Thank you."

"And you said Rosemary Ferrante had a fake ambulance waiting outside the hospital?"

"Her name is Rosemary *Allen,* and her husband, Chad, was in the ambulance, dressed as the driver."

Dane smirked at this information. "More evidence that Ferrante approved the whole thing. Allen would never dare go against his boss."

There was a certain truth to this, so Savannah decided to abandon the subject. "Was it terrible—having to work for Ferrante?"

"Not too bad," he replied vaguely, and she knew he was lying.

"What was the project he was having you work on?"

"There were a couple of people he wanted me to find."

"Did you find them?"

He shook his head.

Before she could question him further, her phone rang, and Dane answered it. After listening for a few seconds, he said, "Roger." Then he closed the phone and put it back in his pocket. "Hack says the hotel room is clear."

Dane pulled the truck up to the hotel's front entrance and parked. He got out and gave the keys to a valet. Then he opened the passenger door and Savannah stepped down. He took her by the hand and led the way into the lobby. They rode the elevator up to the seventh floor, and after inserting the plastic key Hack had given him, Dane opened the door to a sumptuous suite.

He waved Savannah inside and locked the door securely behind them. They moved past a convenient little powder room, through a tastefully furnished sitting area, past a fully stocked kitchenette, and into a bedroom with a huge, four-poster canopy bed. Through the open bathroom door she could see a sunken tub romantically surrounded by candles. Savannah's heart was pounding, but Dane didn't even seem to notice the atmosphere as he looked at his watch.

"Where is Hack?" he demanded as if she had more information than he did.

She didn't even bother to respond.

"He and the guys should be up here by now," Dane continued in irritation. "They know we've got a limited amount of time to figure out our next move."

Savannah was glad for the few minutes of privacy. She stepped forward and wrapped her arms around his waist. "Speaking of limited time, we haven't had a second alone to talk about us and our future."

"We'll find time to do that," he said. "Eventually." Then, instead of returning her embrace, he held the phone over her head and punched a button. A split second later she heard Hack's booming voice.

"Hack."

"Where are you?" Dane demanded. "We're supposed to be meeting."

There was a brief awkward moment of silence, and then Hack replied, "You and Savannah just got married, and you're on your honeymoon."

Savannah felt a blush warm her cheeks, but Dane just looked more annoyed. "We don't have time for nonsense. Get up here and bring the guys with you. We've got a lot to do before Ferrante's lawyers get him released."

She let her arms drop from around his waist and moved to the windows that overlooked the marina. She kept her face averted from Dane as she stared at the waves crashing against the sandy beaches below. Dane was being nice enough—even tender occasionally—but it was like nothing had changed. Yet everything had changed.

She pressed the fingers of her good hand against the cool glass. Dane said they were really married and that he wasn't planning to have it annulled. Doc had procured the license, and she trusted him. But Dane was taking the whole wedding thing too calmly, and he certainly wasn't acting like a groom on his wedding night. So Savannah had to wonder why.

She knew Doc cared for her and wouldn't willingly do anything to hurt her. But if given a choice between her and Dane, he would have to choose his commanding officer. So maybe when he was assigned to get the marriage license, he had done what he thought Dane would want him to—create a fake one. And Dane, knowing Doc so well, probably suspected this. In which case she wasn't Dane's wife after all, and that would explain his odd behavior.

Dane interrupted her troubled thoughts by speaking from very close behind her. "Our lives depend on us making the correct move here. You understand that?"

She nodded. Unfortunately she understood only too well.

"There will be time to talk about things later."

She hoped so, but before she could comment, there was a rap on the door. Then Hack walked in, followed by Doc, Steamer, and Owl—all looking equally ill at ease in the romantic room.

"It's about time," Dane told them. Then he turned to Savannah and grimaced. "Savannah and I need something else to wear besides these formal clothes. Preferably something more comfortable and dry. Steamer, will you see what you can do with the shops here at the Borgata?"

Steamer smiled. "I've died and gone to heaven."

"No, you're not dead, but you're killing me," Hack replied.

"Hurry," Dane told Steamer. "I don't want to be here more than an hour."

"I'm starving," Hack said. "Can Steam pick us up something to eat while he's downstairs acting like a style consultant?"

Dane shook his head. "We're trying to save time. Just call room service and have them deliver some food up here."

Hack pulled out his phone as Dane turned on the gas logs in the fireplace. Savannah stepped closer and rubbed her hands together in front of the flames.

"You'd probably be warmer without that damp coat," Dane said as he gently eased it off her shoulders. "Besides, Giordano might have planted a tracking or listening device in it. Anything we were wearing on the yacht will have to be scanned."

Savannah unhooked the locket around her neck. "Then this will need to be checked again. Ferrante took it while I was in the sanatorium, and Giordano returned it to me right before the wedding."

Just saying the word made Savannah's hands tremble, but Dane seemed unaffected. He handed the locket and the coat to Hack. Then he said, "Scan her."

Hack scanned Savannah and Dane. "Both of you seem to be clean."

"I'll feel better when we've changed into completely different clothes," Dane said. He walked over to the sitting area where the guys were gathered.

He spoke first to the team's most recently returned member. "It's good to see you, Owl."

Owl nodded. "It's a pleasure to be here, sir."

Dane turned to Hack. "I want this place blanketed with security until we get out of here. And make sure the crew you left at my cabin is on full alert."

Hack pulled out his cell phone. "I'm on it."

Savannah was amazed by how quickly and automatically Dane had reassumed leadership of the team. And even more surprised by how glad she was to relinquish it.

"Doc, you coordinate with General Steele. We need to know if the FBI can make their charges against Ferrante stick."

"What do you think?" Doc asked.

"I have no doubts that Ferrante could potentially be back on the street by morning," Dane predicted. "But then I'm a pessimist. He might stay in custody until tomorrow night."

Doc opened his phone. "I'll monitor the proceedings."

"And while you're at it, check on Rosemary Ferrante," Dane requested.

"Rosemary Allen," Savannah corrected automatically.

Dane turned to Owl. "Will you work on our transportation out of here? We'll need a charter plane—nothing too large or too small."

"Where are we headed?" Owl wanted to know.

"We'll fly to Andrews," Dane said. "So get us military clearance. And we'll need a couple of cars once we land for the short drive to Fort Belvoir."

Owl pulled out his phone. "I'll take care of it."

There was a knock on the door.

"That must be Steamer," Hack said as he opened it. But instead they found several waiters pushing carts of food.

"How much food did you order?" Owl asked in amazement.

Hack rubbed his hands together as the waiters arranged the carts in front of the fireplace. "Better too much food than not enough is my motto."

"Don't we all know *that!*" Steamer said as he arrived with his arms full of shopping bags. He held his nose up high in the air and took a deep breath. "This food looks delicious, and the retail piazza downstairs is a shopper's paradise!"

Hack stuck a boiled shrimp in his mouth before muttering a reply, so no one understood him. Which Savannah felt was just as well.

"Here you go, Savannah." Steamer passed several bags to her. "Since I didn't know how long it would be before you get back home, I asked all the store clerks to help me and bought you cosmetics, hair supplies, two pairs of jeans, four sweaters, and some leather loafers. And when I told the girls you were on your honeymoon, they insisted on some lingerie."

Dane looked mildly uncomfortable for the first time since their reunion on Giordano's yacht. "That's enough on the clothing discussion."

"Thank you!" Hack said.

Steamer went on as if neither man had spoken. "I spent so much money that they gave me a free duffel bag." He held up a brown bag with BORGATA COLLECTION printed across the front in gold script letters. "I figure it will come in handy since you don't have any luggage."

"Did you buy anything for me to wear?" Dane asked.

Steamer handed Dane two bags. "Your clothes were less fun to buy, so I didn't spend as much money, and consequently, you didn't get a free duffel. But at least you won't have to go around in that wet uniform."

Dane took the bags Steamer extended to him and pointed at the bedroom. "Savannah, you change in there. I'll use the powder room." He waved toward the little half bath by the door.

Wordlessly, she walked into the bedroom. She shut the door and put the shopping bags on the huge bed. Then she peeled off the ruined wedding dress, which looked as forlorn as she felt. She pressed her cheek to the damp fabric briefly. Then she stuffed it into a shopping bag.

The need to remove the ocean residue from her skin and hair couldn't be ignored. She resisted the urge to take a long soak in the sunken bathtub and took a quick shower instead. Rather than make use of the hairstyling supplies Steamer had purchased, she towel-dried her hair and pulled it back into a ponytail. She pulled a pair of jeans and a lavender sweater from the shopping bags and put them on. After applying a minimal amount of makeup, she returned to the living area of the suite.

Dane was wearing a pair of jeans and a T-shirt that advertised Bobby Flay's restaurant, located on the main level of the hotel.

Savannah had to smile. "That shirt is so you."

Dane glanced up. "At least I'll fit in with the other tourists." His expression warmed. "You look nice."

"Thank you." Steamer took credit for her appearance as he stood and hooked his arm through hers. "Come over here and get something to eat. Hack must have thought he was feeding the whole Army and not just a few of the Army's best men."

Hack waved a shish kebab at him. "Make fun if you will, but at least nobody will leave here hungry."

Savannah handed the bag containing her damp clothes to Hack. "Dane said you would need to scan these or something," she said. "I guess you might as well throw them away. I won't need them again."

Hack took the bag with a wary look. "I'll get rid of them."

She put some food on a plate and walked back toward the fire. She sat on the stone hearth where she could enjoy the warmth while she ate. The meeting that was already in progress continued.

"We need to talk about this latest operation," Dane said. "First of all, why did you give me such lame charges? Tax evasion, bank fraud—people probably think I'm a sissy."

"Sorry, sir," Owl apologized for the group.

Hack scowled. "Yeah, next time we'll have you accused of murder and armed robbery."

"At least I'd get some respect if I ended up in prison," Dane muttered. "Now fill me in on the operation."

The guys took turns telling how they had planned it. Finally Steamer said, "And Savannah gets total credit for the plan's conception, execution, and success."

Dane raised an eyebrow in her direction. "What do you have to say to that?"

"I'm responsible, all right," Savannah admitted. "But it didn't work the way I planned."

"Like you said," Hack contributed with his mouth full, "we got Dane."

"Thanks to you," she said.

"You had a good concept," Owl interjected quickly. "And even if none of your plans was directly responsible for Dane's release, they provided distractions that helped Hack's plan to succeed."

"So we all agree that all's well that ends well," Steamer said.

Dane shook his head. "I don't agree with that. Getting involved with Giordano was an unnecessary risk. Savannah attending a meeting where she knew Ferrante would be present was borderline insane."

Savannah struggled to keep her tone level. "Your life was in danger. I was nearly *insane* with worry."

He ignored this defense and turned to his men. "I hold you all responsible for letting Savannah do such foolish things."

They hung their heads in shame. "Sorry, sir," Owl said for the group.

Savannah was speechless. She knew the operation had been flawed and wasn't expecting praise. But she did think he'd at least appreciate that they'd cared enough to try and rescue him.

"I know how persuasive she can be," Dane continued, and the look on his face was anything but grateful. "So like the closet incident in New Orleans, I'm going to let it go." He swung around to Savannah again. "But I want you to promise me right now that you'll never do anything so dangerous again. In fact, I'm going to have to make that a requirement for your continued membership in the team."

She put her food aside and stood. "You seriously expect me to promise that I won't try to help you?"

Dane nodded. "Once you got away from Ferrante, you should have stayed in a secure situation. I would have found a way to escape on my own eventually."

Savannah decided she'd had enough. Narrowing her eyes at him, with deliberation she said, "Like you found a way to escape from that Russian prison?"

Various degrees of shock registered in the eyes of Dane's men, and the air in the room sizzled with tension.

Dane stood to face her, and when their eyes met, instead of the anger she expected, she found a cold, distant expression. "That was different."

She'd gone too far to back down now. "The only difference is that this time you unwisely surrendered yourself to the enemy. *You* should have remained in a secure situation, just as you advised me to do. But you didn't because you were worried about me."

His lips formed a hard, angry line. "I knew you couldn't free yourself."

"I did get away from Ferrante and without your help!" she reminded him.

They stared at each other, both hurt and furious—both trying to pretend to be otherwise.

Finally Savannah took a deep breath and said, "We considered the options and decided that we didn't want to wait around until Ferrante got tired of your company and had his men shoot you."

"I can take care of myself," Dane insisted. "Now I want you to give me your word that you will never risk your life for mine again."

She waved toward the other members of the team. "Aren't you going to ask them too?"

"I'm not married to them, so it's different," he claimed.

She raised an eyebrow. "Oh, is it?"

Hack intervened. "We're wasting time with this bickering. Let's figure out our next move before Ferrante storms through the door."

Savannah couldn't control a little shudder at the thought of Ferrante, and her anger toward Dane dissipated. She sat back on the hearth and suggested, "Maybe he'll leave us alone this time?"

Dane returned to the couch and leaned his head against the back. As he stared at the ceiling, he said, "We've humiliated Ferrante, so now he has more reason than ever before to come after us."

"No question," Steamer agreed. "He'll come."

"It's just a matter of when," Owl added morosely.

Doc scooted forward onto the edge of his chair. "So what are our options?"

Dane kept his eyes on the ceiling. "The way I see it, we have two. We can take the defensive approach and try to hide from him—"

"For how long?" Savannah asked.

"Indefinitely," Dane replied grimly.

Savannah shook her head. "What's the other option?"

"We can go to a secure location and wait openly for him to come to us," Dane replied.

"Trap him?" Steamer asked.

Doc looked unhappy. "That hasn't worked out too well the past few times we've tried it."

"We did trap him once," Steamer pointed out. "But the FBI let him go."

"The FBI is on our side now," Savannah said.

"We can't count on that too much," Dane said.

"A trap may not be a perfect idea, but it's better than hiding," Owl said. "That gives us more control."

"Yes," Doc agreed, "I hate the idea of always having to look over our shoulders. We want Caroline to live a normal life."

"If we set a trap, we've still got to wait for Ferrante to take the bait," Steamer said.

Dane frowned. "I don't think we'll have to wait long."

Hack slammed one of his huge fists down on the coffee table. "I knew we shouldn't have gotten involved with Rosemary Ferrante. If we'd left his daughter alone, Ferrante might not be so dedicated to this vendetta."

Savannah took his comment personally. "The vendetta started long before Rosemary came to see me at Fort Belvoir," she insisted. "Ferrante kidnapped Caroline. He recruited Cam to spy on the team, and he killed Wes. He came after *us*." She waved around the room to include them all. "We're just trying to protect ourselves."

"You two can continue that debate later," Dane said. "Right now we've got to make some decisions. I agree with Owl. Setting a trap is marginally better than trying to hide."

"Hiding sounds so cowardly." Steamer's expression showed his distaste.

"What will happen when Ferrante comes?" Savannah forced herself to ask.

"Then we'll shoot him," Dane said. "In self-defense."

"We're done with depending on the legal system," Steamer agreed.

Savannah was shaken by this revelation. "What about Caroline?" she asked. "How will we make sure Ferrante doesn't go after her instead?"

"Because she'll be with us," Dane replied.

Savannah felt tears sting her eyes. She missed her daughter terribly, but Caroline's safety was the most important consideration. "Won't that be dangerous for her?"

"As long as Ferrante is breathing, Caroline is in danger," Hack said.

"That's true," Dane agreed. "But no one will protect her better than we will."

"We can't trust her safety to anyone else," Doc confirmed.

"When will we get her?" Savannah asked.

Dane checked his watch. "In a few hours. First we'll swing by Fort Belvoir to ask for the general's help." He looked over at Owl. "Did you arrange a charter plane for us?"

Owl nodded. "It's ready."

"Doc, call the general, and ask him to wait at his office until we can get there," Dane further requested. "I know it's almost time for him to go, but he's worked late before."

Doc walked into the room's kitchenette to make his phone call.

"How much will we involve General Steele and the FBI?" Owl asked.

"Just enough to test his loyalty," Dane replied. "If we set our trap up right, we might be able to snare more than one guilty party."

Savannah frowned. "You're going to set the general up? But didn't he just prove his loyalty by refusing to prosecute Hack and the other guys?"

Dane nodded. "Based on recent events, it seems like the general and Agent Gray are with us, but it's time we knew for sure."

Doc rejoined them. "The general will be waiting for us when we get to Fort Belvoir. And Rosemary Allen is fine. She checked herself in to George Washington Memorial, and she'll be there until her baby is born, which should be any day."

"Thanks Doc," Dane told the medic. "We'll meet with the general and secure the cabin. Then we'll go get Caroline and bring her home."

Savannah was nearly overwhelmed by the thought of a reunion with Caroline and the idea that the three of them actually had a home together now.

"I've got twenty-five employees scattered in various places around Atlantic City," Hack said. "If we're closing things down here, I need to reassign them."

"You do that and then meet us at the airport."

Hack stood, ready to obey. "Where do you want me to set them up?"

"In strategic positions around my cabin," Dane replied.

"We're setting a trap for Ferrante at your cabin?" Savannah clarified.

He nodded. "It's the best place."

Savannah frowned. "But when we were looking for a location to hide Rosemary, you said you wouldn't risk it, since a battle there might destroy your property."

"I said I wouldn't risk my property for Rosemary Ferrante," Dane corrected. "I'd risk most anything for Caroline."

Savannah didn't trust her voice, so she just nodded. He was impossible and incomprehensible, but at least she knew he loved Caroline. And for that she was grateful.

"Go get the new stuff Steamer bought you at ridiculously inflated prices from the trendy boutiques downstairs," Dane said. "Then we'll go."

When she returned with her duffel bag, only Dane remained. He was standing impatiently by the door, waiting for her. As she joined him, she gave the suite one last longing look.

Dane noticed and leaned down to whisper, "I'm not ready for this yet. You'll have to be patient with me."

She stared into his eyes and saw the vulnerability he was usually so careful to hide. Slowly she nodded. "Okay."

He kissed her briefly before leading her into the hallway.

CHAPTER 7

THE SUN WAS STARTING TO SET when they walked out of the Borgata, headed for the Atlantic City International Airport and eventually Fort Belvoir. Now that their course had been determined, Savannah was frustrated by the necessity of going to see the general. She just wanted to collect her daughter and get settled in at Dane's cabin—finally at home with the people she loved.

After the short drive to the airport, they boarded the charter plane and settled into their seats. Dane utilized the flight to discuss the upcoming confrontation.

Savannah watched Dane in confusion, unsure how to behave toward him. She wanted to hold his hand, to discuss their future together, to ask if he planned to adopt Caroline. But such a conversation couldn't take place in front of his men. So she kept her questions to herself.

After the plane landed, Dane ushered her outside. On the tarmac they found General Steele's personal driver and a minivan instead of the vehicles Dane had requested. Savannah could tell Dane was unhappy, but he didn't complain. They all got into the minivan and headed toward Fort Belvoir. Without privacy, they all remained quiet during the drive.

They were dropped off at the Intelligence Center, and Savannah led the way up the steps and into the building. The halls were familiar and comforting. When they reached the reception area in front of the general's office, Savannah stopped and stared at the woman sitting at the reception desk.

"Louise," she breathed.

The general's former secretary looked up and smiled. "Hey, Savannah. I see Major Dane is still getting you into trouble."

"I've missed you too, Louise," Dane replied.

"But what are you doing here?" Savannah finally managed. Louise was retired and had sworn never to darken the door of the Intelligence Center again.

Louise shrugged. "The general needed someone to replace Lieutenant Hardy—for obvious reasons."

Savannah rolled her eyes. "Very obvious."

"Since he's short on time and can't trust much of anyone, he convinced me to come back temporarily."

Savannah was amazed. "I didn't think anything could bring you out of retirement."

"Only the general," Louise replied. "I'll let him know you're here."

Dane knocked on the general's door. "That won't be necessary."

"Well," Louise said, "since apparently you all don't need me, I'll be heading home."

By the time the general opened his door, Louise was halfway down the hall. The general gave Savannah a welcoming hug, which she accepted, feeling a little disloyal since part of the new operation included a test to see if the general could be trusted. But she decided that if he was guilty of betraying Dane, he deserved it. And if he wasn't, then they would all be friends again.

The general and Dane shook hands.

"It's good to have you out of Ferrante's grasp," General Steele said with a smile.

"Thanks for your support," Dane replied.

"I'm glad we were able to help you."

The men took seats around the room. Dane sat in one of the chairs in front of the general's desk and waved for Savannah to take the other one. Once they were all settled, Dane outlined the situation for the general.

"We know that Ferrante will come after us. It's only a matter of time."

The general nodded. "How do you plan to handle that?"

"We're going to set ourselves up at my cabin and wait for him to come."

"I can provide part of the security," Hack interjected, "but we'll need more from the Army. We'll also need specialized equipment like helicopters, night-vision goggles, etc."

The general nodded. "I'll get you whatever you need, but you've got to keep it quiet. The armed invasions we had planned were not popular with my superiors, and if I'm not careful, I'll be demoted and of no use to anyone."

There was general agreement around the room. They might not trust the general completely, but he was definitely better than an untested outsider.

"We're expecting a pretty strong backlash from the press over Savannah's boycott," the general said. "When the paper comes out tomorrow with the wedding photographs, it's going to look like she tricked the media and the public. It could turn nasty."

"So what can we do to counteract that?" Dane asked.

The general leaned forward onto his desk. "Agent Gray is willing to make a public statement saying that Savannah was working undercover for the FBI at the time the pictures were taken—trying to help them collect evidence against Ferrante."

"That's not too far from the truth," Steamer pointed out.

"He'll say that they appreciate the broad support the public has given the boycott, but it has now served its purpose," the general continued. "And then he'll request that all protest against those businesses cease."

"What is his price for helping Savannah?" Dane asked.

"He didn't name one," the general replied. "Maybe he thinks he owes you."

Dane nodded. "He does."

"I say we take that deal," Hack advised. "And if Savannah lies low for a few days, it should blow over."

"Then that's what we'll do," Dane decided.

The general's phone started to ring, and he frowned at the console on his desk. "Someone is calling from the receptionist's desk outside."

"Louise went home," Savannah said. "Do you want me to go out and see who it is?"

Every man in the room shook his head.

The general punched a button and said, "Steele."

"General?" Corporal Benjamin's voice asked tentatively. "I heard that you were meeting with Major Dane, and I have something I need to give him."

"Just a minute," the general said curtly. He disconnected the call. "Benjamin has been hanging around my offices for the past few days. He's becoming a real annoyance."

Savannah waited to see how Dane was going to handle this, since the corporal had been assigned to spy on things at the Intelligence Center and on the general specifically.

"The kid can be a pain," Dane agreed, "but he's a hard worker, and the Army can use more like him."

"He has aspirations to be a part of the team," Savannah explained.

The general raised an eyebrow. "I didn't know you were taking applications."

Dane scowled. "We're not. But the kid has been helpful a couple of times in the past."

"So do you want me to let him in?" the general asked.

Dane shook his head. "Nah. Like you said, he's annoying." He turned to Savannah. "Now you can see what he wants. Hack, go with her."

Savannah stood and walked to the door with Hack right behind her. They found Corporal Benjamin pacing nervously in the outer office.

"Where's Major Dane?" he asked, looking over Savannah's shoulder at the door that Hack was closing firmly behind them.

"He's in an important meeting with the general," she said in an effort to keep from hurting the corporal's feelings.

"Tell us what you need, and we'll pass it on," Hack promised halfheartedly.

The corporal looked down at an envelope in his hand. "I have something to give him. I was told that it was very important and for the major's eyes only."

This sounded mildly intriguing, and Savannah studied the envelope more carefully. It was a standard Army internal mail envelope with Dane's name scrawled across the front. Underneath his name were the words *Operation AWOL.*

Savannah pointed to the name of the operation and asked Hack, "Are we still actively working on this?"

Hack shrugged. "I guess—if we ever have time in between rescue operations."

She held out her hand. "I actually initiated Operation AWOL, so I can take it."

Corporal Benjamin seemed uneasy. "I was told to give it to the major personally."

"That's because he is the CO of the covert operations team," Savannah explained patiently. "But he's busy now, and this relates to an operation that has low priority at the moment. So thank you for delivering it. I'll take charge of it now."

The corporal reluctantly surrendered the envelope. "I also wanted to tell Major Dane that I'm glad he got away from Mario Ferrante."

"I'll tell him for you," Savannah promised.

"They told me to stop monitoring the boycott on Ferrante's businesses." He sounded sad.

"Yes, that operation is over." Savannah was getting impatient.

He lowered his voice. "And I've been keeping an eye on the general like you said."

"We appreciate it," Savannah assured the young man.

"If there's anything else I can do to help the team . . ." he pointed at the envelope, "with that operation or anything else, all Major Dane needs to do is let me know."

"Just keep doing what we told you to do before," Hack said. "Keep your eyes and ears open. If you hear information on Ferrante or anything else you think we should know, call the number we gave you."

With one last longing glance at the general's door, Corporal Benjamin walked away. Savannah did feel a little sorry for him. Not so long ago, she was in his position, and she had resented the exclusion deeply. Now it made perfect sense to her to keep the corporal on the fringes of the operation until he'd proven himself trustworthy.

Her eyes moved from the corporal to the envelope in her hand. Since it was related to the operation she had initiated and funded, she felt completely justified in reading whatever the envelope contained. So as they walked back into the office, she tore open the envelope and extracted a small stack of papers.

"What is it?" Dane asked.

"I'm not sure." She turned the coversheet over and skimmed the first page. "These are the lab results you ordered while trying to find a match to my DNA in the government database." As she continued reading, her heart started to pound. She glanced up at the men who were all staring at her. "It says they found one positive match." Her lips trembled. "You found my father."

Dane stood and started toward her. "Savannah." His tone was a warning and strangely kind. He held out his hand. "Don't waste your time on that now. We've got more important things to worry about."

She gave him an incredulous look. "I think we've got a few seconds to invest in reading a lab report that claims to have found a positive match to my DNA." She returned her eyes to the sheet, and as she read, she could feel everyone staring at her. She sensed their curiosity and their concern.

"Savannah! I'm serious. Give me that." Dane grabbed the papers just as she saw the name listed under "Father—99.93% positive match." The shock was so profound that for a few seconds, she forgot where she was. She seemed to slip into an alternate dimension where she was alone with that hateful, horrible name. Dane's arms surrounded her in a futile attempt at comfort, and she was brought back to the terrible present.

She looked into his eyes and saw anxiety but no surprise. "You knew?" she whispered.

He nodded. "Ferrante told me."

"And when were you going to tell me that I'm the child of a monster?" she demanded. Her voice sounded hysterical even to her own ears, and tears leaked unchecked from her eyes.

"I was going to tell you soon," he claimed, but there was no conviction in his voice.

Savannah was still struggling to get her mind around the horrific news. "All those years I was dreaming of my father as an FBI agent . . . when really he was a super-criminal." She had grown up feeling alone and deserted. Now she knew that there were worse things than belonging to no one.

"Your mother was the FBI agent," Dane said gently. "She was working undercover in Ferrante's organization and provided some excellent intelligence until Ferrante got suspicious. Ferrante didn't say so, but I think he was in love with her and took her betrayal hard. He confronted her, and . . . well . . . he raped her."

"And I was the result." Savannah clutched her stomach. The pain was so acute, she wasn't sure she could survive it. She was not who she thought she was. She was the product of evil—all the way down to a cellular level.

Dane held her tight. "He didn't know about you until he saw you on television, doing one of those ads for the Child Advocacy Center. You look so much like your mother that he realized right away that you had to be her daughter. Then he did some checking, and based on the dates, he realized that you had to be his child. Whether something snapped then or whether he's always been deranged, I don't know. But that's when his evil obsession with you began."

Savannah tried to think. "So it was never about Wes?"

"No," Dane confirmed reluctantly. "It was always about you. He recruited Cam and Wes because of their connection to you. Since then he's developed a grudge against me, but it all started with you and your relationship to him."

Her eyes narrowed. "And why didn't you tell me immediately after we rescued you?"

"During our wedding vows?" he challenged.

"How about on the Coast Guard boat or in the hotel suite or during the plane ride from Atlantic City? It's not like you haven't had a chance."

"I wanted to wait until I was sure that we'd created a safe environment for you and Caroline—"

"Caroline!" she cried as a new wave of agony washed over her. "Because of me, her *grandfather* is Mario Ferrante!"

"The only thing you and Caroline have in common with Ferrante is DNA," Dane replied firmly. "You're making more of this than it deserves."

She looked at him incredulously. "It would be impossible to make too much of this." Suddenly the reason for his odd, ungroomlike behavior became clear. "That's why you're not ready for a *honeymoon*," she whispered. "Because you're afraid you'll father a child that is part monster!"

Dane looked over at his men and General Steele, who had been watching in unified discomfort. "Excuse us, please," he said. Then he led Savannah out into the reception area and across the hall to her office. Once the door was closed behind them, he said, "You need to get a hold of yourself."

Savannah dissolved into tears. He held her while she sobbed. Finally she managed to say, "It's more than just the fact that I'm related to Mario Ferrante. It's the death of the dream that my father was someone good and would one day reenter my life."

He rubbed her back. "I know."

"All these years, I've tried to picture my father. I've given him all kinds of excuses for leaving us and ignored all the bad possibilities. But this is worse than anything I could ever have imagined."

"Yes."

"Ferrante ruined everything."

"He brought us together," Dane reminded her. "And in a way, he's given you your mother back."

"My mother?" she repeated.

"She was a hero," Dane said. "Not just for her country, but for you."

Savannah would need time to rethink her relationship with her mother. And time was something she didn't have now. "My entire existence is a terrible mistake. I'm the result of a *crime*." She forced herself to meet his eyes. "I should never have been born."

He stroked her hair. "I'm sorry for the circumstances of your birth, but I don't regret the fact that you exist."

She shook her head. "I used to feel so sorry for Rosemary because she had to pass the Ferrante legacy down to her children. And now look at me!"

He took her face in his hands. "You're all your mother has to show for her life."

Fresh tears leaked out onto her cheeks. "Are you trying to make me feel better or worse?"

"Better, definitely."

She looked away. "I appreciate you trying, and maybe eventually I'll come to grips with this . . . horror. But right now, nothing can make me feel better."

"Wasn't it you who, just a few days ago, was giving me a lecture about putting the past behind me and living the best life I can? Maybe you should take your own advice."

"You have to deal with what you've done. I have to deal with what I *am*."

"Will you stop that?" he demanded. "Nothing has changed about you. You're the same person you were a few minutes ago—before you knew."

She narrowed her eyes at him. "So you don't mind being married to Mario Ferrante's daughter?" Just saying the words made her shudder.

"Your biological relationship to Ferrante does change things," he admitted. "It makes your life more dangerous. And if you're married to me, you are entitled to the Army's protection—both officially and unofficially."

She was thankful for the numbness that kept this new emotional blow from hurting too much. "So you want to stay married for safety reasons, but you want to keep our relationship as it is? You'll still sleep in your room, and Caroline and I will sleep in the guest room?"

"Yes," Dane confirmed as if this were the most logical thing in the world. "Once the situation is settled, we'll contend with my nightmares, and then maybe things can change."

Savannah turned away so he wouldn't see the tears in her eyes. The only thing worse than not having him at all would be having him under these limited circumstances. "I appreciate the gallant offer of your name and your protection," she told him. "But no thanks. I don't need your pity."

"I don't pity you." It was an obvious lie.

"Then say you married me out of love," she demanded.

"I participated in Giordano's impromptu wedding so we could get safely away from Ferrante."

She shook her head. "If that was true, you would have accepted my offer of an annulment. You didn't want to marry me before, because you felt like you would make me worse by association. But now, knowing who I really am, you're willing to be married to me, but only in a limited way."

"No." But she saw the truth in his eyes. Because she was Ferrante's daughter—and therefore the lowest form of life—he didn't have to feel guilty about including her in what he considered his miserable life.

"I don't need another buddy or another bodyguard," she told him. "I need a husband."

He stared back. "I don't know what you want me to say, Savannah."

"I don't want you to say anything," she told him. "I just want to get out of here and collect Caroline before her psychotic grandfather finds her."

CHAPTER 8

SAVANNAH WALKED ACROSS TO GENERAL Steele's office, but she didn't go inside. She knew the team and the general would accept her and love her in spite of her disgraceful genealogy. But she just wasn't quite ready to face them yet.

Dane came to a stop beside her and opened his mouth to say something. Then he thought better of it and just walked by her and into the general's office. He left the door open, and she assumed this was so he could keep an eye on her. Whether he was trying to prevent her from being abducted or from running away was anyone's guess.

"Let's wrap this up quickly," Dane said to the others in the room. "Hack, Savannah and I are going to get Caroline. I'd like you to come with us."

"I'm ready to go," Hack replied. "Savannah's Yukon is parked in front with two escort cars."

"Everybody else knows what to do?" Dane asked the others.

Savannah heard a series of affirmative murmurs.

"Then let's get busy," Dane said.

The men all kept their eyes averted from Savannah as they walked out of the general's office. She didn't hold this against them. She knew they were just trying to keep from picking sides in this new war between her and Dane.

As Dane passed her, he grabbed Savannah by the cast-free hand and pulled her down the dark hallway. The other team members fell into place behind them.

When they got to the curb in front of the Intelligence Center, Savannah jerked her hand away and asked, "Wasn't it risky to let General Steele hear our plans to get Caroline?"

"It would have been if that was really the plan," Dane replied. "We're sending a decoy team in your Yukon to my sister's house in Tennessee, where the general and everyone else thinks Caroline is staying. Once we're sure all attention is directed there, we'll go get Caroline."

"At the secure, secret location where I stashed her," Hack offered hesitantly.

Savannah gave him the closest thing to a smile she could muster. "Thank you."

Hack nodded and then asked Dane, "Which car do you want me to take?"

"You ride in the escort car," Dane said. Then he waved toward the Yukon. "Savannah, you ride here with me."

She was mentally and physically exhausted and didn't want to discuss her father or her mother or her loveless marriage or her messed-up life anymore. So she shook her head and said, "I'd rather ride with Hack."

When Dane spoke, his tone was steely. "You were in charge while I was gone, but I'm back, and now I give the orders. You're riding with me if I have to pick you up and carry you to the Yukon. I hope you won't force me to inflict that indignity on you—again."

Savannah clenched her good hand into a tight fist and was trying to think of a suitable response when Hack inserted himself into the conversation.

"Savannah did do a good job of running the team while you were gone," he told Dane. "Thanks to her, you're a free man right now. And while you are in charge of the team, with all due respect, sir, she can ride wherever she wants to."

Savannah watched the two men face off with a sad sense of déjà vu. This wasn't the first time she'd come between Dane and one of his men. Anxious to avoid similarly catastrophic results, she stepped between them.

"Thanks, Hack," she told him sincerely. "But Dane is in charge, and it was childish of me to disobey an order. I'll ride in the Yukon."

The big man looked uncertain. "As long as it's what you want."

"It is," she assured him. Then she climbed into the Yukon.

A few seconds later, Dane slipped in under the wheel and started the vehicle. During the drive to Tulley Gate, he stared straight ahead and maintained an icy silence. At the gate, the MPs made a show of searching the vehicles. Dane and Hack used this opportunity to switch cars. A few minutes later, the Yukon proceeded west toward Tennessee while Savannah and Dane, now in a gray sedan with tinted windows, followed a FedEx truck driven by Hack, headed east.

Savannah wanted to know Caroline's exact location, but since Dane was still giving her the silent treatment, she decided her curiosity could wait. So she turned away from him, snuggled against the upholstery, and closed her eyes. Moments later she was sound asleep.

Dane awakened her later by shaking her shoulder. As she returned to consciousness, she remembered the earlier events of the evening. The knowledge that Ferrante was her biological father was still there like a cancer, but she felt more comfortable with her own identity—more ready to fight for her life and her daughter's.

The clock on the dashboard glowed in the darkness. It was five o'clock in the morning. "Where are we going, and how long will it be before we get there?"

"We're going to Fort Hamilton in New York," Dane replied. "And we should be there soon. I'm going to take the next exit so we can get some gas and eat."

Savannah hadn't even realized she was hungry until he mentioned food. Apparently now he could read her stomach in addition to her mind.

When they parked in front of a truck stop, she opened her door and walked into the restaurant. She had expected Hack to join them, but he remained in the FedEx truck. Whether this was a security precaution or just a chance for him to avoid more interpersonal conflict, she didn't know.

Savannah visited the restroom, and when she returned, Dane waved for the waitress.

"We'll order now," he said. He ordered a breakfast sampler for himself and then gestured to Savannah. "Go ahead."

She ordered French toast with hot chocolate. They didn't make small talk while waiting for the meal to be prepared. Dane continually scanned the restaurant, always on guard for an attack. She continually scanned him, always on guard for a sign of how he really felt about things.

When the food arrived, they ate quickly and silently. Afterward, Savannah felt less discouraged. Dane paid the bill and then led the way out to the car. Savannah settled into the front seat and waited for him to bridge the communication gap.

Finally he said, "We'll need to tell Caroline that we're married first thing—before she sees our wedding pictures in the newspaper."

Savannah shook her head. "I don't want her to get her hopes up, since it's not permanent."

Dane looked annoyed. "I told you I'm not going to have the marriage annulled."

She glared at him. "*I'm* going to have it annulled. I won't live a lie."

She saw him stiffen.

"That's up to you, I guess. Just make sure she doesn't see the paper."

"If she does, I'll let you make up a cover story," Savannah told him. "You're good at that."

"If she sees the pictures, we'll tell her the truth—that the wedding was planned just to get me released from Ferrante. And then we'll ignore the subject until we have eliminated the threat Ferrante poses to Caroline. As soon as Ferrante is taken care of, you're free to do whatever you want to about our marriage."

She nodded but took no satisfaction from his comment.

"Unlike Caroline, my sister does read the morning papers."

"Lucky for you, you've already got an excuse ready."

"I'll tell Neely the truth about the wedding, but I won't tell her there's a chance it will be annulled. You might change your mind after you've had some time to think. Like I said before, there are a lot of advantages."

The major advantage was that, as Ferrante had pointed out, the marriage gave Dane legal rights to Caroline. Her resentment grew. "I've had plenty of time to think. I don't want to be married on your terms. If you decide you want a real marriage—not one based on duty and pity and tax breaks—then let me know."

He apparently had no response for this, and they continued their journey in silence.

When they were a few miles outside of Fort Hamilton, Dane called ahead and told his sister that they would be arriving soon. At the fort's gate, Savannah and Dane were both required to show their military ID. They were allowed to pass on into the post, but Hack and his men were required to get out of their vehicles and submit to a search. Under other circumstances, Savannah would have been amused by the look of frustration on Hack's face as they passed by.

Caroline and Neely were staying in a small house near the officer's club that was normally reserved for VIPs. The first light of morning was just beginning to penetrate the darkness when Dane parked in front of the house. Soldiers were standing guard around the grounds, and a guard that looked like one of Hack's men was standing by the front door.

One of the soldiers approached the car when Dane parked at the curb. Dane showed his ID again, and after making a quick phone call, the soldier let them proceed up the sidewalk toward the house. Hack's guard nodded to Dane, obviously recognizing him.

Dane rang the doorbell, and they heard small, running feet from inside.

Then Caroline threw the door open and cried, "You're here!"

Savannah stepped forward and clutched her daughter in a desperate embrace. "Oh, Caroline." She couldn't stop the tears or hide her anguish.

Caroline frowned. "What's wrong, Mama?"

"She missed you," Dane said.

Savannah couldn't speak. She just kept her face buried in Caroline's clean, soft hair and wept. She felt closer to her mother in that moment than she ever had in her life. She wanted more than anything to provide only the best for her daughter. But through simple biology, she had managed to do Caroline a terrible disservice.

"Mama," Caroline said gently. "Don't you think you should let Major Dane get a hug too?"

Savannah pulled back and looked at her daughter. It seemed impossible that something good could come from someone like Mario Ferrante, but Caroline was living proof. And love for her child helped Savannah overcome the debilitating guilt. After taking a deep breath, Savannah smiled and said, "I'm sorry to be such a stingy crybaby. I did miss you, but of course Major Dane wants a hug."

Caroline smiled. "I missed you too. But Neely is pretty fun. She says I'm a lot like her daughter used to be when she was little."

Dane reached down and disengaged Caroline from Savannah. Then he lifted the child into his arms. "I'll take that hug now."

As Savannah watched them together, fresh tears poured. Dane loved Caroline. There was no question of that. Maybe it was selfish of her to deny them the opportunity to be together as a family.

Dane's sister interrupted Savannah's unwelcome thought. She had been standing in the doorway watching the reunion. Now she stepped forward and held out her hand. "It's nice to see you again, Savannah." Dane's sister might not share Dane's dour personality traits, but with her dark hair and eyes, she looked a lot like him. Neely glanced from Savannah to her brother, obviously curious about their relationship.

Savannah stood and accepted the handshake but didn't assuage Neely's curiosity. "Thank you for taking such good care of Caroline."

Dane's sister smiled fondly at the child. "It was a pleasure. I didn't think anyone could live up to Christopher's glowing description. But Caroline does."

"It's cold out here," Dane said, looking around nervously. "Let's go inside."

Neely led the way into their temporary quarters. "Caroline and I have already eaten breakfast, but I can get the cereal out again if the two of you are hungry."

"We stopped a little while ago," Savannah said.

"We're here to get you and take you back to my cabin," Dane told Caroline. "So you need to go pack up your stuff."

"Are all the guys going to be there too?"

"Hack is with us," Dane said. "He's at the front gate and will follow us home. The others will be there by the time we get back."

"Then I'd better go pack my stuff!" Caroline exclaimed.

After Caroline ran toward the back of the house, Dane reached over and hugged Neely. "When you see the morning papers, you'll find out that Savannah and I got married yesterday."

Unlike Dane, Neely hadn't been trained to hide her emotions, so her feelings on the subject were immediately obvious. She looked completely dismayed.

"Don't worry," Savannah said. "It's just a temporary thing. We'll have it annulled as soon as we get the chance."

Dane shot her a cross look, and Neely didn't seem relieved.

"I guess you don't need me to watch Caroline any longer, then?" Neely asked.

Dane nodded. "I'll have a couple of Hack's men take you to the airport so you can catch a flight home."

"To Tennessee?" Savannah confirmed.

Dane nodded again.

"Where you had the decoy car lead Ferrante?"

Neely looked upset. "But if I go home, I'll be alone." She turned to Savannah. "My husband, Raleigh, is out of town on business until the end of next week."

"That won't work," Savannah said.

Dane frowned. "No, it wouldn't be safe for you to be there alone."

"Why doesn't she just come to the cabin with us?" Savannah suggested.

"I guess that's the best thing to do," Dane agreed reluctantly. "Although we've got more people than we can comfortably accommodate already."

This didn't concern Neely. "I'll take your room. You don't sleep anyway."

Hack arrived at this point, complaining about the MPs at the entrance to Fort Hamilton. "They treated me like a criminal," he railed.

"You should be glad they're thorough," Savannah said. "That's what made this a safe place for Caroline during the past week."

Hack scowled. "I'm not complaining about their thoroughness—just their inability to judge character."

"As soon as Caroline gets packed, we're headed back to the cabin," Dane told Hack.

"I'll need to get packed too," Neely realized belatedly and started down the hallway.

Dane gave Hack an exasperated look. "We're going to have to keep my sister for a few days since we led the criminals to her house."

Hack nodded. "Very wise."

Savannah stood and moved toward the hall. "I'll go help Caroline pack."

She found her daughter haphazardly stuffing clothes and toys—most of which Savannah didn't recognize—into a large suitcase.

"So what have you and Neely been doing?" she asked as she stretched the bag open to make room for Caroline's new belongings.

"We've been doing lots of stuff," she reported. "We've gone to movies and shopping."

That explained all the unfamiliar clothes and toys.

"We visited a planetarium and ate at restaurants," Caroline continued. "Neely said if it got warm enough, we'd go to the beach, but it didn't."

"I'm glad you had fun."

"Did you have fun, Mama?"

Savannah pasted on a smile. "Yep. I did get to go to the beach, and I rode on a big boat called a yacht."

"Wow."

Before Savannah had to say more, Dane came to stand in the doorway. "Are you ready to go?"

"I can't really fit all my new stuff into my suitcase," Caroline explained.

Dane frowned at the large but still inadequate suitcase and hollered over his shoulder. "Neely, we need another suitcase."

Neely joined them almost immediately with several bags clutched in her hands. "I didn't realize we'd bought so much."

"We did go shopping a lot," Caroline reminded her.

Neely laughed, and Savannah watched in fascination. Her features were so similar to Dane's, but he never expressed carefree emotion the way she did.

"Yes, we do like to shop," Neely agreed.

While Savannah helped Caroline pack the rest of her things in the shopping bags, Dane arranged for Hack's men to take his sister's things to the car.

"What about the food and stuff?" Neely asked.

"Just leave everything. We'll have a crew come in and clean the house," Dane told her.

Neely looked around anxiously. "We're leaving in such a hurry, I'm afraid I've forgotten something."

"If you've left anything of importance, I'll have the cleaning crew send it to us," Dane said. "Now let's get out of here fast."

Neely seemed a little alarmed but nodded. "I'm ready."

When they got outside, Savannah climbed into the backseat with Caroline, leaving the front for Neely to sit by her brother. Once she had Caroline secured in the seat belt, Savannah glanced at Dane. His jaw was clenched, and she knew he was angry with her for taking the backseat. But she had missed Caroline and didn't have any desire to resume their earlier discussion. And they could argue from different seats just as well as they could side by side. So he could just be mad if he wanted to.

During the drive back to Dane's cabin, Caroline watched a DVD while Neely and Dane talked about their family. Savannah listened with envy, wondering what it would be like to have cousins, aunts, uncles, and parents. At least ones she wasn't afraid of.

They stopped right outside of Washington, DC, for lunch. Hack made a huge production out of checking the McDonald's before allowing them to come inside. Then he rushed them through their meal.

"Has the FBI released Ferrante already?" Savannah finally asked.

"No, but that doesn't mean he doesn't have some of his guys looking for you. So the longer we're out in the open, the more dangerous it becomes."

Savannah reached over and pushed the long blond strands of hair back from Caroline's face. She was so tired of hiding and running from danger. She wondered if her life and Caroline's would always be interrupted by Ferrante and his twisted obsession with them. If so, she wondered if she could stand it.

It was midafternoon by the time they drove through Tylerton. Savannah noticed a few soldiers milling around town and assumed they were part of the security detail General Steele had sent to protect them. She spotted more along the road, and once they turned onto the gravel road that led up to Dane's backyard, there were soldiers interspersed with Hack's employees every few feet.

Hack made them wait in the car until he checked out the cabin. Then he waved for them to come inside. Doc, Steamer, and Owl were waiting in the living room, where a fire was blazing.

Caroline greeted everyone enthusiastically and then offered to show Neely all her Christmas gifts. "This is my new train!"

"It looks a lot like the one Christopher used to play with when he was little," Neely said. "You couldn't walk through our house without tripping over some tracks."

Savannah tried to picture a small Dane playing with his train. Finally she shook her head in defeat. It was impossible to imagine Dane other than how he was now.

"He said he's going to ask his mom where his train is so we can set it up and have races," Caroline told Neely.

"I know where it is," Neely said. "It's in the attic at Mom and Dad's house. There's all kinds of stuff up there. They never throw anything away."

Savannah imagined going through all the paraphernalia, looking at mementos from Dane's childhood and youth. She imagined the insights this would give her into his complicated psyche. Then she wondered if she'd ever get a chance to meet his parents or explore their attic or be a real part of their family.

"There are a bunch of pictures too," Neely said. "It might be fun for you to look at them. Christopher was a bratty kid, but he was cute."

Savannah nodded. "I'd like that."

"Me too," Caroline said. "Especially if there are any pictures of his train."

Caroline drafted Doc to play with her, and soon the medic was connecting track and setting up fake trees and railroad-crossing signs.

"You need groceries," Neely told Dane. "Are you going to assign a regiment to take me to the grocery store in Tylerton?"

Dane shook his head. "No, a platoon should do."

Neely rolled her eyes.

"Hack, will you get an escort group together?"

"I'll go with her myself," Hack replied. "And I'll bring a few guys along, just for show—although all she needs is me."

Neely smiled and patted one of Hack's arms. "I do feel safe in your company." Then she turned to Dane. "While I'm gone, get what you need out of your room so I can move in."

Savannah watched in fascination as Dane nodded. She'd never seen him get bossed around before—and she liked it.

"Can we get you anything at the store, Savannah?" Neely asked.

Savannah shook her head. "No, I'm good, thanks."

"How about you, Caroline?"

The child looked up from the train set long enough to say, "Just doughnuts and hot chocolate."

Once Neely and Hack were gone to the grocery store, Dane sat down at his desk and turned on his laptop. Savannah surveyed the room, looking for an activity to fill her time and finally settling on the dried-up Christmas tree.

It took her nearly an hour to remove all the icicles, ornaments, and lights. During the process, almost every brittle needle fell to Dane's wood-plank floor. After packing away the ornaments and wondering if they would be needed the next year, Savannah swept up the needles. She needed help to get the tree itself outside but didn't want to interrupt Caroline and Doc.

There was no way she was asking Dane to do anything for her. So she walked into the kitchen, where Steamer and Owl were working. Both men looked up from their laptops when she walked in.

"Could one of you to help me get the Christmas tree outside?"

"What's the rush?" Steamer asked.

She shrugged. "There's just something about a Christmas tree after the holidays are over that seems depressing."

"Maybe it's because the dead tree is a reminder that Christmas is over and you have a whole year to wait before it comes around again," Steamer philosophized.

She gave him an exasperated look. "Will you just help me drag it out so we can stop being reminded that all the fun is over?"

He smiled. "I will as soon as I get through with this email."

"I'll help you," Owl surprised her by offering. "I'm not busy."

She gave him a grateful smile. "Thanks."

She led the way into the living room and pulled on her coat while Owl lifted the tree. She opened the front door and followed him to the edge of the woods where he threw the tree into its final resting place. Then they walked back toward the cabin together.

"Doc says you're one of the best snipers in the Army," she said, just making conversation.

Owl nodded.

This was not a promising beginning for a heart-to-heart talk, but Savannah persevered. "Have you always been a good shot?"

"Always," he confirmed. "I used to win all kinds of awards when I was a kid. It didn't matter what kind of contest I entered—I always won. I could win shooting targets or small game or large game. My dad was so proud."

"But you didn't enjoy it," she guessed.

"No, I hated every minute of it. I begged my dad to let me stop, but his theory was that if you're that good at something, you would eventually learn to like it. Otherwise it wasn't natural." He turned brooding eyes to her. "I guess I'm not natural."

"Why did you join the Army if you hated shooting?"

"I wanted to be a pilot. I figured the military was manly enough to please my dad, but I wouldn't ever have to fire a gun again. I got accepted into flight school, but then they found out how good I could shoot."

"And they made you change?"

"Yeah, and compared to the Army, my dad didn't know the first thing about applying pressure."

"I'm sorry."

"Yeah," he agreed, "me too. I tried to keep track of the people I killed at first, but somewhere along the line I lost count."

"You were defending your fellow soldiers and your country."

"That doesn't make it any easier for me to sleep at night. Only God has the right to take a life. How many more people have to die just because I was given this awful talent?"

She didn't have an answer for him, so they stood in silence for a few minutes. Finally she suggested, "Maybe you could quit the Army altogether."

He gave her a quizzical look. "I don't know who I am if I'm not a soldier."

She was saved the necessity of answering when Caroline called to them from the door. "Come in and see the train. Me and Doc have it all fixed."

Owl led the way to the door and stepped aside for Savannah to pass through first. Then they settled down to watch as Caroline played with her train.

Hack and Neely returned with so many groceries that the cabin's limited cabinet space couldn't accommodate them all. Doc and Savannah left the train exhibition to help organize food. Savannah heard Caroline invite Owl to play trains with her. She waited for Owl's polite refusal, but it never came. She walked to the door and looked into the living room. Owl was on his hands and knees, helping Caroline put together a bridge for the train to cross. For the first time since she'd met him, Owl seemed relaxed.

Neely and Doc began preparations for dinner. Savannah offered to help, but Neely said they had it under control. So Savannah walked into the living room. She watched Caroline and Owl for a few minutes, but they didn't need her either. Finally she drifted over to Dane's desk.

"What are you doing?" she asked him.

He glanced up at her. Dark circles framed his eyes, and she knew he was exhausted, but she steeled herself against sympathy.

"We can't remain here indefinitely, so I'm setting up an escape to another country in case it becomes necessary."

It was an intriguing thought. "Where would we go?"

He gave her a long look. "Italy."

She pulled up a chair and sat beside him. "Mind if I watch?"

He shrugged. "Suit yourself."

For the next hour, she watched him make airline reservations and inquire about hotels and tour guides in Milan—all under assumed names. Every once in a while her mind would drift into the realm of fantasy, and she'd pretend that they were a real family and that there really was a dream vacation in their future. Then she'd remember the events of the past twenty-four hours, and reality would come crashing back. She was the daughter of Mario Ferrante—Dane's mortal enemy. There could be no happily ever after for them.

Dane worked steadily and made no attempt at small talk.

Finally she said, "Maybe hiding was a better option than sitting here waiting for Ferrante to attack us."

"That's assuming that there's anywhere on earth Ferrante can't find us," he replied.

"This is just so boring," she said. "It makes me nervous."

"Things will happen soon enough," he assured her. "You won't be trapped here forever."

He'd misunderstood her, but she couldn't think of a way to correct him without taking the conversation to a level where she'd be uncomfortable. So she turned and looked out the window at the setting sun reflecting in the creek. There was a time when she had thought all she wanted from life was to be married to Dane and live in his cabin. The thought that she would leave soon and might never come back was almost unbearably painful. "I'm not in a big hurry to escape," she admitted.

He looked up from the laptop, and their eyes met. He opened his mouth to say something, but Owl came up and interrupted.

"Can I take Caroline outside for some fresh air?" he asked, oblivious to the tension between Dane and Savannah.

"As long as you stay on the porch," Dane permitted as if he were Caroline's parent.

"And as long as she wears her coat," Savannah added, trying not to be resentful of Dane's assumption of her parental authority.

Once they were gone, she said, "Did you know that Owl wanted to be a pilot when he joined the Army?"

Dane frowned. "I knew he was in flight school for a few days after enlistment, but I figured he ended up there by mistake. Owl was born to shoot."

"He hates it," Savannah divulged.

"Hates what?"

"Shooting," she clarified. "You should see if you can get him reclassified and retrained."

"Owl is a talented misfit just like the rest of us," Dane said. "The world doesn't know what to do with us, but the Army needs us. That's especially true of Owl's shooting ability. He has an incredible gift."

"But he *hates* it," Savannah reiterated. "And how he feels should count for something."

"More than duty?" Dane asked.

She nodded. "He's fulfilled his duty many times over, and now he deserves to be happy. He can still serve the Army—just not as a sniper."

At this point their conversation was interrupted again, this time by Neely.

"Dinner's ready, and I made your favorite," she told Dane. "Chicken and dumplings." Neely turned politely to Savannah. "Do you like them?"

"I don't think I've ever eaten chicken and dumplings," Savannah said.

Neely looked appalled. "You don't know what you've been missing."

Everyone gathered around the table, and Neely started serving. The food was wonderful, and Dane's sister seemed to enjoy having a crowd to feed. After they'd finished eating, Neely passed out pieces of homemade pecan pie—which she claimed was also a favorite of Dane's—and instructed the group to move to the living room, where they could enjoy the fire. There she entertained them with stories from her childhood. Everyone seemed to enjoy the stories—except Dane, who claimed that his sister's memory was faulty.

When Caroline fell asleep, Dane leaned over Savannah to pick the child up. "Party's over," he announced.

"We ladies will retire and leave you men to . . . whatever it is you do at night instead of sleep," Neely said.

"That would be guard you and keep you safe," Steamer provided.

Neely included them all in her smile. "Thanks!"

Savannah trailed behind Dane as he carried Caroline up the stairs. When they reached the guest room, she ducked in front of him and turned back the covers on the bed under the window. She smiled, thinking how happy Caroline would be the next morning when she saw the familiar sunrise.

Dane put the child on the bed and stepped back to watch while Savannah tucked the covers securely around her daughter. When she was finished, she stood and faced Dane. Their eyes met and held. He reached out a hand, and Savannah wanted nothing more than to slip into the comfort of his arms. But he had to commit to her and a real marriage first.

So she ignored his hand and said, "Thank you for bringing Caroline up."

He nodded and let his hand fall to his side. "Good night." He walked out into the hallway, closing the door firmly behind him.

The closed door seemed symbolic of her relationship with Dane, and Savannah collapsed onto her bed, too tired and discouraged to even cry.

CHAPTER 9

THE NEXT TWO DAYS PASSED in simple routine. Neely prepared the meals and managed the household with minimal assistance. Caroline played with her toys, and Dane and his men worried about safety and waited for word that Ferrante had been released from federal custody. Only Savannah had no task, no purpose.

In the evenings they gathered around the fire after dinner to eat dessert. Dane excluded himself from these gatherings by sitting at his desk—close enough to hear everything his sister disclosed, but far enough away to claim nonparticipation.

One night Neely divulged that she was planning to start her own business.

"Now that my kids have left the nest, I find myself with a lot of extra time on my hands," she told the group. "My husband travels constantly with his job, and, well, you can only dust and vacuum just so much."

"Why don't you go with Raleigh when he travels," Dane suggested from his desk, proving that he was paying attention to their conversation.

Neely looked aghast. "You think sitting alone in a hotel room would be better than being alone at home?"

Dane shrugged. "I guess not."

"So what is this business you're starting?" Savannah asked, partly to be polite and partly because she could tell it annoyed Dane.

"I'm calling it Dinner in a Cup."

Dane's expression was comical. "What?"

"I was at the airport a few months ago and noticed how people look so stressed and how the food options are unhealthy and unappetizing," Neely explained. "So I thought you could take a Styrofoam cup and put potatoes or rice or pasta on the bottom. Then add some type of meat with gravy. Then a vegetable as the next layer and top it with a roll. That would be a healthy meal that would stay warm while airline passengers were standing in line or waiting to board. So what do you think?"

"I'm not sure about it, Neely," Dane said. "It doesn't sound all that appetizing to me."

"It sounds delicious to me!" Hack disagreed.

Neely beamed at him. "Good, because I've already hired a lawyer to help me incorporate, and I've arranged with the Nashville airport to rent me some space. I've made a logo—it's a cup with *dinner* written inside it. I've met with a food supplier and plan to open for business on February first."

"You're serious about this?" Dane asked.

"Completely," she assured him.

"What does Raleigh think?"

Neely shrugged. "He said to do whatever makes me happy."

"I'm going to buy a plane ticket and fly to Nashville on February first just to eat one of your dinners in a cup," Hack said. "Or two or three."

Neely gave him a hug. "Your first one will be on the house."

The subject changed, and finally the evening ended. Dane carried Caroline upstairs as usual. Then he left Savannah alone and miserable as was also becoming standard practice.

Savannah's only defense against the pain was to keep her distance from Dane, emotionally as well as physically. Sometimes she would see him watching her, but she avoided his gaze. At times she wondered if they could ever work through their problems. Maybe she could accept her parentage and he could stop feeling sorry for her and want a normal marriage relationship instead of one based on his misguided sense of duty. Tears burned her eyes, and she realized that she missed him. It was odd that they could be in the same small house but not together at all.

On the third day, close-quarter confinement and sleep deprivation started to take a toll on everyone. The men became short tempered and argued with each other over inconsequential issues. Caroline begged continually to be allowed to fish or go for a walk or to a movie. Savannah didn't complain openly, but her resentment toward Neely grew as the other woman continued to act like lady of the house and relegated Savannah to the role of tolerated houseguest.

The only good thing about having so much time and so little to do was that it gave Savannah the opportunity to think. She was able to come to terms with herself—at least to some extent. And rather than brood about her father, she decided that she wanted to learn more about her mother.

So on the fourth day of their very unsolitary confinement, Savannah broke her self-imposed gag order and spoke to Dane privately.

She walked over to his desk and said, "Everyone is getting a little stir-crazy, and it's only a matter of time before personality conflicts occur."

He glanced up. "What do you suggest to avoid this?"

"I was thinking we could revive Operation AWOL," she proposed. When he didn't discard the idea offhand, she continued. "We already know who my father is." Saying this didn't hurt as much as she thought it would. "But I still know almost nothing about my mother, and I'd like to know more."

Dane considered this for a few seconds and then nodded. "A project would help take our minds off of the boredom."

"And now that we know she was an FBI agent, it shouldn't be too hard to get some details about her. I'm hoping that my mother has some surviving relatives, even if her parents aren't alive. Which means Caroline has a family. I grew up without roots, and I want to avoid that for Caroline if I can."

Dane nodded. "It's a good idea. We'll gather the guys after lunch and make assignments."

True to his word, as soon as they finished their midday meal, Dane told the team they needed to meet. While Caroline helped Neely with the dishes, Savannah joined the rest of the team around the kitchen table.

"What's up?" Hack asked.

"Savannah has made a good suggestion," Dane replied. "Since we have some spare time . . ."

Steamer laughed. "Spare time is all we got, baby!"

Dane continued as if Steamer hadn't spoken. "Savannah would like to learn more about her mother."

"You sure about this?" Hack asked. "What we've turned up so far isn't great news."

Savannah shrugged. "I don't think it could get any worse, so I'll take my chances."

"Since the circumstances have changed slightly, I'll redo the assignments," Dane told them. "Doc, pressure the FBI into giving you Hope Williams's file." He turned to Hack on his left. "Hack, infiltrate the secret service's systems, and get everything you can about her."

"It will be a pleasure," Hack replied.

"During her adult life she went by the name Karen Laney," Dane continued, "but her real name was Hope Williams. Check under both names and collect every bit of data—even if it seems unimportant. We're trying to get a complete picture of the woman she was, so nothing can be considered insignificant."

Hack nodded. "I've got it."

"Steamer, contact everyone you can find who knew Hope Williams—before and during her short career with the FBI. I want you to talk to former teachers, classmates, coworkers, supervisors, and—most importantly—any surviving relatives. We'll review your notes and decide if there are any leads worth pursuing. This will be a big project, so Savannah can help you with it."

"What about me?" Neely asked from the sink as she was washing dishes. "Do I get an assignment on this operation like Savannah?"

Dane shook his head. "Savannah is a member of the team, so she gets an official assignment."

Neely frowned. "So you've got me here just to cook, wash dishes, and do laundry?"

"You're here because you were scared to go back to Tennessee," Dane reminded her. "Anytime you're ready to go, I'll have Hack take you home."

Neely narrowed her eyes at her little brother. "I'm going to forget you said that this time, but you'd better start showing me a little appreciation, or I'll tell Mother!"

Dane apologized immediately. "We do appreciate you, and I'm sorry if you feel taken for granted. But you still don't get an assignment on my operation. Working with relatives always turns out badly."

Neely shrugged. "I guess I don't really have time to do more than my housekeeping duties anyway." She turned to Caroline. "Would you like to watch a movie with me?"

Caroline accepted this invitation, and after they left, Owl asked, "What about me? What's my assignment?"

"I've got an assignment for you, but it's not specifically related to this new operation," Dane told him. "It will have a broader effect."

Everyone was paying attention now.

"What is Owl going to do?" Steamer asked. "Sneak into the federal prison and shoot Ferrante?"

Dane smiled. "That's not a terrible idea, but it's also not Owl's assignment. He's going to learn to fly a plane. His first lesson is at the Fredericksburg airport in two hours."

Owl seemed stunned, and if Savannah hadn't been trying to convince Dane she didn't want to stay married to him, she would have kissed him.

Hack scowled. "Owl's going to learn to fly?"

"Why?" Steamer asked.

"Since Cam's gone, I'm the only pilot on the team, and you know how I hate to operate without a backup," Dane explained. "Owl was in the Army's flight school before they plucked him out to be a shooter, so he's the obvious choice."

"I'm taking flight lessons?" Owl repeated.

Dane nodded. "Starting today."

"Why are you having him take lessons at Fredericksburg instead of at Fort Belvoir?" Steamer wanted to know.

"Because if the Army finds out he can shoot *and* fly, they'll take him away from us in a heartbeat," Dane responded.

Hack grinned. "Yeah, being too talented can have its drawbacks."

"They're already trying to reassign him without flying skills," Doc said. "We get three or four inquiries about him every day. I keep replying that he's on medical leave, but it's only a matter of time . . ."

"We'll figure that out later," Dane said. "But for now Owl is going to learn to fly. Are you okay with that assignment?"

"Yes, *sir!*" Owl managed.

Dane smiled, and Savannah's heart beat a little faster.

"Then make sure you're at hangar six at the Fredericksburg Airport at three o'clock." Dane looked up at the rest of the group. "Everyone has their assignments. Let's get busy."

Savannah enjoyed the rest of the afternoon. Working with Steamer was always entertaining, and they made remarkably good progress. They found an online site that listed the students who graduated from high school with her mother. Then they were able to track down phone numbers for a third of them. The rest Steamer turned over to the company Dane used for background checks in hopes that they would be able to get contact information.

"It was a fairly big senior class, and they graduated over thirty years ago, so a lot of people probably didn't even know her, and some of the ones who did won't remember her," Steamer warned.

She nodded. "I don't have my hopes up too high." She pointed to the first name on the list. "Make the call."

Steamer called a man named Jason Alexander. He claimed to have been Hope's high school sweetheart. He said they dated steadily until the middle of their senior year. "All of the sudden, Hope lost interest in me," he said. "We were supposed to go to the prom together, but she said she'd changed her mind and didn't even want to go. I'm pretty sure she'd met someone else. The rumor was that she was seeing a married man, maybe an FBI agent. But I never knew for sure. Right after graduation, she left town, and I never saw her again."

Steamer asked a few more questions and then got contact information from Mr. Alexander before disconnecting the call. He turned to Savannah and said, "I'm not sure we can trust that guy."

"Why not?"

He tapped the computer screen, where a picture of the senior class was displayed. "Hope was gorgeous."

Savannah looked at the picture of her mother, young and carefree, smiling at the camera.

"And Alexander wasn't." Steamer moved his finger to the face identified in the caption.

"Maybe she saw something else in him—besides looks."

"Or maybe he dreamed of a girl like Hope being interested in him, and now all these years later—when she's dead—he figures he can claim association even if there wasn't one."

"What about his mention of the FBI agent?"

"Apparently that was a pretty widely known rumor," Steamer said. "Anyone could have heard that."

Savannah stared at the faces on the computer screen. "How will we know for sure?"

"We'll ask the other people we interview if they remember the two of them being a couple."

Steamer tried two more men who didn't remember Hope, and left messages on several answering machines. He handed the phone to Savannah. "Now it's your turn. You get the idea."

She nodded, unaccountably nervous. She would be talking to people who knew her mother back when she was young and had a future in front of her. She dialed the first number on the list. When a woman answered, Savannah asked to speak to Leslie.

"This is Leslie," a wary voice replied.

"My name is Savannah McLaughlin, and I'm researching a story about a woman who went to high school with you. I was wondering if you had time to answer a few questions."

"Who are you researching?" Leslie asked, sounding vaguely curious.

"Hope Williams."

There was a brief silence. Leslie said, "Hope is dead. Why are you doing research on her?"

"We're doing a story about former FBI agents," Savannah improvised. "Did you know she was an agent?"

"No," Leslie replied. "I knew she wanted to be one. It was all she talked about during our senior year of high school. She'd met a recruiter at a college fair, and he convinced her to apply for some college scholarships that the FBI offers."

"Do you remember his name?"

"Of course not," Leslie replied. "That was thirty years ago."

Savannah tried not to be discouraged. "Were you and Hope close?"

"We were good friends in high school, but we didn't keep in touch after graduation."

"Did she date a guy named Jason Alexander?" Savannah asked.

"Yeah, she and Jason were inseparable until she became obsessed with the FBI."

Savannah phrased her next comment carefully. "He said there were rumors that she was involved with a married agent."

"I think she had a crush on the guy who recruited her," Leslie said. "But the rumors were exaggerated. She just met him for dinner a few times."

Steamer scribbled furiously on a piece of paper and then showed it to Savannah.

"Did you ever meet the FBI recruiter, and could you give me a description of him?" Savannah read.

"I never met him."

Savannah sensed that Leslie's cooperation was waning, so she thanked her for her time and hung up the phone. Her hands were shaking.

"Whew," she told Steamer, "that was more intense than I had expected."

"Put a star by her name," Steamer suggested gently. "Later on you might want to call her back and tell her that you're Hope's daughter. She might even have some pictures or something she'd be willing to email you."

Savannah nodded. "That's a good idea." She squared her shoulders. "Now on to the next name."

The other women on the list didn't remember Hope. One said her name sounded familiar, but she couldn't remember anything specific.

"Now we'll call the teachers," Steamer said.

They only found two teachers who remembered her, and neither of them knew anything about a connection to the FBI.

When they finished, Savannah was disappointed.

"Maybe some of the people we left messages for will call back with details," Steamer encouraged her when they'd called everyone. "Or maybe the background checks will turn up contact information on more of her classmates."

Savannah nodded. "Maybe."

Hack walked over and asked, "How's it going?"

"Savannah's disappointed because we only found three people who knew her mother."

Hack waved a hand. "We're just getting started. We'll find a ton of stuff."

"Try the churches in the area around the school," Dane suggested.

Savannah was surprised. "The churches?"

"You said your mother taught you to pray. Maybe she went to church as a child. If so, the church where the Williamses attended might have records of—or even remember—the family."

"Not a bad idea," Steamer said as he started typing commands into his laptop.

Savannah was suspicious that Dane might be giving them busy work as he had been known to do in the past. But soon Steamer had a list of churches, and they began making phone calls. Finally they spoke with an elderly church secretary who remembered the family.

"I worked with our youth ministry back in those days," the secretary explained, "so I got to know the teenagers quite well. Hope was a pretty girl and friendly. She also had a beautiful singing voice. She did a solo every year in the Christmas service."

This was news to Savannah. She didn't remember her mother ever singing.

"The parents were in poor health and weren't able to attend regularly. We had an outreach bus that would go by and pick Hope up. She was one of our most reliable participants until about the middle of her senior year. That's when she started having an affair with a married man."

"What was his name?" Steamer asked.

"Oh, I don't know that," the woman said. "She never brought him to church or anything. In fact, once she took up with him, she stopped coming to church altogether. I saw her on graduation night and invited her to come to a party I was having for all the seniors at my house, but she said she already had plans. I never saw her again. We later heard that her married boyfriend had gotten her pregnant and then left her. But I can't say that for sure."

Savannah felt fury rise up inside her. People were still telling unsubstantiated rumors about her mother years after her death.

Steamer gave the woman a number to call with additional information and then ended the call quickly. "Maybe we've made enough calls for one day," he said.

Savannah nodded. "I need to go check on Caroline."

She found her daughter playing checkers with Owl in the kitchen.

"How was your first flying lesson?" she asked him.

He grinned. "It was even better than I thought it would be. We're going to do two lessons a day starting tomorrow, so I can get my license quicker."

Savannah was happy for him. "That sounds like a good plan." She glanced at the checker board. "Who's winning?"

Caroline gave her an incredulous look. "Me, of course."

Savannah laughed. "Of course."

After dinner, Savannah gave Caroline a bath and settled her on the couch beside Neely to play Old Maid. Neely looked a little sad, and Savannah remembered what it felt like to be excluded by the team. So she took the time to sit with them for a few minutes.

"You said your husband is out of town on business?" she asked.

Neely nodded. "Raleigh's an accountant for a big firm and has to go around auditing books at their various offices."

"Is he gone a lot then?"

"You have no idea," Neely confirmed. "It didn't bother me too much when the kids were little, because I was so busy. But now my son is in college, and my daughter . . . well, she's grown too. So when my husband travels, I'm alone. I'm not bored," Neely said. "I work part-time at the local library, and I stay busy with church service. But at night, when I come home to a dark house . . . it's lonely. And I feel like I'm just passing time instead of really living and accomplishing something. That's why I decided to create Dinner in a Cup."

Savannah nodded. This she could understand. "My husband died shortly after Caroline was born. It's been very lonely since."

Neely raised an eyebrow. "Your first husband."

Savannah asked Caroline to get some more firewood from the stack on the back porch. Once the child was gone, she said, "Yes, my first husband."

"Do you love him?" Neely angled her head toward the kitchen. "Christopher, I mean?"

"Yes," Savannah admitted.

"And yet you're planning to cancel the marriage?"

"He thinks it's his duty to protect us," Savannah forced herself to say. "And that he can best do so as my husband and Caroline's father."

Caroline walked in with an armload of wood. "Did you call me?"

Savannah smiled at her. "No. Get a little more firewood."

Once Caroline was gone again, Neely whispered, "He loves you."

Savannah nodded. "I know. But I'm beginning to think it's not enough."

Neely didn't have an answer for this. Caroline returned, and they stoked the fire. Then they sat in silence for a few minutes until Dane asked Savannah to join the rest of the team in the kitchen. "We need to have a little meeting."

Savannah stood. "Can you keep an eye on Caroline?"

Neely nodded, and Savannah walked into the kitchen.

"Thanks for waiting for me," she muttered, noticing the meeting was already underway.

"Don't worry, we haven't discussed anything important yet," Owl said.

"Hack just reported that amazingly enough, the FBI is still holding Ferrante," Doc told her.

"But that can't last." Owl's tone was grim.

"When he gets out, I'd bet everything I own that he'll come here," Steamer predicted.

"And if Agent Gray doesn't warn us when he gets released, he could be here without our even knowing it." Hack waved to encompass the area around them.

Savannah shuddered.

Owl smiled in an attempt to comfort her. "And Doc was about to give a report on what he found out about your mother."

"Hope's parents were both retired schoolteachers," Doc told them. "So the family's resources were limited, but they managed. Hope was a good student and had a chance at several academic scholarships. But during her senior year, she developed a sudden interest in working for the FBI."

"After attending a college fair at the beginning of her senior year?" Steamer guessed.

Doc nodded. "The FBI recruiter arranged a scholarship for her, contingent on her joining the bureau upon graduation. She completed the four-year program in three years and then was hired by the FBI."

"The question that keeps nagging at me is why she was recruited in the first place," Steamer said. "She had good grades but not overly impressive."

"No, her grades alone wouldn't have attracted the FBI's attention," Doc agreed.

"Maybe the recruiter was just a rogue agent who used his position to attract beautiful girls," Hack suggested.

"Let's find out who the recruiter was," Dane said. "The FBI is bound to have records."

"I'm already working on that," Doc replied. "And I have a theory about why Hope Williams was targeted and tenaciously recruited."

"What's your theory?" Savannah asked, although she was pretty sure she didn't really want to know.

"I think the recruiter was looking for a specific type," Doc said.

"Ferrante's type?" Dane asked.

"Yes," Doc confirmed.

Hack used his fingers to count off Hope's physical attributes. "Blond, beautiful, Southern."

"With elderly parents who couldn't provide much in the way of support—financial or otherwise," Steamer added.

Owl nodded. "That sounds like FBI criteria."

Dane looked unhappy as he said, "So it's probably safe to assume that she was recruited by the FBI because they thought she would appeal to Mario Ferrante, and nobody would miss her if she disappeared."

"She trained at Quantico for twelve weeks and was then assigned to work undercover in Ferrante's organization," Doc continued.

Steamer whistled. "Just twelve weeks' worth of training for an assignment like that?"

"Maybe they'd been grooming her while she was in college," Savannah suggested hopefully.

Dane frowned. "Or maybe they were negligent."

"Unless Savannah plans to sue the U.S. government in her mother's behalf, this whole discussion is pointless," Hack pointed out. "Let's concentrate on what happened and not who is to blame for it."

"How did they slip her into Ferrante's organization?" Hack asked.

"Yeah, what was her cover?" Steamer added.

"She went in as a computer rep," Doc told them. "This was back when computers weren't widely used and expertise was limited. So when Ferrante purchased PCs for his businesses, he got Hope Williams as part of the deal—temporarily, just until they got the computers up and running."

"It was a perfect way to integrate her into Ferrante's organization without causing suspicion," Owl said.

"According to the FBI files, Ferrante was immediately fascinated by her," Doc reported. "He convinced her to quit her job with the computer company and hired her as his personal assistant. She went everywhere with him."

Hack sighed. "And because of that, she was able to give the FBI all kinds of incredibly sensitive info."

Doc pushed his glasses into place. "It was great for awhile, but then she started asking to be pulled out. She said he was pressuring her constantly to take their relationship beyond the professional level."

"But the information she was providing was too valuable, so they made her stay?" Dane guessed.

Doc nodded. "Finally she got caught trying to pass on information. We know the rest."

"What we don't know was what kind of information she was passing to the FBI," Dane said quietly. "If the FBI was willing to keep Hope in a dangerous situation, I have to believe that the information she was providing was saving other lives. Maybe a lot of other lives."

Savannah turned on him. "You're saying that my mother *had* to be sacrificed?"

"We're soldiers," Dane replied simply. "We understand that our value is not greater than that of those we serve. Maybe your mother felt the same way."

This was a new perspective, and Savannah frowned as she considered it. "If my mother felt that way, why was she so bitter and unhappy?"

"Her life was hard, but maybe she didn't regret what she did for the FBI and for her country," Steamer said. "And I'm sure she didn't regret having you."

Doc nodded. "She was probably worried for you, not wanting you to have to pay the price for her choices."

Savannah could certainly relate to that.

"She had to know that Ferrante was still looking for her," Dane agreed. "And if he found out she had a child—his child . . ."

"Hope would have found herself in the situation we have now," Hack muttered.

"Only she didn't have the team to help her," Owl pointed out.

Savannah felt a sudden surge of warmth toward the men around her— even Dane. It was very good not to be alone.

Dane turned to Steamer. "Okay, now it's time for you to report on your assignment."

Steamer summarized the telephone calls they'd made earlier, but his information was anticlimactic compared with Doc's.

"Everyone who remembered Hope also remembered rumors about her having a relationship with an FBI agent," he said. "That could mean it was true, or it could mean it was a rumor started by the FBI to cover her disappearance."

Dane shrugged. "Either way, it doesn't help us much. Hack, what did you find out?"

Hack had tracked Hope from the time she left the FBI until her death. He had a list of all her addresses and all of Hope's unimpressive jobs.

"The FBI did offer to put her in their witness protection program," he informed them, "but she declined."

"That was the smartest thing she could have done," Dane said approvingly.

Owl nodded. "She knew Ferrante had employees within the FBI, and he would have found her."

"By not using her degree and instead working at low-paying jobs and living in crummy apartments, she stayed just below Ferrante's radar," Dane said.

"For over twenty years." Hack was obviously impressed.

"That's not bad for a girl from Georgia with only twelve weeks of FBI training," Steamer pointed out.

Savannah smiled with pride. And in that moment everything changed again. The constant moves from one dreary apartment to the next were no longer acts of desperation, but calculated parts of a master plan. Her mother was no longer a poor woman beaten down by life but a skilled FBI agent, hiding her daughter from terrible danger.

She looked up and saw Dane watching her closely. He understood the significance of what had been said. A suspicion began to grow. Did Dane and the guys fabricate all this just to make her feel better about herself and her mother?

"I'll need to see all the reports and collaborative evidence you have to support this theory," she said flatly.

Dane raised his eyebrows. "You don't trust us?"

She smirked. "Of course not."

She waited for Dane to make some defensive or deflective remark. But Doc spoke first.

"I swear to you that what I've told you is true," he said.

She looked at Doc. The lenses of his glasses magnified his eyes and seemingly his sincerity as well.

"Me too," Steamer added.

Hack just nodded.

Savannah turned to Dane. "What about you?"

"Everything I've told you about your mother is correct."

She studied them all. She did not doubt their loyalty—or their willingness to lie to protect her. She had trusted them often enough with her life. She decided to trust them with her past. Nodding, she said, "I won't need corroborative reports after all."

The guys all beamed at her—except Dane, who still looked mildly irritated, as if in spite of his tendency to lie to protect those he cared about, he thought it completely illogical for someone to question his integrity.

"So are we closing down Operation AWOL?" Steamer asked to end the awkward silence.

"I think we've got the basic story," Dane said. "Hack, you can stop your research and just concentrate on monitoring Ferrante and keeping this place secure. Doc, you keep digging at the FBI. I'd like to know for sure how Hope was recruited. If an agent involved her in an unprofessional relationship it might not be too late to have him reprimanded. And Steam, you and Savannah keep working on the personal contacts. You might not learn much that can help us clear up the specifics of Hope's association with the FBI, but it will be information that interests Savannah and eventually Caroline."

This sounded suspiciously like busywork to Savannah, but she didn't complain.

"What about me?" Caroline asked as she breezed into the kitchen, followed closely by Neely.

Dane pulled her up onto his lap and said, "I thought you were in the living room." He gave his sister a disapproving look.

"Caroline wanted to eat dessert before bedtime," Neely defended herself.

"We made a cake and we've been saving it," Caroline added. "Neely said everybody can have some."

Hack rubbed his midsection. "Sounds good to me.

Dane nodded. "I guess we've talked enough for tonight."

Neely smiled. "Then everybody come get a piece of cake and meet in front of the fire. I've thought of several more funny stories to tell on Christopher."

Dane groaned, and Caroline laughed with delight.

Savannah waited her turn in line for a generous slice of chocolate cake from Neely and then hurried into the living room—anxious to hear the new disclosures.

CHAPTER 10

DANE JOINED THE OTHERS BY THE fire while they ate their dessert and listened to Neely tell childhood memories. Dane even participated to some extent—mostly to correct his sister when he felt her memory was faulty. When Caroline fell asleep, Dane used this as an excuse to end the embarrassingly personal discussion.

He carried the child to the guest room and watched while Savannah tucked her in. Then, as usual, he said good-night and walked back down the stairs.

Savannah collected her personal items and went into the bathroom, where she took a nice long shower. Afterward she dressed in her pajamas and a warm robe. She intended to go back upstairs and get some much-needed sleep, but she glanced into the living room and saw Dane sitting on the couch, staring into the fire. It was a lonely picture, and she felt compelled to join him, just for a few minutes.

He looked up warily when she sat beside him. "I thought you were going to bed."

"I am," she confirmed. Then she looked around. "Where are the guys?"

"Doc and Steamer are sleeping on cots in the utility room," he said. "Hack's on guard duty."

"So you have the living room to yourself?"

He shrugged. "For what good it will do me."

"How long has it been since you had any significant sleep?"

He glowered at the fire. "I can't remember."

"If you don't sleep, you'll be useless to the team."

"I'm fine," he muttered.

She didn't want to argue, so she didn't reply. Instead she sat on the couch and tucked her feet underneath her. She watched the fire and tried to ignore him.

"What are you doing?" he asked.

"Nothing," she replied as the flames engulfed a log and sent sparks flying.

"Why don't you go to bed?"

"I'm not sleepy," she lied. "I thought I'd sit here and watch the fire for awhile."

From the corner of her eye, she saw him frown. "Suit yourself."

"I will."

For the next several minutes, the only sound that broke the silence was the popping of the fire. Soon she saw him relax against the couch. His head leaned back, and finally his eyes fluttered closed. And he slept. She remained completely still, knowing that the slightest movement might wake him.

For the next several hours she sat beside him, getting up only to put more logs on the fire. He shifted positions occasionally and snored softly but didn't open his eyes until the first light of early dawn began to seep in through the windows.

Dane looked startled when he saw her curled into the corner of the couch, wrapped in an old afghan. "I've been asleep?"

She nodded.

Now he looked angry. "Why didn't you wake me?"

"Because you were tired," she replied. "But don't worry—I kept my distance, just in case you had a psychotic moment and tried to kill me."

She could tell he didn't want to ask but had to know. "Did I?"

"You might have had some psychotic moments," she replied, "but you didn't try to kill me."

"You were lucky," he muttered. "Don't risk it again."

"I'm not afraid of you," she said as she rose from the couch. "Asleep or awake. And now that you're rested, I'm going to bed." She walked toward the stairs. She was halfway up before he spoke.

"Thank you."

She nodded without turning around. "You're welcome."

* * *

When Savannah woke up later that morning, the sun was streaming through the window, and Caroline was not in her bed. Savannah dressed quickly and went downstairs. She found Caroline in the kitchen with Neely, working on a puzzle Caroline had received for Christmas.

"I'm sorry I slept in," she apologized, mostly for Neely's benefit.

"Christopher told me the two of you were up late," Neely replied, a little too casually. "So he wanted to let you sleep as long as you could."

"He hadn't slept in days," Savannah defended herself. "He fell asleep on the couch, and I sat by him. It seems to help the nightmares if I'm there."

Neely nodded. "That's what he said. Not that he owed me an explanation. After all, the two of you are legally . . ."

"So," Savannah interrupted with a pointed look at Caroline, "you're making good progress on this puzzle."

Neely looked abashed. "Sorry," she muttered.

"Owl was helping us before he had to go to his flying class," Caroline said. "Did you know his real name is Kevin Robinson?"

Savannah shook her head. "No, I didn't know that."

"He said I could call him Kevin if I want. Is that okay?"

"It's fine," Savannah said.

"We saved you some breakfast." Neely pointed to a foil-covered plate on the stove.

Savannah retrieved it and got a fork from the drawer. "Thanks. I'm starving."

She removed the foil and dropped it in the garbage can then walked into the living room, where the guys were gathered. As she curled into a corner of the couch and balanced her plate on her lap, she noticed that Owl had returned from his first flying lesson of the day. Apparently he had slipped in to avoid being drawn into puzzle-making again.

All conversation had stopped when she entered the room, and she glanced up from her breakfast to ask, "What's up?"

The men exchanged a concerned look, and her anxiety level rose.

"It's Ferrante, isn't it?" she forced herself to ask.

Dane nodded. "Agent Gray called. Ferrante's legal staff got the charge of harboring a fugitive dropped."

Savannah's heart pounded. "So they're letting him go?"

No one seemed anxious to answer. Finally Dane sighed and said, "Not yet. There's one other charge the FBI can still use to hold him."

"What is it?" she asked.

"Kidnapping," Dane said.

Savannah's heart pounded. "Caroline's?"

Dane shook his head. "Yours."

"That deal with the White House protects him from prosecution for all his many crimes," Doc explained. "Since your kidnapping happened after the deal was reached, it wasn't included."

"A conviction for kidnapping could put Ferrante away for the rest of his life," Owl said.

She was relieved. "Okay. That's good."

"Don't speak too soon," Dane warned. "In order to get him indicted, they want you to testify before a grand jury."

"Because your testimony is all they've got," Hack said.

"So I have to do it?"

Steamer winced. "You don't have to. But if they don't pin something on Ferrante this time, they might not ever catch him again."

Savannah clasped her hands together to keep them from shaking. "Will he be there when I testify?"

Doc nodded. "I'm sure he'll insist."

Savannah looked away. "I'm not sure I can do it," she whispered, feeling like a coward. "Face him again, I mean. Especially now that I *know*."

"You don't have to do anything," Hack growled. "If you can't testify, then the FBI can figure out another way to keep Ferrante in prison."

"Maybe they really can undo that deal with the White House," Steamer suggested, "and recharge him with all those old crimes."

Doc shook his head. "Agent Gray didn't hold out much hope for that when we were trying to figure out a way to free Dane."

"Hey, if she can't do it, then she can't," Owl said. "Don't feel bad, Savannah."

Surprisingly, Doc expressed a different, less sympathetic opinion. "If Ferrante is in prison, the world will be a better place. And it will be much easier for us to safeguard you and Caroline. I'm sorry, but I don't see how you can miss this chance."

Savannah looked at Dane. "Is that how you feel too?"

He nodded. "I think it's something you should do—to ensure a better life for yourself and Caroline."

"Well, then," she said and hoped they couldn't hear the tremor in her voice, "I'll do it . . . somehow."

"We'll be there," Steamer said. "Right beside you all the way."

She gave him a weak smile. "Thanks."

"There's no point worrying about whether Ferrante will be at the hearing or not," Dane pointed out. "We won't know that until Savannah is actually called as a witness."

"I can't help it," Savannah said as Dane's cell phone started to ring.

They all watched as he answered it. "Dane." He listened for a few seconds and then closed the phone. "Time to worry," he said.

Savannah could barely breathe. "When do they want me to testify?"

"Ferrante's lawyers are screaming foul since they think he's immune from prosecution. So the FBI will have to present evidence to back up their charges fast. Agent Gray says they are negotiating with a superior court judge now and hope to bump another case that was about to go to a grand jury."

Savannah could tell he was stalling. "When?" she repeated.

He frowned. "Tomorrow."

The room reeled around Savannah, and she was afraid she was going to be sick. How could she sit in the same room with Mario Ferrante? How could she look at his face, knowing that he ruined her mother's life and wanted to destroy hers as well? Yet how could she refuse and let him continue to go unpunished? How could she let her cowardice put Caroline at risk?

"I don't know if it would be wise to let Savannah testify," Hack said.

She wondered if he had a legitimate concern or if he was trying to give her a way out. "We know Ferrante has employees in the FBI," Hack continued. "Maybe this is an elaborate way of getting to Savannah."

"What do you mean 'getting to her'?" Dane demanded.

"I mean as soon as she shows up to testify, they grab her," Hack explained. "And without her testimony, the FBI has no case against Ferrante, so he goes free."

Steamer paled visibly. "We'll have to be sure that doesn't happen."

"If Savannah testifies, security will be a major concern," Owl agreed.

"But how can we let this chance to get Ferrante pass us by? We'll have to confirm the charges against Ferrante from several different sources and make sure they're legitimate," Doc said.

"And we'll have a large security presence at the courthouse," Hack said. "Inside and out."

"That could be a problem," Dane said. "They are very sensitive about firearms and such in courthouses."

This didn't seem to bother Hack. "So we'll have an unarmed presence at the courthouse and armed guards outside. And Savannah will be wearing Kevlar."

"Bulletproof vests don't cover enough vulnerable areas to suit me." Dane stood and started pacing. "She'll be at risk from the minute we leave the cabin, the whole time we're at the federal courthouse, and while traveling between the two."

Even Hack was daunted by this thought. "That's a lot of time and distance to provide adequate security."

Dane stopped pacing for a moment and turned to Savannah. "Aren't the Child Advocacy Center offices just a couple of blocks down from the federal courthouse?"

She nodded.

"Are the offices still vacant?"

"As far as I know," she replied.

Dane stopped in front of her. "Do you still have keys?"

"Yes," she said. "Why all this interest in the CAC offices?"

Dane turned to Hack. "Will you take Savannah's keys and drive to the CAC offices and scout out the situation? See if the keys still work and if we can get in without making a fuss."

Hack nodded, but Savannah spread her hands. "Why?"

"We could move you to the CAC offices without anyone knowing," Dane explained. "That would eliminate all but a couple blocks of vulnerability when you go from the CAC offices to the courthouse."

"And we could set up our equipment there." Hack looked encouraged. "We'll set up cameras so we can monitor everything that goes on in a four-block radius."

"It will be our command center." Steamer smiled. "Nice and secure."

"It's the perfect place to swap out our personnel," Dane noted.

"And when it's time to take Savannah to the courthouse, nobody will be expecting her to leave from the CAC," Doc said. "We'll have the element of surprise for a few yards anyway."

Hack grinned. "I like it."

"Then go see if Savannah's keys still work," Dane suggested. He turned to Owl. "I'll need you on the roof across the street—just in case."

"Of course," Owl agreed, and Savannah felt terrible. Owl hated shooting people, and yet he would to save her. And the worst part was that she *wanted* him to be on that roof, ready to protect her if the need arose. Because he was the best.

"Will we leave Caroline here while Savannah testifies?" Steamer asked.

Dane didn't have to think before giving his response. "No. If it's a trap, coming to get Caroline would be next on Ferrante's to-do list. We'll move Caroline to another location—one that we'll decide on just before we leave to avoid the remotest possibility of a leak."

Hack took Savannah's keys and headed for the door. "I'll let you know as soon as I can determine the feasibility of the CAC offices."

Dane nodded. "We'll wait to hear from you."

After Hack left for Washington, DC, Dane and the others went to work drawing up their security plan for the federal courthouse. Savannah didn't ask how they obtained a detailed map of the courthouse showing exits and restrooms and all other locations that needed to be covered. She sat in the corner of the couch, wrapped in the old afghan, trying not to show how terrified she was.

Finally Dane got the call from Hack.

"Well?" Savannah asked when Dane closed his phone.

"The keys work, and Hack says it's the perfect location," Dane informed them. "The offices are vacant but still furnished. Apparently the rent was paid through the end of the year, so the owner hasn't been in a hurry to get new tenants."

"I think the owner was hoping someone would step in and revive the CAC now that Doug Forton is gone," Savannah said.

"Well, for whatever reason, the offices are sitting there ready and available for us," Dane said. He turned to Doc and Owl. "I told Hack to stay there and start collecting equipment and getting things set up. Will you two go help him?"

Owl nodded and Doc stood. "Of course."

"Be prepared to spend the night there," Dane warned. "And once we get the go-ahead and a time, Steam, you will be on babysitting duty."

"Hey!" Caroline said as she walked in from the kitchen.

"Kid-sitting," Dane amended.

Steamer nodded. "That's my favorite kind of duty."

"Then this meeting is adjourned."

As men left, Caroline said, "We finished the puzzle."

Savannah pulled Caroline onto her lap. "I'll come see it in a few minutes. Right now I just need to sit here and think about how much I love you."

"Can you think about how much you love me while I move my train tracks over by the stairs?" Caroline asked.

In spite of her anxiety, Savannah laughed. "I can think about how much I love you no matter what we're doing."

Caroline wiggled out of her mother's embrace. "Good, 'cause I'm tired of the tracks being where they are."

"I can see why," Dane remarked. "You've had this particular arrangement for at least two hours."

The sarcasm was wasted on Caroline. "So, Steamer, you'll help me fix them?"

He stood. "I guess that's part of kid-sitting." He followed her to the corner of the living room dominated by train tracks and accessories. While Steamer and Caroline disassembled train tracks, Neely joined Savannah and Dane by the fire.

"Is the meeting over?" Neely asked.

"For now," Dane confirmed.

"What's going on?" his sister wanted to know.

"Savannah is going to testify before a grand jury tomorrow," he replied softly. "You and Caroline will wait in a secure location during her testimony. Then, if the grand jury indicts Ferrante, this encampment will be over."

Neely nodded. "And not a minute too soon. We're running out of food *and* ways to distract Caroline. There are only so many configurations for these train tracks."

"And I'm sure you have a lot to do to get ready for your new business to open in February," Savannah said. "I can't thank you enough for putting your own life on hold to help me with Caroline."

Neely leaned forward and patted Savannah's hand. "That's what families do."

"I'm kind of new to the whole family thing," Savannah admitted. "But so far I really like it."

"Wait until our parents get home and Mom starts bossing you around," Neely warned. "Then you might reconsider your opinion on families."

"I doubt it." Savannah was careful to keep her tone light, but this was a painful topic for her. She wanted more than anything to be a part of a real family—Dane's family—but it seemed that this was not to be.

She felt him watching her and met his gaze. His eyes were solemn, but she couldn't tell if he'd read her mind or just sensed her sadness.

"Neely!" Caroline called. "Will you come help us?"

"Can't anybody do anything around here without my help?" Neely acted exasperated, but Savannah suspected that Dane's sister enjoyed the feeling of being needed.

Dane gave his sister a rare smile. "It looks like there are a few track configurations left to make."

Neely laughed. "Maybe, but I'm too old to be crawling around on the floor."

"Neely!" Caroline called again.

With one last look at her brother, Neely walked over and joined Caroline and Steamer.

Once Neely was gone, Savannah lowered her voice and asked Dane, "What will I tell the grand jury?"

His eyes focused first on her mouth, then her eyes. Finally he said, "The truth."

"Of course I'm going to tell the truth," she replied. "But I thought you might have some helpful advice."

"Just answer their questions," he told her. "Answer them as briefly and honestly as you can. Ferrante will try to rattle you. You'll have to be strong."

She nodded and leaned a little closer. In spite of her simmering anger toward him, she wanted more than anything to bury her face in the crook of his neck and gain the comfort she knew he could provide. But Mario Ferrante was still firmly between them. It was ironic that she had once considered Wes the insurmountable obstacle to her happiness. If only she'd known.

"You can do it," Dane encouraged her.

"I dread seeing him again," she confided.

"I know." His hand was moving toward hers when his cell phone rang. After a brief conversation, he closed the phone and said, "That was Agent Gray. The grand jury will convene at nine tomorrow morning, and since you are the only witness, you can expect to be called shortly thereafter. We'll plan to leave here just before dawn—before anyone expects it."

"Okay."

"You will be answering questions related only to your kidnapping—not Caroline's."

Unable to force her trembling lips to form words, she just nodded.

"The prosecutor has been advised of the situation and is sympathetic to your position. We want to keep it that way, so you'll need to follow his instructions exactly."

"I can follow instructions."

He held her gaze. "You can do anything you want to."

She wasn't sure if he was referring to the grand jury testimony or their temporary marriage or her relationship to Mario Ferrante. But she didn't feel like discussing any of those topics, so she remained silent.

Finally Dane said, "I'll need to let Hack know what's going on." He called over his shoulder. "Steamer!"

"Do you need me?" Steamer asked when he arrived seconds later.

"The grand jury convenes tomorrow. We'll take Savannah to town just before dawn, but I want to move Caroline tonight under the cover of darkness."

"I've got that." Steamer pulled out his phone and started making calls.

Savannah shivered and wondered if the nightmare would ever end.

CHAPTER 11

SAVANNAH COULDN'T BEAR TO THINK about her looming confrontation with Mario Ferrante—so she chose denial instead. She approached the rest of the day as if it were any other. She worked on the train-track reorganization with Steamer and Caroline for a while. Then they got a call from the preacher Steamer had talked to the day before. He said he'd found some pictures of her mother that he'd be glad to put in the mail to her. She gave him the address for the Intelligence Center on Fort Belvoir and thanked him for his trouble.

At noon she helped Neely fix lunch. Then she did laundry and packed Caroline's clothes as if the child was going on a vacation instead of into deep hiding—again. She comforted herself that hopefully this was the last time it would be necessary to stow Caroline away. But that brought her thoughts too close to Ferrante. So she cleared her mind with an effort and concentrated on folding clothes.

She was putting towels in the bathroom cupboard when she heard Dane invite Caroline to go fishing. She walked into the kitchen, where they were gathered around the table, and asked, "You're going to go fishing in January?"

"The weather is nice," Dane pointed out. "And we'll put on coats."

Caroline looked so delighted by the prospect that Savannah couldn't refuse. "Okay, but don't stay out long." She had turned to go back to her self-imposed laundry duties when she heard Dane speak to Caroline.

"Your mom might want to come fishing too," Dane surprised Savannah by suggesting.

"But she doesn't know how," Caroline pointed out.

"We could teach her."

Caroline gave her mother a speculative look. "We tried that before, and she couldn't do it."

Dane smiled at Savannah over Caroline's head. "We could give her another chance to prove she's not a failure at fishing."

Savannah rose to the challenge. "If Major Dane can do it, I definitely can."

Caroline laughed as she crossed the room and took her mother by the hand. "Then come on."

As they put on coats and headed outside, Savannah had to wonder if she'd been duped.

Savannah spent the next two hours sitting on the bridge while Dane and Caroline fished. They made a token show of trying to teach her, but despite her claims, she had no aptitude, and their attention quickly turned to the activity they both loved. Savannah didn't mind since she had little interest in the whole fishing process. But she did enjoy watching them together and the almost springlike weather.

When the sun fell beneath the horizon, the temperature dropped as well. Dane stood, lifted the bucket that contained the day's catch, and pronounced the fishing expedition over. Caroline looked disappointed, but she was also tired and a little cold, so she didn't argue.

When they got back to the house, Steamer helped Dane clean the fish while Savannah and Caroline helped Neely in the kitchen. They ate a simple meal of fish and coleslaw and slices of white bread. When dinner was over, Dane suggested that Savannah go ahead and give Caroline a bath. Since she knew this was a necessary preparation for Caroline's departure, she accepted the assignment without much enthusiasm. But Caroline danced happily all the way to the bathroom.

As Savannah worked shampoo through her daughter's long, blond hair Savannah couldn't control a few tears, anticipating the separation. Noting her mother's distress, Caroline reached up and put two wet hands on Savannah's cheeks.

"What's wrong, Mama?"

"You're going to have to go on a little trip tonight." Savannah tried to sound cheerful but knew she failed. "Steamer and Neely are going too."

Caroline's expression became solemn. "But not you?"

Savannah shook her head. "No. Major Dane and I have to stay."

"Is that bad man trying to get me again?"

Savannah didn't want her daughter to be terrified, but she did want her to be cautious. So she said, "The FBI arrested Mario Ferrante, and they think they can put him in jail for a long time. But they need me to help them by telling a judge some of the things Mr. Ferrante has done. If everything goes well tomorrow, they will keep him in jail, and he won't be a danger to us anymore. But while I'm talking to the judge, Major Dane wants you to be in a very safe place."

"Where?"

Savannah shrugged. "I don't know. But I trust Major Dane."

Caroline grinned. "Me too. And I'll have Steamer and Neely with me."

Savannah did her best to smile. "Yes."

"And you'll come get me as soon as you're finished."

"I will," Savannah promised.

"So don't cry," Caroline said.

Savannah wiped her eyes. "The water's getting cold. It's time to get out."

She toweled Caroline dry and dressed her in warm pajamas.

Caroline was confused by the choice of clothes. "I thought you said I was going somewhere tonight. So why am I wearing my pajamas?"

"I want you to be able to sleep comfortably in the car."

Caroline accepted this explanation. "Can I take some DVDs with me?"

Savannah pulled Caroline's hair into a ponytail and secured it. "Of course."

By the time they returned to the kitchen, Neely had it cleaned up from dinner, and three overnight bags were stacked by the back door. Savannah thanked Neely again for being willing to care for Caroline while Savannah couldn't do it for herself. Neely kindly assured her that it was not a problem.

"I've had more fun the last few days than I have since my kids grew up and left home," Neely said. "Thank you for sharing Caroline with me."

Savannah knew this was just good Southern manners, but she appreciated it just the same. She walked down to Steamer and was surprised by the strength of emotion she felt as she thanked him. He'd only been a part of their lives for a few weeks, but now she couldn't imagine operating without him.

"I hope the Las Vegas real estate market doesn't improve anytime soon," she told him as she wiped at tears. "We need you here."

He grinned. "I'm sure the millions of people in Nevada who want to buy or sell property appreciate that selfish wish."

She smiled back. "You know what I mean."

Steamer laughed as he carried the bags outside and loaded them into a green Honda CR-V parked right by the porch. Dane picked Caroline up into his arms and carried her outside. Savannah and Neely trailed behind.

"New car?" Neely asked.

"The Yukon is in Nashville, so we had to get something else," Steamer explained.

"Let me guess," Savannah said when she saw the new vehicle. "Steamer got to pick the mode of transportation."

Dane nodded, looking irritated.

But Steamer was all smiles. "I don't know why some folks think driving stodgy old cars makes you inconspicuous. There are way more flashy new cars on the roads than grandma-style clunkers." Steamer waved at the new CR-V. "We'll fit right in driving this baby."

Savannah ran a hand down the sleek side. "I like it," she said. "Maybe when this is over I'll sell the Yukon and keep this."

"You'd better check that out with Hack first," Dane advised. "Security is much more important than style."

Then he opened the passenger door and situated Caroline inside. Once the seat belt was secured, he stepped back and allowed Savannah into the small space. She put *Sleeping Beauty* into the built-in DVD player attached to the back of the driver's seat and handed Caroline the set of headphones then tucked a blanket around her.

"All cozy?" Savannah asked as Steamer and Neely climbed into the front seat.

"I'm cold." Caroline snuggled down into the blanket. "And could you turn the movie up a little?"

Savannah adjusted the volume, and Steamer turned up the heat.

"It will be warm in here soon, baby!" he promised.

"Be good," Savannah instructed, fighting tears.

Caroline reached up and stroked her cheek. "I will, Mama."

Left with nothing else to do, Savannah kissed her daughter and stepped back. Dane leaned in and whispered something to Caroline. Then he closed the door, and Steamer pulled away.

"Where are they going?" Savannah asked as the red taillights disappeared into the darkness.

Dane's breath stirred the hair around her ear when he whispered, "General Steele has a condo in Washington, DC. The housing complex has an excellent security system, and Hack has improved upon that considerably. They'll take a circuitous route—which means they'll be driving for a couple of hours—but in the end, they'll only be a few miles away from the CAC."

Savannah was confused. "We trust the general now?"

He shook his head. "I said the general owns the condo. I didn't say he knew we were using it for the next few hours."

Dane led the way back inside. He passed through the quiet kitchen, headed toward the living room. He paused at the foot of the stairs and turned to Savannah. "You need to get to bed so you'll be at your best tomorrow morning. And remember we're leaving early."

Savannah didn't want to go upstairs alone, but she really didn't want to argue with him. So she nodded, stepped over Caroline's train tracks, and walked up the stairs. The second floor of Dane's cabin was even quieter than the kitchen below, and Savannah felt loneliness descend. Over the past few days, she'd grown used to the bustle of too many people living in too small a space. Adjusting to too few people was more unpleasant than she would have expected.

Out of boredom, Savannah looked through her limited wardrobe to find an outfit for her court appearance the next day. She still had one of the outfits Steamer had purchased that she hadn't worn—complete with matching shoes and a handbag. She fingered the plum-colored fabric of what would be her courtroom outfit. Her gratitude and appreciation for Steamer grew yet again. He had not only impeccable taste, but also amazing foresight. When she'd sent him to the boutique on Pennsylvania Avenue in search of one outfit and he'd come back with three, she'd thought him extravagant. She'd worn one outfit to meet Giordano and another to the yacht. Now she'd be wearing this last one when she testified against her father.

Unable to deal with the painful emotions, she closed the door and changed into her pajamas. She climbed into the bed closest to the window and snuggled down under Caroline's covers. Despite her exhaustion, she found it difficult to sleep. She tossed and turned for almost an hour and finally got up and walked back downstairs.

She found Dane in the living room, staring at the fire.

"You're back," he said.

She plopped down beside him. "Yeah, I figured you'd be missing Caroline, so I came down here to comfort you."

He smiled. "I'm definitely missing Caroline."

"Have you heard from Steamer?"

He nodded. "They've arrived, and all is well."

Savannah felt some of the tension leave her shoulders. Caroline was safe. That was something.

"We never did have a chance to go over my," she took a deep breath and forced herself to go on, "testimony."

"I told you to tell the truth. What else is there to go over?"

She shrugged. "I thought you would want me to practice it a few times—to make sure I say the right things."

"We don't want your testimony to sound canned, so we won't rehearse it. Just keep it simple. Try to avoid being too emotional. Be sure to mention Ferrante's personal involvement frequently—the live camera shots, hearing his voice, etc. We have to prove that he was personally behind the kidnapping. We don't want him to be able to blame someone else—and that is his most likely defense."

"I think I understand."

He turned toward her. "Can you do it?"

She dragged her eyes up to meet his. She knew he could see all the fear and uncertainty registered there. But she whispered, "Yes."

He covered her hand with his. "I know you can."

Afraid that if she kept looking into his eyes, she'd end up in his arms, Savannah turned back to stare at the fire. Soon her eyes drooped closed. Just before she drifted off to sleep, she heard Dane's voice in her ear.

"Do you want me to watch guard over you tonight while you sleep?"

It was tempting. But she'd made her terms clear, and he had not accepted them. So she shook her head and forced herself to stand. "No, I'll go back to bed." She paused, giving him the chance to redefine their relationship.

But he just nodded. "Tomorrow is going to be a big day. Get all the rest you can."

She turned away to hide her disappointment and retreated up the stairs.

Savannah climbed back into Caroline's bed and tried to sleep, but her mind wouldn't rest. Nothing was as it should be. She was a mother without her child, a wife without a husband, a daughter who would have to send her father to jail. She searched for an answer—or at least a reason for the confusion—but couldn't find one

She slept fitfully for a few hours and finally got up to prepare for what she hoped would be the last time she'd ever have to see Mario Ferrante. She took a shower and fixed her hair and makeup as well as the cast would allow. She dressed in the plum suit and went downstairs.

Dane was in the kitchen, standing in front of the stove. He turned when she walked in. He was breathtakingly handsome in the shirt and pants of his blue dress uniform. The coat, with its complement of impressive ribbons and medals, was draped carefully over an empty chair. It didn't look any worse for their time spent on the Coast Guard boat, so Savannah assumed he had somehow managed to have it dry-cleaned. Or maybe he had a spare.

He didn't seem to notice the effect he had on her as he waved toward one of the two mugs he had arranged on the table. "There's your hot chocolate."

"What about doughnuts?" she managed.

He lifted a skillet from the stove and brought it to the table. He slid half of an omelet onto each of two plates. "You need protein."

"I'll probably throw it up when I see Ferrante," she predicted as she sat down. She kept her eyes away from Caroline's empty seat and her thoughts away from the upcoming courtroom confrontation.

"Then don't eat much," he advised. He put the hot skillet on the stove and then sat in his regular seat at the table. He ate hungrily while she picked at her food. When his breakfast was gone, he took his plate to the sink and rinsed it. He looked back at her nearly untouched food.

"Are you finished?" he asked.

She nodded. "Except for my hot chocolate." She drank the last of the sweet, hot liquid and took her dishes to him, watching while he washed them.

Once he was done, he said, "Time to go."

She nodded wordlessly.

"It's going to be okay," he promised.

"Let's get out of here before I lose my nerve," she replied.

They drove to Washington, DC, in one of the nondescript sedans that Steamer had deemed "conspicuously inconspicuous." Four cars filled with Hack's men and soldiers from Fort Belvoir accompanied them, but Savannah still didn't feel safe until they reached the CAC offices. Dane and her armed escorts rushed her inside, and once they were in the elevator, she was able to take a deep, relaxing breath. She'd made it that far alive.

Stepping off the elevator into the hall that led to the CAC offices increased her sense of well-being. She had done the same thing hundreds of times, and there was comfort in the familiar. They walked through the smoked glass that separated the reception area from the rest of the building, and despite the bodyguards and soldiers milling around, it felt like home.

She saw Dane watching her and wondered if he had chosen the CAC offices for the calming effect he knew they would have on her as much as for their proximity to the federal courthouse. If that was the case, she decided to be grateful instead of resentful. She gave him a little smile, and he smiled back.

Hack and Doc walked into the lobby and greeted her enthusiastically.

Savannah hugged them each in turn. "Where's Owl?"

"Owl is already positioned on a building across from the courthouse."

Savannah frowned. "What if there's trouble behind the courthouse?"

"Owl can move easily from rooftop to rooftop," Hack told her. "Kind of like Batman."

"You're kidding?"

Doc shook his head. "We wouldn't kid about something as serious as your safety."

"I know you're all amazingly talented," she replied, "but I didn't realize you were superheroes."

Hack grinned. "That's us. Superheroes."

Dane killed the happy mood quickly. "We may need everyone's super powers to make it through today."

All vestiges of humor left Savannah as the anxiety returned.

Doc seemed to sense her feelings and tried to distract her. "I guess it was quiet at the cabin last night."

"Yeah," Hack said. "Just the two of you alone—sounds nice and romantic."

Savannah carefully avoided Dane's gaze. "It was just like any other night."

Doc glanced between Dane and Savannah then said, "Would you like to see how we've got things set up?"

"Definitely," Dane confirmed.

Savannah couldn't tell whether he was really interested in seeing how the equipment was arranged or if he just wanted to end the current discussion. But Doc looked pleased by Dane's interest, so she nodded too and followed them down the hall and into what had at one time been Doug Forton's office.

Doug's office was completely transformed. Most of the antique furniture had been removed, and what remained was pushed against the walls. The room was now dominated by computers and video monitors. Doc pointed out all the different locations outside and within the federal courthouse that they would be able to watch.

"If there's trouble, we'll know it," Doc told them. "And then we can move our personnel to the appropriate places."

Dane circled the room and then nodded. "This looks great."

"Very impressive," she agreed.

"We're ready for anything," Hack said. "Ferrante won't trick us this time."

Seeing all their cautious preparations did make Savannah feel a little better.

"We can handle anything Ferrante throws our way," Doc assured her.

Savannah didn't share their confidence completely, but she kept her doubts to herself. "We'd better get out of here before we break something."

This possibility alarmed Hack. "Yes, everybody out, and don't touch anything!"

Savannah and Dane passed through the office doorway at the same time. The small space required them to almost touch. The close proximity caused Savannah's heart to pound and her breath to come in short gasps. Annoyed with herself for being so affected by Dane, she hurried down the hallway and into the lobby.

When Dane arrived there a few seconds later, he said, "It'll be a while before you're needed at the courthouse. You might be more comfortable waiting in your office."

She considered this for a few seconds and then nodded. "I'll be there when you need me."

She started down the hall. Upon hearing footsteps behind her, she turned, hoping that Dane had decided to accompany her, but it was Hack.

"You mind if I come too?" he asked.

She smiled. "I'll be glad to have your company."

She opened the door to her office, and they stepped inside. The room was just as she had left it. The vacuum marks on the carpet and the absence of dust indicated that the cleaning crew was still making regular visits, but otherwise it seemed untouched by time.

"You got anything to eat in here?" Hack asked.

She sat at her desk and opened the drawer where she'd kept snacks for Caroline. "A few candy bars, some crackers, and a bag of fruit snacks," she itemized. "And they may all be expired."

Hack held out one of his hands. "I don't even care."

She piled the questionably fresh food on his outstretched palm and then turned on her computer. Her old password brought it quickly to life. Then she glanced through the files on her desk. It felt strange to read the names of children she had been closely involved with a few months before but hadn't even thought of recently.

"You want this?" Hack asked, holding up a Hershey bar with a suspiciously tattered wrapper.

"No thanks."

He shrugged, tore it open, and ate the whole candy bar in one bite. Then he pulled up a chair and cleared his throat, acting uncharacteristically nervous. "I've been meaning to talk to you about something."

She turned her gaze to him, wary. "What?"

"Do you ever watch those shows on TV like Dr. Phil or Oprah?"

She shook her head. "I don't watch much TV."

"Well," he continued, still fidgeting. "On those shows sometimes they have what they call an intervention. That's when two people have what seems like an unsolvable problem. But they sit down and talk it through and come up with a way to make it work." He paused and looked up.

Savannah nodded in encouragement. "Go ahead."

"The guys and me, well, we've all noticed that your new marriage isn't exactly going great," Hack continued. "So I thought maybe what we need is an intervention."

Savannah controlled a smile. "If we're going to have an intervention about my marriage, shouldn't Dane be here too?"

Hack waved this remark aside. "Dane's not very good at talking through his feelings. So I figured I'd better just intervene with you."

She took a deep breath. "Okay, so what do you think I should do differently in my impossible marriage?"

"You should love him," Hack said, "just like you always have."

"It's not that simple, Hack," she told him. "Marriage is a serious commitment, and it involves not only me and Dane, but Caroline too. If he can't commit to us permanently, then we're better off on our own." Just saying the words made her heart ache.

"Dane is committed," Hack replied. "I don't think that's an issue. He just hasn't committed on your terms."

She frowned. "You think I'm being unreasonable because I want him to say he loves me? Because I want him to tell me that our marriage is worth more to him than a tax break?"

"Tax break?" Hack repeated in confusion.

"That's why he said he wasn't going to annul our marriage," she informed him. "Because there are lots of advantages to being married—like better insurance coverage and tax breaks. He wants to stay married to me for all the wrong reasons."

Hack shook his head. "You know Dane loves you, and he's never cared anything about money or tax breaks. No marriage is perfect, and maybe yours is stranger than most. But if you'll give up your romantic fantasies and commit yourself to making it work, I think you two have a chance to be very happy together."

Savannah was mildly offended by Hack's remarks. "Are you saying I'm the problem?"

He shrugged. "You are partly to blame, yes."

Hack's intervening skills left something to be desired, but there was some wisdom buried deep in his words, and she began to feel a glimmer of hope. "You really think our marriage can work?"

He nodded. "If you'll accept him as he is and quit expecting him to turn into Prince Charming."

She had to laugh. "I guess you're right. My expectations were a little high."

Hack leaned back in his chair and sighed. "Well, I think my first intervention went pretty well."

She raised an eyebrow. "Are you planning more?"

"Hey!" he said. "If guys like Dr. Phil can make a living at it, why not me?"

Before she could answer, Dane appeared in her office doorway. Based on his grim expression, she knew her reprieve was over.

He confirmed her suspicions by saying, "Agent Gray is here."

She stood and circled around to the front of her desk. "We might as well go ahead and get it over with."

She joined Dane by the door. "I can do this, right?"

He nodded.

Deciding to take Hack's advice, she reached for Dane's hand. He encircled her trembling fingers in a tight grip. At least she didn't have to do this alone.

Agent Gray and several other men she didn't recognize were waiting in Doug's conference room. Two were FBI lawyers, and the others were agents, there to provide additional security during the trip from the CAC offices to the federal courthouse. Agent Gray introduced them, but Savannah didn't even try to remember their names.

"Do you have any special instructions for Savannah before we go?" Dane asked them.

One of the lawyers stepped forward. "The most important thing to remember is that you cannot mention any crime except the one the grand jury has been called for."

"If you do," the other lawyer said, "you'll taint your testimony, and it won't be admissible in a future trial."

"Ferrante's lawyers will be hoping for something like that," Agent Gray added. "Let the federal prosecutor lead you."

"She knows what to do," Dane told them. "Let's go."

"You'll need to surrender your weapons," Hack said.

Dane frowned.

Hack held out his hand. "You can either give them to me or one of the guards at the courthouse."

With obvious reluctance, Dane lifted his uniform jacket and removed a revolver from the holster, putting it into Hack's hand.

"Your backup too," Hack insisted.

Dane looked angry as he pulled a small gun from a pocket near his waist. "Are you satisfied?"

Hack nodded as he put the weapons in his own pocket. "I'll take good care of them for you."

When they got to the building's exit, Hack helped Savannah put on a Kevlar vest. "It's bulky and uncomfortable," Hack acknowledged, "but it might save your life."

"I can deal with uncomfortable," she assured him.

Once she was strapped into the coat, the FBI agents and Hack's men combined to create a human barrier between Savannah and anyone who might wish her harm. Hack hurried her outside to a black Hummer parked at the curb. After Savannah and Dane were safely settled in the backseat, Hack climbed behind the wheel.

"Where did this Hummer come from?" Dane asked.

"The Yukon is still in Nashville," Hack said.

"I liked that CR-V Steamer picked out," Savannah told him. "I was thinking that when this is all over, we might trade in the Yukon and get one permanently. It's cute and gets great gas mileage."

"The most important things in picking a vehicle are safety and seats big enough for me to sit comfortably in," Hack replied. "So forget about a cute CR-V and learn to love this Hummer."

They arrived at the federal courthouse, and Hack pulled the Hummer to a stop by a side entrance. Savannah noted a significant police presence around the building and on the street. Dane climbed out first and walked around to open the door for her. As she climbed out, she glanced up. Even though she couldn't see Owl, she knew that his protective presence loomed above them.

Dane squeezed her fingers, and she garnered her courage. She could do this. For Caroline. For her mother. For a chance at a normal life.

They walked quickly into the courthouse, through the marble-floored lobby and to the doorway of a moderately sized meeting room. Dane helped Savannah remove the Kevlar vest, and they put it on a chair by the door.

"This is as far as we can go," Agent Gray said. "We'll be waiting in here in case you need us. Just tell the prosecutor you want to consult with us, and they'll pause the proceedings."

"Okay," Savannah said.

"Major Dane is being allowed inside only because he's also on the witness list," Agent Gray continued.

Savannah's eyes swung back to Dane. "You're testifying too?"

He shook his head. "They just put me on the list so you wouldn't have to go in alone."

She turned to the FBI agent and whispered, "Thank you."

He smiled. "I do what I can."

Dane opened the door and ushered her into the room. Several people were sitting in folding chairs arranged in rows to their right. They all looked up when Savannah and Dane walked in. To their left was a table with a court reporter sitting at one end. A laptop and a feminine-looking briefcase dominated the other end of the table. Ferrante was nowhere in sight, and there was a casual atmosphere in the room that Savannah hadn't expected. She felt herself begin to relax.

An attractive woman in a black business suit walked over to them and introduced herself as the federal prosecutor. She was younger than Savannah had expected, with long dark hair and green eyes. She was beautiful and just Dane's type.

"My name is Portia Campbell," she said, "and I'll be conducting the grand jury questioning today." She gave Savannah a passing glance and then settled her gaze on Dane with more interest. Savannah watched as the woman took in his spiky dark hair, his unreadable brown eyes, and the impressive number of medals pinned to his blue dress uniform. "Thank you for coming today," she added, more to Dane than Savannah.

"I can't say it's a pleasure," Savannah replied, recapturing Ms. Campbell's attention.

The prosecutor pulled her eyes reluctantly from Dane. "We've saved a seat for you here in front." Ms. Campbell waved at a chair near the center of the room. Then her eyes dipped to Dane's nametag. "Major, you can sit at my table." She pointed to the laptop and briefcase.

Dane smiled. "Thank you."

Savannah had an immediate and unwelcome reaction to Ms. Campbell's flirtatious behavior. And there at the federal courthouse in a room surrounded by strangers, she had to accept the disturbing truth. She loved Dane. She wanted to be his wife. Not just on her terms—on any terms. Even if all he wanted was a marriage of convenience, she'd never have the strength to leave him. Maybe Hack did have a future as Dr. Hack, after all.

Shaken by the moment of self-discovery, Savannah crossed to the middle of the room and sat down in the chair the prosecutor had indicated.

Ms. Campbell waited until Dane was settled by the table before she walked over to stand in front of Savannah. "As you know, Mrs. McLaughlin—"

A voice from behind them interrupted. "Her name is Dane."

Savannah and Ms. Campbell both looked toward the table.

"I beg your pardon?" Ms. Campbell asked.

Savannah's eyes locked with Dane's. She saw possessiveness in his gaze, and her heart pounded.

"Her name is really Savannah Dane," he repeated. "We were married recently."

Ms. Campbell seemed flustered. "Oh, well, I didn't realize." Her disappointment was obvious, and Savannah had to work hard to control a smile.

The prosecutor turned to the court reporter. "Please correct the court records to reflect that change." She turned back to Savannah. "We are here today to determine if there is enough evidence to indict Mario Ferrante on the charge of felony kidnapping. Your testimony will be crucial to this process. Do you understand?"

Savannah nodded.

"I will ask you to say yes or no, so your response can be recorded."

"Yes," Savannah said.

"Now, please begin by telling us, in your own words, the events of December 26th. Once you finish your account, I will ask a few questions. Then we will take questions from the jury."

"Okay," Savannah replied.

"You may begin."

Savannah took a deep breath, organized her thoughts, and opened her mouth to speak. But before she was able to begin her testimony, the door opened and two men walked in. The first was a man she'd never seen before. The other was Mario Ferrante. He was wearing a prison jumpsuit, and his hands were cuffed in front of him, but his arrogant attitude remained. He claimed Savannah's eyes and smiled.

Savannah glanced at Dane. He was staring at Ferrante with loathing, his lips pressed together in a hard line.

Ms. Campbell crossed the room in an ineffective attempt to block Ferrante's entry. "What are you doing here?" she demanded. "This is most irregular."

"But not illegal," Ferrante said. "I have the right to be here if I choose."

Ms. Campbell addressed Ferrante's lawyer. "You've agreed to this?"

"I've warned Mr. Ferrante about the risks involved in being present during grand jury testimony," the lawyer replied. "He's chosen to ignore my advice."

"Is your client going to testify before the grand jury?" Ms. Campbell asked.

"Definitely not," the lawyer replied. "We're here in an observation capacity only."

"You need to get some seats brought up," Ferrante told the prosecutor. "I want to sit right here." He pointed to the area across from Savannah.

Ms. Campbell asked the guard at the door to bring some chairs up from the back. The atmosphere in the room was now anything but relaxed.

Once Ferrante and his lawyer were seated, Ms. Campbell tried again to discourage him from staying. "If you say something incriminating, it *will* be part of an official court record that can be used against you during a trial."

Ferrante waved this aside. "I understand all that, and I don't care."

Ms. Campbell seemed astonished. "Mr. Ferrante—"

"We're wasting time," Ferrante interrupted. "Let's get on with it. I believe you were about to question your witness."

Ms. Campbell looked uncertainly at Savannah. "Yes."

"Good," Ferrante said, "because I want to object."

"You can't object," Ms. Campbell said.

Ferrante ignored this and said, "She shouldn't be allowed to testify against me since she's my daughter."

All the color drained from Ms. Campbell's face as murmurs erupted around the room and Ferrante smiled at Savannah.

"I said you can't object." There was now a strident edge to Ms. Campbell's voice. "And if you keep interrupting these proceedings, I will have you removed."

"You can try," Ferrante taunted her.

Ms. Campbell smoothed her skirt and moderated her tone. "Only spouses and minor children are excused from testifying—even in a court of law, which this is not. If the witness wants to testify before the grand jury, she has a perfectly legal right to do so."

Ferrante didn't argue, and this told Savannah that he wasn't actually trying to block her testimony. He just wanted their relationship in the court record—which would lead to an announcement in the press. He was publicly disgracing her and Caroline.

The door opened, and four more armed guards filed into the room.

"You *will* sit quietly while Mrs. Dane testifies," Ms. Campbell told Ferrante, emboldened by the extra security personnel. "If you cause another disruption, you *will* leave."

Ferrante shrugged. "Then I'll be quiet." He winked at Savannah. "Because I definitely want to stay."

"Why?" Savannah asked, honestly confused by his insistent presence.

He leaned toward her and said, "Because when I'm near you, I can feel your mother's anguish. It's my only source of revenge against her."

"That is it!" Ms. Campbell declared. "Mr. Ferrante, you will leave this room immediately, or I will have you removed."

Ferrante's lawyer stood. "We should go now."

Ferrante slowly rose to his feet. "I've done what I came to do." He gave Savannah one last unpleasant smile and then led his lawyer from the room.

As the door slammed behind Ferrante, Dane walked over and crouched down beside Savannah's chair. "Can you go on, or do you want to ask for a postponement?"

Savannah took a deep breath. "I want to get this over with."

He patted her knee and nodded at the prosecutor. "She's ready."

Ms. Campbell, who seemed as shaken as Savannah, said, "Continue, please."

Savannah slowly related the events of the day she was kidnapped. She didn't hypothesize about anything she didn't know—like how she was transported from the hospital at Fort Belvoir to the sanatorium in Pennsylvania. She made sure she mentioned frequently the constant and personal surveillance Ferrante kept her under while in the sanatorium. She spoke clearly and was careful to make eye contact with each of the jurors during her testimony. When she was finished, she felt drained but satisfied that she had done the best she could.

Ms. Campbell stepped forward and said, "Thank you for your testimony, Mrs. Dane. I think you have been very thorough." She turned to the grand jury seated in the folding chairs. "Do any of you have questions for our witness?"

A man toward the back raised his hand. "Are you really that guy's daughter?"

It was the first time Savannah had ever had to admit this horrible truth. But she forced herself to nod. "Yes. I just found out a few days ago myself."

"Why did he want to kidnap you?" a woman on the front row asked.

"I know why," Savannah said cautiously, "but I can't explain without tainting my testimony. The important thing is that he did kidnap me and held me against my will."

Ms. Campbell nodded approvingly. "That is the important thing. Are there any more questions?" She paused only a few seconds before declaring, "In that case, we'll excuse you, Mrs. Dane. Thank you for your time."

Savannah stood and walked over to Dane. He took her arm, and together they left the room. Agent Gray and the FBI attorneys were waiting in the hall.

"How did it go?" the agent asked.

"She did great," Dane replied for her.

"What happens next?" Savannah asked.

"We wait and see what the grand jury decides," Agent Gray replied.

"But we don't wait here," Dane said as he pulled out his cell phone. "I want to get back to the CAC offices as soon as possible. But first I've got to call Hack and find out where Ferrante is."

After a brief consultation with Hack, Dane closed the phone. "Ferrante is in a holding cell in the basement," he informed them. "Hack has some guys watching the door, and as soon as we're safely away, Owl will come in and watch Ferrante. I've asked him to let us know when they move him."

"So we can leave?" Savannah asked.

Dane nodded as he helped Savannah put the bulletproof coat back on. "Hack is bringing the car around. Let's go."

CHAPTER 12

THEY WALKED QUICKLY DOWN THE hall, through the lobby, and to a different side entrance. Two of Hack's men were standing inside the door. They walked out, checked the area, and then waved Dane and Savannah out. Surrounded by FBI agents and Hack's men, they walked out and climbed into the car.

Hack was behind the wheel and pulled away from the curb as soon as Dane closed the door. He passed Dane his guns, and Savannah watched as he returned them to their concealed locations.

"Heard you did a great job," Hack told Savannah.

"I did the best I could," she replied. "We won't know if it was enough until we find out what the grand jury decides. How is Caroline?"

"Fine," Hack said. "Steamer says she's having the time of her life."

Savannah smiled. Hopefully the whole experience would be over soon, and for Caroline it would be nothing more than a good memory.

They returned to the CAC offices, and once Savannah was safely ensconced in her office, she removed the Kevlar vest and collapsed into the chair behind her desk.

Owl called a few minutes later to report that he was inside the courthouse and was watching Ferrante.

"I want to talk to him," Savannah told Dane when they'd completed their business.

Dane passed the phone to her, and she said, "Thank you for protecting me. And I'm glad you didn't have to shoot anyone."

She heard Owl laugh. "Me too."

After closing the phone, she asked Dane, "What's going on at the courthouse?"

"Not much," he replied. "They've got Ferrante in a holding cell awaiting the grand jury's decision."

"How much longer will it be?" Savannah asked.

Dane shrugged. "There's no way to know for sure."

After an excruciatingly tedious hour, the door finally opened, and they all looked up. Doc walked in, and his grim expression telegraphed impending bad news.

"The grand jury voted not to indict?" Savannah whispered.

"We haven't heard from the courthouse yet," Doc said.

Savannah felt relieved, but the feeling was short lived.

"I just got word from my source inside the FBI," Doc continued reluctantly. "He said it was the most difficult research project he's ever had, but he was finally able to get the name of the agent who recruited your mother."

She took a deep breath and nodded to let him know she was ready.

Doc looked so sad as he said, "It was Agent Gray."

Tears filled Savannah's eyes. Hack cursed under his breath, and Dane's lips pressed into an angry line.

"You're sure?" Dane verified.

"Yes," Doc confirmed.

There was a commotion in the outer office, and the men all stood.

"Stay here," Dane instructed Savannah. Then he turned to Hack. "You wait with her." The command to kill to protect her if necessary was implied.

Hack nodded, and Dane stepped into the hall, followed closely by Doc.

Savannah stood and moved toward the window, but Hack shook his head.

"You need to stay out of sight. Over here would be best." He pointed to the corner of the room. She had just taken a seat on the couch when Dane and Doc walked back in. Agent Gray was right behind them.

"I've got great news!" the agent announced. "The grand jury voted to indict Ferrante. The government has frozen his assets, seized his properties and is in the process of arresting his employees. Since he no longer has an army of mobsters to protect him or his interests, he's finished in the DC area."

No one spoke.

Agent Gray frowned. "I expected you all to be more excited by this news."

Dane moved over to sit beside Savannah on the couch. "Forgive us for our lack of enthusiasm, but we've just gotten some shocking news."

The agent's expression became wary. "What kind of news?"

"Regarding the agent who recruited Hope Williams."

Agent Gray sighed. "I was going to tell you," he claimed.

Hack grinned without a trace of humor. "I guess you were just waiting for the right moment."

"Actually, I was," Agent Gray replied. Then he turned to Savannah. "Could I talk to you privately?"

She shook her head. "Anything you have to say to me can be said in front of the team."

Agent Gray nodded in resignation. Doc and Hack moved over to stand on either side of the couch, discreetly offering support and protection for the ordeal that was to come.

Savannah focused on the FBI agent. "Tell me," she commanded.

"I wanted to talk to you sooner," he said, "but I felt like it would be better to wait until your grand jury testimony was over."

"You were afraid that if I knew, I wouldn't testify and help you get Ferrante?" she asked.

He shook his head. "I just didn't want to confuse the issues."

"Everything's pretty clear right now," Hack pointed out, "so go ahead and explain how you tricked Savannah's mother into working with Ferrante and ruining her life."

Agent Gray flinched, and Savannah almost felt sorry for him. Almost. He sat down—careful to choose the chair that was farthest away from them—and began.

"I wasn't her first contact. She met a recruiting agent at a college fair and expressed interest. He was impressed with her and gave her information to his superior. After doing some checking, they decided she'd be perfect for Ferrante and wanted to pull her in. I was twenty-five years old and working my first assignment in the field office in Charleston. I was anxious to prove myself and establish some job security."

"You were ambitious," Dane said.

The agent put a hand to his forehead and rubbed. "Ambition isn't a bad thing."

"Unless you hurt other people in your climb to the top," Dane countered.

Savannah leaned forward to put herself in the agent's line of vision. "Please continue."

"The special agent in charge called and said he had an easy job for me," the agent said.

"And you jumped at the chance to impress the higher-ups," Hack guessed.

"They wanted you to recruit a new agent," Savannah prompted with an annoyed look at Hack.

"Yes," Agent Gray confirmed. "I thought he meant they wanted me to find someone to recruit, but when I got to his office he said that the Bureau had already identified the person they wanted. They'd done all the background work, etc. All I had to do was hook her. They sent me to Savannah, Georgia, to meet with Hope. She was so young and beautiful."

"Didn't you feel a little guilty?" Hack asked.

"Maybe a little at first," he admitted, "but she wanted to be an FBI agent more than anything, and the Bureau needed her. So I did what I was told. You understand about following orders."

Dane nodded, but it was more of a prompt to continue than a gesture of agreement.

"She was easy to recruit," the agent told them. "The family didn't have money for college, so we set up a scholarship for her. She breezed through college in three years. After graduation, the FBI hired her, and she went through a basic training course at Quantico."

"You were still working with her?" Dane asked.

Agent Gray nodded. "They moved me to Atlanta, put me on the organized-crime task force, and made me her handler."

"Let me guess, a promotion," Hack sneered.

The agent didn't deny it. "It was a great position that under ordinary circumstances would have taken me years to qualify for. I was grateful for the opportunity, and Hope was happy to have me as her handler. It was a win-win situation. We worked well together, and she wanted her first assignment to be a success."

"Ferrante," Savannah forced herself to say.

"Yes," he said. "We set her up with a computer company that was installing hundreds of units for Ferrante. It was a pet project of his, so we knew he'd be personally involved with the process."

Dane looked more grim than usual. "And you knew once he saw Hope Williams, he'd be smitten."

"We hoped so. The plan worked perfectly. Ferrante was fascinated with Hope. He hired her away from the computer company, and soon she was never far from his side. During the year we had her in place, she provided us with the best intelligence we've ever gotten from inside his organization. She was able to give us names and dates and other specifics that took all the guesswork out of our arrests. She saved so many lives—took so many criminals off the street.

Savannah nodded. "You don't have to convince me that she was a hero."

"More than that—she was so perfect, so successful as an agent. Her data didn't have to be analyzed or researched. She knew exactly what information to get and how to pass it on. We could take what she gave us and act on it. It was that pure."

Dane said, "That's why you left her in even when it got dangerous for her."

The agent's eyes dropped to the floor. "Yes."

"Tell me what happened," Savannah insisted.

Agent Gray took a deep breath. "She'd been begging to be pulled out for almost a month. She said he was getting insistent about a romantic relationship, and she didn't know how long she could hold him off. In the defense of me and my superiors, it's somewhat understood that at this level of undercover work, an agent has to be prepared to do whatever is necessary to maintain their cover. So while none of us wanted her to have to be romantically involved with Ferrante . . ."

"Don't lie," Dane said harshly. "She was chosen specifically because she was his type. It was part of the plan all along for Hope Williams to sleep with Ferrante."

"We thought she understood," Agent Gray said softly.

"It may be a harsh reality," Doc said, "but it's one she should have been warned about."

"They probably went over it during that 'extensive' twelve-week training she was given," Hack said sarcastically.

Agent Gray looked up. "We send plenty of agents into the field with less training than Hope received."

"Not against Ferrante you don't," Dane argued. "It was her innocence that you hoped would attract him."

Agent Gray was not willing to concede the point. "While Hope was young and inexperienced, she was prepared as well as anyone can be for an assignment like that. She had a natural gift for assuming a role and sticking to it. I feel bad about a lot of things that happened with Hope, but not her preparedness. She was ready for Ferrante, and she beat him. We've never had another agent do half as well with him. And she was specifically warned about the possibility of a physical relationship with Ferrante. I told her myself. So intellectually she was aware that it might be necessary to sleep with him. But when the time came, emotionally she couldn't do it."

"So why didn't you just pull her out?" Dane asked.

"There was a big drug bust in the works at that time. We had the chance to get a whole slew of criminals, and we were working on the operation with several other agencies. Like us, all of them had a lot of time and money tied up in it. We needed her to hold out just a few more weeks." He looked up at Dane. "I don't expect you to understand that. If one of your people was in a dangerous situation, you would go in and get them regardless of the cost. Unfortunately, I didn't have that much power or courage."

"That's true," Dane acknowledged. "If she'd been part of my team, I would have moved heaven and earth to get her out. It's understood that members of my team are totally committed to each other. If someone gets in trouble, they know the others will come after them. Even if they die trying to free them."

Savannah turned slightly so Dane could see her face and raised an eyebrow in his direction. He ignored her.

"I had orders," Agent Gray tried to explain. "And following the rules is what separates us from the bad guys."

Dane shook his head. "Following the rules is what makes you predictable and your operatives vulnerable."

The agent spread his hands. "I thought I was doing the right thing— protecting the operation. I thought Hope could handle it."

"So she stayed until the big operation was complete?" Savannah said.

He nodded. "Yes, it was a huge success. Everyone was very pleased."

"Who got Hope out?" Dane asked.

"I did," Agent Gray said. "We were able to keep Ferrante in jail for a few days, and that was my opportunity to extract her." He paused, obviously reluctant to go on.

"Tell me," Savannah said.

With a sigh, he continued. "She wouldn't even look at me. During the entire drive to Atlanta, she didn't say a word. I talked a lot. I tried to explain and apologize, and she just sat there and stared out the window. When we got back, they had her examined mentally and physically. That's when we found out that she'd been raped." Agent Gray's voice took on a dull, monotonous quality as if he were repeating facts that had no personal connection. "The Bureau gave her a desk job and arranged some counseling sessions. I thought that given enough time she'd get over it."

Hack scoffed. "Something like that you never get over."

"I know now that I was naïve," Agent Gray said. "But remember, I was young and inexperienced too. And I paid a personal price as well. My wife was pregnant, and there were complications. She felt like I wasn't being supportive and moved back home with her parents. She filed for divorce a few weeks later, the same day Hope disappeared."

"You'll understand if we can't muster much sympathy for you?" Hack asked.

Agent Gray met his gaze. "I'm not asking for your sympathy. I just want you to know that I didn't come out of this unscathed."

Savannah was frustrated by all the interruptions. She gave Hack a stern look and then asked, "You say my mother just disappeared?"

The agent nodded. "She still wasn't talking to me, so I didn't find out until a little after the fact. They called me when she didn't show up for work two days in a row and missed a counseling session. I checked her apartment and found it empty. The manager said Hope's rent was paid through the end of the month, but she'd put her keys in the drop box and moved without leaving a forwarding address. I called her parents, and they'd heard from her but didn't know where she was."

"You didn't try to find her?"

"I did for a while, but I finally decided that if she wanted to disappear, I should honor her wishes. I hoped that maybe she could start over somewhere new, with a different career and find happiness."

"She didn't," Savannah said. "Find happiness, I mean."

He nodded. "I know. However, she did hide you from Ferrante for over twenty years." There was pride in his voice when he added, "Like I said, she was good."

"And I guess all this helped you move up the FBI chain of command?" Hack asked.

"It should have," the agent agreed. "But after Hope disappeared and my wife left, I struggled with alcoholism and depression. I almost lost my job completely, but then I realized that all I had to live for was to bring Ferrante down. And the only way to do that was to clean up my act. So that's what I did. I've been tracking him and his activities ever since. I've come close to getting him a few times." He looked over at Savannah. "Isn't it fitting that it took Hope's daughter to finally put him away?"

Savannah cleared her throat before speaking. "I feel differently than I thought I would," she began. "Of course I'm sorry for what my mother went through, but I'm proud of her too. And I feel a sense of connection with her—that in a way we worked together to punish Ferrante for all his many crimes." She looked over at Dane. "And I'm determined not to let bad things that happen make me bitter and ruin my ability to enjoy life. And enjoy my daughter."

Dane took her hand in his. "I think you're looking at this in exactly the right way. What's done is done. There's nothing we can do to change the past. We should concentrate on the future."

She managed a small smile. "Where have I heard that before?"

He ignored this and turned back to Agent Gray. "What's going on with Ferrante now?"

"He's in a holding room at the courthouse waiting to be taken before a judge. Because of the security issues that surround moving him, they have arranged a hearing for today. He'll be notified of the indictments against him, they'll set a trial date, and then he'll have the opportunity to request bail."

"Which will surely be denied," Doc said. "I can't imagine a greater flight risk."

Agent Gray nodded. "Bail will be denied, and Ms. Campbell will petition the judge to make Savannah's grand jury testimony admissible as evidence in his trial. This is an insurance policy of sorts, and it won't guarantee Savannah's safety, but if they know that her testimony is already a matter of record, there's less reason to kill her."

Dane winced.

"I'm sorry," the agent apologized. "But that's the best I could do. We'll push for a quick trial . . ."

Dane squeezed Savannah's hand. "I understand. Security is our specialty. We'll keep Savannah and Caroline safe until Ferrante is convicted."

Agent Gray stood. "I need to get back to my office now."

Savannah rose as well and took a step toward the agent. She had conflicting feelings regarding him and knew that she'd need time to sort them out. "Maybe we can talk again," she said.

He nodded. "I'd like that."

Hack was less forgiving. "I'll show you to the door," he offered.

The agent took this dismissal in stride. With a small wave to Savannah, he followed Hack out of her office and down the hall toward the front entrance.

"Well," Doc said after the agent was gone, "that answers a lot of questions."

"Slowly we're filling in the gaps of my mother's life," Savannah agreed. "Eventually we may know the whole story."

Hack returned, muttering under his breath, and Savannah didn't even try to understand what he was saying.

"So what do we do next?" she asked Dane.

"We'll collect Caroline and go home," Dane said as he pulled out his cell phone.

Tears stung Savannah's eyes. "Home." It had always seemed like an impossible dream. Now maybe it had a place in her reality.

"I'm going to have Owl stay with Ferrante and monitor everything that goes on with him." Dane walked into the hall while making a call to Owl and waved for them to follow him.

They stopped at the smoked-glass doors that separated the CAC offices from the fourth-floor hallway.

"Savannah and I are going to get Caroline," Dane told them. "Doc, you'll come with us. Hack, we'll need a few of your guys too."

Savannah frowned. "You heard Agent Gray. Ferrante is headed to prison, and his organization has been dismantled. We don't have anything to fear from him now."

Dane shrugged. "It's force of habit. I have to be cautious—even when there's no apparent danger."

She knew it was pointless to argue, so she smiled at Doc. "Even if we don't need protection, we always enjoy your company."

Doc smiled back.

Dane continued his assignments. "Hack, you stay here and dismantle all the security equipment."

Hack nodded.

"When you're done, come to the cabin. We'll meet you there."

As they walked out into the empty hallway, Savannah felt a sense of sad relief. She had left the CAC offices many times, but today it felt final. Perhaps she was finally leaving the past behind her and moving forward.

Dane walked as briskly as his bad leg would allow to the elevator. There he punched the down button with more force than necessary.

"You seem to be in a big hurry," Savannah said. "Is something wrong?"

He shook his head. "I'll just be glad when all this is over and we have Caroline back with us."

Savannah couldn't argue that. "How long will it take us to get to the general's condo?"

"About thirty minutes," he replied. "Depending on traffic."

They were stepping onto the elevator when Doc's cell phone rang. He listened for a few seconds and then held up his hand. "Wait!" he commanded, and they stared at him in alarm.

"What's wrong?" Dane demanded.

"Nothing's wrong," Doc assured them, and Savannah watched as the tension drained out of Dane's face. "Well, there's no danger," Doc amended. He turned away and completed his conversation. Then he closed his phone and addressed Dane and Savannah. "General Steele just patched a call through from George Washington University Medical Center. Rosemary Allen is having her baby."

Dane waved his hand impatiently. "That's her business, not ours."

Doc persevered. "Her husband was just arrested in the labor room."

"As part of the FBI's roundup of Ferrante's employees?" Savannah guessed.

Doc nodded. "That leaves her there alone to deliver her baby."

Dane put one foot into the elevator. "I'm sorry, but that's what she gets for marrying a criminal."

Savannah gave him a disappointed look as Doc continued. "Savannah was listed as a relative on Rosemary's hospital admission papers. So when they arrested Chad, one of the nurses called information at Fort Belvoir trying to contact her." He turned to Savannah. "The nurse said they'd like for Rosemary to have someone there with her when the baby comes."

Savannah turned to Dane and clutched his arm. "I have to go."

Dane shook his head. "No way."

"You said yourself that security should be sufficient," she reminded him.

"I don't remember saying that exactly," Dane hedged. "And Rosemary Ferrante has always been trouble for us."

Savannah had already made up her mind. She was going to the hospital whether he chose to come along or not. But she decided to try negotiation before she issued an ultimatum. "She's my sister."

"She's a woman you barely know who shares some of the same DNA," Dane argued. "The nurses at the hospital will take care of her. Now let's go get Caroline."

"I can go to the general's condo and wait with Steamer and Neely and Caroline while you and Savannah go to the hospital." Doc joined Savannah's persuasive effort. "When the baby is born, we'll bring Caroline to your cabin and meet you. No time will have been wasted, and Rosemary won't have to have her baby alone."

"And what if some of Ferrante's diehard employees haven't gotten the word that he's finished yet and follow us to the hospital?" Dane demanded.

Doc had an answer for that too. "Hack can send a security detail to the hospital to make sure it's safe before you get there."

Dane gave them an exasperated look. "And why should we change our plans to help Rosemary Ferrante?"

Savannah was composing a response, but Doc was quicker.

"Like Savannah said, she's her sister and she's alone," he said quietly.

"When Caroline was born, there was no one there with me," Savannah added in an effort to gain sympathy for Rosemary. "And it was hard. There was no one else to be happy with me and tell me what a beautiful baby Caroline was. I don't want it to be that way for Rosemary."

"Sometimes it takes days to have a baby," Dane muttered, and Savannah could tell he was weakening.

"The nurse said the baby will be here within the hour," Doc was pleased to report.

Dane didn't look happy. "It's still a risk—and an inconvenience."

Doc smiled. "Nothing we can't handle."

Dane sighed as he pulled out his phone and called Hack. He explained the situation and then said, "Send an advance team over to the hospital to make sure we won't receive an unpleasant welcome."

"I'll do better than that," Hack's voice blared from the phone. "I'll come along myself. I can pack up computers later."

"Come on," Dane agreed. "We'll wait for you."

"Do you want me to head to the general's condo?" Doc asked.

Dane shook his head. "Just call Steamer and let him know to be on high alert." Dane frowned at Savannah. "I don't like us all being spread out like this."

"You worry too much," Savannah told him.

"It's impossible to worry *too* much," he replied as Hack arrived.

"I've got a team headed to the hospital," Hack informed Dane. "They should have the area secured by the time we get there."

Once they were all inside the elevator, Savannah leaned against the wall and thought about Rosemary. Being related to Mario Ferrante was unquestionably a bad thing—but Rosemary was the silver lining. Savannah liked the idea of being an aunt and knew Caroline would be excited to know she had a cousin. She hoped that her presence at the baby's birth would signify the beginning of a new stage of life. A life where she had a sister but was free of Ferrante and the danger he posed.

When the elevator reached the first floor, they exited through the heavily guarded front entrance and walked out onto the sidewalk. Dane led the way to the Hummer and opened the front passenger door for Savannah. Once she was settled, he climbed in under the wheel while Hack and Doc got into the truck parked behind them. They waited for their escort cars to move into position. Then Dane pulled out into the street and headed toward George Washington Medical Center.

The drive to the hospital was short, but once they arrived at the sprawling campus, it took a few minutes to find a place to park. Then they had to wait in the Hummer until Hack's advance team gave them the all-clear signal. Dane fidgeted and sighed during this process—as though he'd never wasted a minute before.

To distract him, Savannah said, "I like this Hummer, but it's so big and conspicuous. If Hack won't let me get a CR-V, maybe he'll consider other options."

"You'll have to discuss that with Hack." He glanced in his rearview mirror. "But maybe safety won't be such an issue in the future. I hope that our hiding days are almost over."

Finally Hack and Doc walked up to the Hummer.

"My men are finished with their search," Hack reported. "Everything looks fine."

"Then let's hurry and get this over with," Dane said as he climbed out and opened Savannah's door.

When they walked inside the Women's Center lobby, Dane asked a woman at the information desk where they could find Rosemary Allen, and she directed them up to the third floor. As they rode the elevator, Savannah started to feel a little anxious. Having only been involved in one birth—Caroline's—she was far from being an expert. She didn't know Rosemary well, and much of what they had in common was painful history. She slowed her pace as the reality of the situation became apparent to her.

Dane sensed her hesitation and put a hand on her elbow, propelling her forward. "Let's hurry. We wouldn't want you to miss a single minute of the blessed event."

At the nurses' station, Savannah identified herself, and they were informed that they had already missed the entire birth. Rosemary had delivered a seven-pound baby girl fifteen minutes earlier.

Savannah tried to hide her relief, but she saw Dane's knowing smile. Ignoring him, she asked the nurse how Rosemary was doing.

"Both mother and baby are fine," the nurse said. "I'll check and see if she's ready for visitors." The nurse walked across the hall and into a room identified as MATERNITY SUITE FIVE by a little sign on the door.

As Savannah stood nervously beside Dane, she noticed that all the other maternity suites had wreaths on the door, announcing whether the mom inside had delivered a boy or girl. But Rosemary's door was ominously unadorned. "It's a shame that Rosemary doesn't have a wreath," she told Dane. "It makes it look like nobody cares about her. Maybe I could go to the gift shop and get her one . . ."

Dane shook his head and pointed as the nurse emerged from Rosemary's maternity room and waved them forward. "No time for shopping now."

"I'll go get a wreath for the door," Doc offered kindly.

Savannah smiled at him. "Thanks."

"And I'll stand guard out here." Hack took a position in front of Rosemary's door with easy access to a waiting room with vending machines.

Left without any more excuses, Savannah pushed open the door and walked into the maternity suite.

The only light on in the room came from a fluorescent fixture right over Rosemary's hospital bed. The effect was lovely—as if heaven were illuminating the scene. Rosemary looked tired but beautiful as she held her new daughter.

Savannah felt a sense of reverence as she approached the bed and had to struggle to contain her emotions. Dane stayed near the door—obviously designating himself as an observer, not a participant.

Savannah stepped into the little circle of light and said, "Hi."

Rosemary looked up. "Thanks for coming."

Savannah shrugged. "I'm new at being a sister, but I think attending the births of my nieces and nephew is required."

Rosemary smiled. "I'm glad you're here, and I'm sorry that you're a part of the dreaded Ferrante family."

"How long have you known?"

"For about a year," Rosemary said.

"So you knew when you came to Fort Belvoir to ask for my help?"

Rosemary nodded. "But I swear I wasn't working with my father to hurt you. I just needed help. I planned to tell you about our relationship—eventually."

Out of the corner of her eye, Savannah saw Dane's expression harden, and she knew he didn't believe Rosemary's claim. Savannah wasn't completely convinced of Rosemary's innocence herself, but she didn't want to accuse the new mother of lying. So instead she said, "We both had it rough. I grew up with no father and a paranoid mother. You grew up with no mother and a psychotic father."

"Is there any hope for us?" Rosemary whispered.

Savannah nodded. "Yes, because of your daughter and mine."

Rosemary seems cheered by this. She lifted the baby slightly and said, "Would you like to hold her?"

Savannah accepted the tightly wrapped bundle. "What's her name?"

"I think I'm going to name her Rene after my mother," Rosemary said. "It's not much of a connection, but it's the best I can do."

At the time Caroline was born, Savannah had still been resentful of her own mother and had therefore carefully avoided any association when she picked a name for her new daughter. "I think that's nice," she told Rosemary. "If I could go back and do it again, I'd name Caroline after my mother too."

Rosemary cut her eyes toward Dane. "Maybe you can name your next daughter after your mother."

Savannah's heart pounded at the thought of a baby in her future. Ever since New Orleans and her fake pregnancy there, she'd been longing for another child. "Maybe."

"So your testimony was enough to finally put my—our—father in jail," Rosemary remarked.

"Yes," Savannah confirmed, "but I'm sorry Chad got arrested too."

"We'll sort it out," Rosemary said. "Maybe he can make a deal or something to avoid prison time."

"Is that what you want?" Savannah asked, trying to keep the frustration from her voice. "I thought you wanted to start a new life away from all that."

"I love him," Rosemary said simply. "If he'll promise to stay away from illegal activities from now on, then I want us to be a family."

Savannah couldn't argue with this. She knew how love could overwhelm rational thinking. So she just said, "I hope he can be the kind of husband you want him to be."

Rosemary smiled and pointed at the baby. "You can kiss her if you want."

Savannah pressed a quick kiss on the baby's forehead. The newborn skin was soft and smelled incredibly sweet.

"I'm sorry to interrupt," Dane said from the door, "but we need to leave."

"Dane thinks my being here is a security risk," Savannah told Rosemary.

Rosemary nodded. "I understand. Maybe you can bring Caroline to see the baby sometime. I want them to be friends."

"I'd like that too." Reluctantly Savannah returned the baby to her mother. "Where will you go when you leave here?"

"There's a hostel attached to the hospital with rooms you can rent—kind of like a hotel. I'll stay there for a week or so while General Steele helps me petition the court for some of my father's assets. Once that's arranged, I'll be able to buy a place of my own. Then I'll hire Chad a good lawyer and see what happens."

"The general is a good person to help you," Savannah said. "And you know I'll be glad to do anything I can. I'd give you my cell phone number if I had a cell phone." She gave Dane a look over her shoulder.

"If you need us, call this number." Dane walked forward and put a small card in Rosemary's hand.

Savannah glanced at the card and saw that Dane had written both his temporary cell phone number and his more permanent home number. She was touched by this seemingly sincere offer of assistance.

"But now we really do have to go," he prompted gently. "Until Ferrante is safely behind bars, having the two of you together is just asking for trouble."

Rosemary gave them a tremulous smile. "Thank you for coming."

Savannah bent down and gave the girl an awkward half-hug. "We'll be checking in on you again soon." Then she allowed Dane to lead her from the room.

"Is she okay?" Hack asked as they walked into the hall.

"Considering all she's been through," Savannah began, "I'd say she's doing amazingly well. And the baby is beautiful."

"Does she look like Caroline did?" Hack asked.

Savannah shook her head. "No, Caroline looked like Wes."

Doc arrived during the awkward silence that followed this remark carrying a huge pink wreath. "It was the biggest one they had," he said unnecessarily as he hung it on the door.

Hack grinned. "I couldn't have done better myself."

Savannah blinked back tears. "It sure doesn't look like nobody cares about Rosemary and her baby now!"

Dane took Savannah by her good hand and pulled her toward the elevators. "Let's get out of here. It's lunchtime, and I'm starving."

"They've got ham salad sandwiches in the vending machines," Hack told him as they walked down the hall.

"I can't imagine eating ham salad under any circumstances," Dane replied. "But certainly not when it's been in a vending machine for who knows how long."

Hack laughed. "What do you think preservatives are for?"

They walked through the hospital's crowded hallway toward the row of elevators that would take them back down to the lobby.

"So was that all you hoped it would be?" Dane asked.

"It's nice to have a sister," Savannah admitted.

"Which means Caroline has an aunt and a cousin," Doc contributed.

Savannah grimaced. "And a grandfather."

Hack shrugged. "Nothing's perfect."

Just before they reached the elevators, a door to their left crashed open. Dane and his men acted instinctively to protect Savannah. Dane pushed her down and against the wall as they all pulled out weapons. Savannah glanced around Dane to see several hospital employees emerge with a patient on a gurney. As they hurried by, Dane helped Savannah to her feet and then stowed his gun.

Savannah pressed her good hand to her pounding heart. "You scared me to death!"

"Better safe than sorry," Dane replied. Then his eyes moved to a small alcove across from the elevators. He stared at the little room for a few seconds and then made a decision. "Hack, you and Doc wait here. I need to talk to Savannah for a minute." He pulled Savannah gently across the hall and into the waiting area.

* * *

Once they were inside the little room, Dane closed the door and turned off the light. Whether this was a security precaution or an attempt to get maximum privacy, Savannah couldn't tell. Then he pulled her into his arms, and she didn't care.

He pressed a kiss to her forehead and whispered, "I'm sorry that I criticized your rescue attempt."

Nothing he could have said would have surprised her more. She pushed back a little so she could think more clearly and said, "You're not mad at me anymore for trying to rescue you?"

He shook his head. "It's what any member of the team would do for another. I realized what a hypocrite I'd been when I was telling Agent Gray how committed we all are to each other. I shouldn't have expected any less. My only excuse is that I value your life much more than my own. If one of us has to die, I want it to be me."

She frowned. "So intellectually you agree with the all-for-one-and-one-for-all concept? But when you're the one who needs us all, you have trouble accepting our help?"

He shrugged. "I guess you could say I'm more comfortable with the role of knight in shining armor than the damsel in distress."

"Me too," she agreed. "Rescuing you was exhilarating."

He smiled. "I hope you don't get another opportunity to experience that particular kind of exhilaration. Anyway, I know you feel that I betrayed you, and you're uncertain about my feelings. So before we go any further I think I need to clarify things."

"I'm listening," she said anxiously.

He took a deep breath and then continued. "I really was planning to tell you about your relationship to Ferrante, and I admit now that I should have made the time rather than wait for an opportunity to present itself."

This was a major concession on his part, and she felt better already. "Thank you."

"And it's true that when I found out you were Ferrante's daughter, it did make a difference to me."

She stiffened.

"But not the difference you think," he was quick to add. "Before, when I thought Ferrante was only after me, I felt that marriage would make your life more dangerous. Once I knew that Ferrante had a personal interest in *you* and would never stop his pursuit, I realized that proximity to me would actually make you safer. That meant I could marry you with a clear conscience." He gave her a half smile. "Relatively speaking."

"That's why you wouldn't return my calls or let me be a part of your life?" she demanded. "Because you thought it was too dangerous?"

He nodded. "It would have been selfish.

"So you really do want to be married to me?"

He stroked her cheek. "Yes."

"You really do love me?" she pressed.

After the slightest hesitation he said, "Yes."

"Even though I'm Mario Ferrante's daughter?"

He nodded.

"Even though I married Wes when I thought you were dead?"

He closed his eyes briefly. "Yes."

She grabbed a fistful of his shirt with her good hand. "And how do I know you're not lying to me?"

He pressed his lips to hers. Several minutes later he whispered, "Some things can't be faked, even by experts like me."

She weakly acknowledged this with a nod.

"So everything is settled between us?" he confirmed.

"Yes," she agreed. "Now kiss me again."

He smiled. "There'll be time for that later. Right now we need to get out of this hospital." He took her hand and led her out of the little waiting room to the elevators where Hack and Doc were patiently waiting for them.

"It's about time," Hack said. "I was headed down the hall to get another ham salad sandwich."

Dane pushed the down button on the elevator. "I'm glad we saved you from that culinary mistake."

Hack laughed. "It wouldn't have been my first."

Doc was quietly watching Dane and Savannah. He seemed to sense that there had been yet another shift in their relationship. "Is everything okay?" he finally asked.

Savannah nodded. "Everything is fine."

Doc looked relieved as the elevator arrived and they all climbed inside.

"So," Hack said as they rode down to the lobby, "we're going to get Caroline?"

Dane nodded.

"Is it safe?" Savannah had to ask.

Dane put a hand on her elbow and guided her off the elevator. His eyes were moving constantly, on the lookout for trouble. "Ferrante is in custody, and all his people are being rounded up. He shouldn't pose a threat anymore."

Just as they reached the exit, Dane's cell phone rang. He pulled it from his pocket and answered. He listened for a few seconds and then closed the phone.

"That was Owl," he told them. "Ferrante's request for bail was denied as we expected. But he told the judge that his youngest daughter had just given birth and petitioned the court to allow him to visit her in the hospital before he was taken to prison to await trial."

"Ferrante is coming here?" Hack said.

"That's strange," Doc said. "I don't think he cares anything at all about Rosemary or her baby."

"Then why would he want to come here and see her?" Savannah asked.

The men exchanged a look, and then they all moved for the door at once. "We need to get to Caroline," Dane said. "Fast!"

* * *

Two of Hack's men were standing guard at the hospital entrance. Hack instructed his employees to follow them, and they all walked outside. Savannah had to run to keep up with Dane as he hurried to the Hummer.

"You think Ferrante just used Rosemary as an excuse to get out of the courthouse?" she asked Dane breathlessly. "But really he's going to try to escape and get to Caroline?"

"I think it's a very good possibility," Dane acknowledged as he opened the passenger door for her. "There's only one way to find out."

While sliding under the wheel, Dane called Steamer. After a brief conversation, he returned the phone to his pocket. "Steamer says they haven't seen Ferrante yet," he reported to Savannah.

"Shouldn't we call the police?"

"Not until we know for sure what's going on," he said. "Besides, they might send cops who are on Ferrante's payroll."

She turned to stare out the windshield. "Drive as fast as you can."

It took less than twenty minutes to reach the condominium complex where General Steele's unit was located. Savannah knew she should be happy that Dane was able to negotiate the traffic so quickly, but she was too nervous to feel anything besides anxiety.

"I'm calling Owl." Dane pulled out his phone and called. A minute later he said, "No answer."

Dane turned in to the parking deck and pulled the Hummer to a stop. Savannah watched in the rearview mirror as one of Hack's men climbed out of the escort car and took up a guard position by the parking deck's entrance. Once he was in place, Dane eased the Hummer forward.

Dane found three empty parking spaces together on the third level. He pulled in to one and turned off the Hummer as Hack parked the pickup truck beside them and the escort car took the third space. Dane climbed out and walked around to the back of the vehicle, leaving Savannah to get out on her own. He opened the back hatch, and she joined him in time to see him pull out two Kevlar vests. He draped one over his shoulders and passed one to her.

"Put this on," he commanded. "Just in case."

She didn't argue.

Dane helped her to put on the vest correctly, and then he tightened the straps on his own. Once the vests were in place, Dane pulled a small handgun from his pocket and pressed it into her open palm. "Promise me you'll use this only as a last resort?"

She nodded and tucked the gun into the pocket of her coat. When Hack and Doc walked over to them, both men were wearing vests as well. The driver of the escort car was standing behind his vehicle, looking alert.

"The general's condo is on the fifth floor," Dane said. "We'll use the stairs as a security precaution. Hack, you go up first. We'll wait here until you tell us that everything's clear."

Hack and Doc nodded in unison.

Dane turned back to Savannah. She held up a hand to stop him. "I know what you're going to say, and I don't want to hear it. I'm part of the team too. I'll take the same risks as the rest of you."

"You are a part of the team," he began diplomatically, "but you aren't as well trained as the rest of us. And you're Caroline's mother. Those two things make a huge difference in the risks we're willing to allow you to take."

Savannah looked from Dane to Doc to Hack. They were all regarding her with the same stubborn expression. She couldn't fight them all. Besides, Dane was right. So she agreed. "Okay. What am I going to be *allowed* to do?"

Dane's obvious relief was mirrored on the faces of both Hack and Doc.

"I want you to stay behind me as we walk up," Dane began. "And then follow every command I give you quickly and without question."

She considered this for a few seconds and nodded. "I'll do what you say."

Satisfied, Dane turned to Hack. "Hack, go on up and see if it's safe for us to bring Savannah inside."

Hack pulled a gun from his shoulder holster and moved into the stairwell.

As the door closed behind him, a cold wind whipped through the concrete columns that dissected the parking area. Savannah shivered, and Dane put an arm across her shoulders to help ward off the cold.

Doc moved up beside her, providing a partial windbreak. "It shouldn't be long," he told her.

She moved closer to Dane and was enjoying the pleasure of his proximity so much, she might not have noticed the two soft popping noises from behind them if Hack's guard hadn't crumpled forward onto the asphalt. Savannah stared at the fallen guard in confusion for a split second before Dane yanked her behind the nearest concrete column. Dane and Doc drew their guns and then stood close together, using their bodies to make a shield for her.

"What's happening?" she whispered.

"Ferrante," Dane guessed grimly.

They didn't have to wait long before his prediction was proven correct. A few feet away, Mario Ferrante stepped out from behind a concrete column. He was still wearing his prison jumpsuit, and his handcuffs dangled harmlessly from one wrist.

Raul Giordano and Chad Allen moved into place beside Ferrante, and several armed men who had previously been hidden moved forward as well.

"You are separated from all your loyal soldiers," Ferrante yelled. "The guard you left at the entrance is incapacitated, and the men Raul posted upstairs are detaining your huge bodyguard. They report that sadly my granddaughter is not in General Steele's condo as we had been told. But that's only a minor inconvenience. We'll collect her later."

Savannah glanced at Dane.

"Caroline is safe," he whispered. "Steamer moved her."

Relieved, she looked back at her father and managed to ask, "How?"

He gave her one of his nasty smiles. "How did I know about the general's condo and Dane's plan to stash your daughter here? I knew because I have an inside man at Fort Belvoir—a very reliable spy. He's just an unassuming, innocent-looking little corporal who no one would suspect but who has access to all kinds of sensitive information. And he passes everything he learns right along to me."

Savannah was stunned. "Corporal Benjamin works for *you?*"

"He does," Ferrante confirmed. "So don't feel too badly about choosing Lieutenant Hardy over him during your kidnapping. Either way you would have ended up in my custody."

Rather than try to process this disturbing information, Savannah asked, "How did you get away from the authorities?"

"The U.S. marshals made the mistake of underestimating me," he said. "They thought that with my organization dismantled and my employees arrested, I wouldn't be able to escape. But they didn't count on my friends." He nodded toward Giordano, who stood stoically beside him. "All I had to do was make was one simple phone call."

Savannah turned disappointed eyes to the man she had thought they could trust, but he wouldn't meet her gaze.

"If you've escaped, shouldn't you be running away instead of playing hide-and-seek in parking decks?" Dane asked.

"The marshals think I'm at George Washington Memorial, so they have dedicated all their manpower to searching that particular area. By the time they realize their mistake, I will be headed to a safe location outside the U.S. So if you'll send Savannah over to me, I'll be on my way."

"Why do you want to take your daughters and grandchildren?" Doc asked. "We all know you don't love them."

"They're insurance against retaliation," Ferrante said. "Kind of like reverse hostages. And company for my old age."

"You know I can't let you take her," Dane said simply.

"I know you can't stop me," Ferrante returned with a sneer. "If you want to die trying, that's up to you."

Savannah's mind was in turmoil. Hack's guard was wounded and needed medical attention. An extended conversation with Ferrante would decrease his chances of survival. Hack was Giordano's prisoner. Dane and Doc were poised and ready to defend her with their lives. She felt a surge of love for them and an overwhelming hatred for the man who had fathered her.

Desperate, she turned to Raul Giordano. "You said family was off limits in business matters," she called to him. "Why would you help him kidnap me and Rosemary and our children? I thought you could be trusted."

Giordano did not look sympathetic. "I thought, too, that we had a mutual understanding, of an unusual sort. But then Mario called me with proof that the charges against Major Dane were fabricated as well as your incriminating testimony. You used me and lied to me. That's not very trustworthy, now is it?"

A knot of dread began to form in Savannah's stomach, but she didn't deny it. "You can't blame me for wanting to free Dane."

"I can blame you for lying to me," Giordano said coldly. "For using my emotions against me. For convincing me to betray a friend, all on false pretenses."

They had known from the beginning that Giordano would not take it lightly if he found out that he was being used. Once they got Dane back, Savannah had considered the risk to be over. Now she saw her mistake, but it was too late. "I'm sorry."

Dane interrupted by saying, "Don't apologize to him. He's a criminal—just like Ferrante."

"You also failed to mention that you are Mario's daughter," Giordano continued.

"I didn't know," Savannah yelled earnestly. "I only found out a few days ago myself."

"I find that hard to believe," Giordano replied.

"Would you advertise a relationship to a snake like Ferrante?" Dane asked. He seemed to be purposely antagonizing Ferrante, and Savannah couldn't begin to understand how that would help them.

"We've wasted enough time," Ferrante said finally. "Send my daughter to me."

"I am not your child," Savannah declared vehemently.

"Of course you are," Ferrante taunted. "And you look just like your lovely mother."

Savannah shook with fury. "Don't you dare talk about my mother!"

Ferrante laughed. "You remain so bold in such a vulnerable situation. Now step away from your *husband* before I ask Raul's men to shoot him."

Savannah wasn't sure what to do. She didn't want to go with Ferrante. She couldn't even imagine being under his control again. But if she didn't go, Dane and Doc would surely die. She looked to Raul Giordano. The fading afternoon light was insufficient for her to read his expression, but the gun in his hand spoke volumes.

Dane seemed to sense her intentions. He spoke over his shoulder and said, "You promised to follow orders, and I am commanding you to stay right where you are."

"He won't kill me," she said. "But he will kill you and Doc. I have to go."

"No." Dane shook his head. "This is between me and Ferrante." Dane pointed his revolver at Ferrante.

"It was never just between you and Ferrante," Savannah said. "I'm involved too—because of my mother."

Ferrante laughed. "That's right, dear. Talk them out of resistance. If they don't cooperate, Raul's men will kill them before they can get off a single shot."

Doc dropped onto one knee and aimed his gun in Ferrante's direction as well. "Savannah's not going anywhere with you," the mild-mannered medic said.

Ferrante looked incredulous. "Do you two think you are a match for Raul and all his men?"

"We don't have to be a match for them," Doc said coldly. "All we have to do is put one bullet in your black heart."

Raul Giordano shook his head. "You don't have many friends here, Mario."

Ferrante shrugged. "Just have your men shoot them. All I want is the girl."

Savannah's heart pounded. She knew she was going to have to leave the security that Dane and Doc were providing in order to protect them. And she knew Dane was going to be furious at her for disobeying an order. But it was better for them all to live to fight another day. She pressed her cheek against the cool concrete column and prayed for strength. Then she put her good hand into her pocket and let her fingers take command of Dane's extra gun.

"No, Savannah!" Dane whispered.

She ignored him and spun into the open with the little gun concealed behind her back.

"Hold your fire!" Giordano commanded his men.

"That's a good little girl," Ferrante said. "Come to your daddy."

Tears blurred her vision, but she blinked them back and took another step toward him. She could do anything for Dane.

When she was only a few feet away from Ferrante, he said, "Raul, point your gun at Savannah, and if these gentlemen don't do exactly as they're told, shoot her."

Giordano changed the angle of his gun as Ferrante had requested until it was pointing directly at Savannah's heart.

"Now," Ferrante said to Dane, "you and the medic drop your guns, or Raul will shoot."

With dismay, Savannah heard the sound of two guns clattering to the ground. Dane and Doc were disarmed and completely vulnerable. Now she was the only armed member of the team.

Ferrante turned to Giordano. "Once I leave, have your men kill Major Dane and the medic. The fat man and the guy from Las Vegas, too."

"You promised that if I came with you, they'd be okay!" Savannah cried.

Ferrante grinned. "I lied."

She stared at him with something approaching wonder. He really didn't have a single redeeming quality. With deadly determination, she pulled the gun from behind her back and pointed it at her father. "I will kill you."

Ferrante laughed. "You won't. You can't kill your own flesh and blood." He held up his empty hands. "I'm unarmed. It would be cold-blooded murder."

"Don't do it, Savannah," Dane begged her earnestly. "You don't want that on your conscience."

"If you kill me, Giordano's men will kill you," Ferrante said.

She took a step closer. "This does have to end. If I kill you and they kill me, at least it will be over, and the people I love will be safe."

"Put down the gun, Savannah." Now Ferrante sounded testy. "You're embarrassing yourself."

She released the safety and cocked the trigger, just like Dane had taught her years ago on the practice range at Fort Belvoir.

All traces of humor left Ferrante's expression. "Savannah."

In her peripheral vision, she saw Chad Allen pull out his gun and spin around. If she didn't shoot Ferrante before Chad shot her, all would be lost. She was out of time and out of options.

"This is for my mother," she hissed, forcing her finger to move.

Shots echoed through the parking deck, and the gun flew from Savannah's hands as Dane tackled her to the ground. When her cast hit the asphalt, sharp pains radiated up her arm, and she screamed in agony.

"Are you shot?" Dane asked.

She shook her head. "It's just my arm."

"I'm sorry!" Dane he rolled over to ease the pressure on her arm.

Slowly the pain receded, and she lifted her head. Giordano and his men had disappeared, and Ferrante was lying facedown on the asphalt a few feet away. His orange polyester jumpsuit was marred by a growing circle of red near his left shoulder.

"I killed him," she whispered.

Dane shook his head. "I think Owl got him."

Savannah frowned. "Owl?"

Dane pointed to the upper deck, where Owl stood with his rifle.

"What was Owl doing here?" Savannah asked.

"Protecting you from Ferrante," Dane said as he stood. Then he leaned down and helped her to her feet.

"But you said he wouldn't answer his phone."

"He turns off his phone when he's tracking someone," Dane explained. "A phone call could give his position away."

"So you knew Ferrante was coming here?" she asked.

"I was pretty sure," Dane said as Hack rushed out of the building and ran toward them.

"Is everybody okay?" he hollered.

"We're fine," Dane said, "but you've got a man down."

Hack ran over to his fallen guard. Doc was already there.

"He's alive," Doc told him, "and I've called for an ambulance."

Hack nodded. "Thank you, little man."

Dane approached the lifeless body of Mario Ferrante, and Savannah followed reluctantly. As Savannah stared down at the man who had been both her father and her tormentor, she felt nothing but relief. Doc hurried over to Ferrante, and after a quick examination, he pronounced the crime boss dead. "He was hit three times," Doc told them. "But the bullet through the heart killed him." Doc looked up at Dane. "There are powder burns around the fatal wound."

Dane frowned. "Ferrante was shot at close range?"

"Who?" Savannah asked.

"Giordano," Chad said. "I saw him shoot Ferrante right in the chest. I got him in the shoulder, and the sniper caught him in the neck."

Owl looked embarrassed. "Sorry, boss. I guess I'm a little out of practice."

Savannah felt tears sting her eyes. "Giordano was our ally after all."

Dane didn't look as sure. "Or he saw this as a good opportunity to get rid of Ferrante and take over organized crime in the Washington, DC, area."

"Either way, he helped us," Savannah said.

"Ferrante is dead, and Savannah's safe. That's all that matters," Hack muttered.

Savannah turned to Chad. "You shot Ferrante too?"

Rosemary's husband nodded. "I guess you could say it was my way of telling him I quit."

Savannah looked back at the building with worry. "Where is Caroline? And Steamer?"

"They're at the Naval Academy."

Savannah frowned. "Did we switch branches of the armed forces?"

Dane nodded. "Just temporarily. Hack figured nobody would think of that—even Corporal Benjamin."

Savannah smiled at Hack. "Hack is almost always right." Then she looked back at Dane. "Did you know Corporal Benjamin was working for Ferrante?"

"I had my suspicions."

Savannah waved to take in the parking deck. "So this was a setup all along. You meant for Ferrante to die here, today."

Dane nodded. "We couldn't risk turning him over to the justice system again."

"And why didn't you tell me?" she asked. "Didn't you trust me?"

"I trust you," Dane said. "But some things can't be said out loud. You never know who is listening. Some things you just have to know."

"How could I have known that Caroline wasn't really here?" Savannah asked in frustration.

He pulled her close. "I would never bring trouble near Caroline or leave her underprotected. As soon as you heard me tell Hack and Doc to stay with us instead of going to reinforce Steamer, you should have known Caroline was not at this condo."

Savannah nodded. It was true. "You're right. There were plenty of clues. I just didn't pick up on them. And thank you—for protecting Caroline, I mean."

He nodded. "You're welcome."

"Are we going to get her now?"

He whispered, "She's on her way to Fort Belvoir. We'll pick her up there."

The sound of sirens rent the air, and Savannah stepped closer to Dane.

"How are we going to explain all this?" Hack asked Dane as an ambulance and two police cars pulled up.

"Let me handle it," Chad said. He pulled something from his coat pocket and approached the first police car. After a quick conversation, he returned and waved toward the Hummer. "I told them I was taking you back to FBI headquarters for questioning. Let's get out of here quick before they change their minds about letting us go."

"I'll stay here with my man," Hack said.

Dane nodded. "Meet us at Fort Belvoir when you've got him settled."

The rest of them piled into the vehicle, with Dane behind the wheel, and once they were driving down the parking ramp, Savannah asked Chad, "Why would the police believe that you were taking us to FBI headquarters?"

Chad pulled a badge from his pocket and handed it to Savannah.

She studied it briefly and then turned her eyes back to stare at him. "You're an FBI agent?"

"I'm Agent Gray's inside man," Chad told them. And before Savannah could recover from the shock of learning this, he added, "And I'm also his son."

"His *son!*" Savannah and Dane chorused in unison.

Chad smiled. "My parents divorced when I was a baby, and I never had much contact with my dad until I went to college. Then I looked him up, and we got pretty close. I had an interest in working for the FBI, and he helped me get hired. When he told me about Ferrante and his lifetime of futile efforts to put Ferrante in jail, I offered to help."

"And he agreed to that?" Savannah asked.

"Not at first," Chad said. "He resisted for awhile. He was afraid that Ferrante would find out about our relationship and kill me. But since my mother reverted to her maiden name after the divorce and didn't list a father on my birth certificate, there was no official connection between the two of us. All my father had to do was clear their marriage and divorce off the records, and then I was clean. He put me in touch with the right people, and I became a part of Ferrante's organization. We didn't expect the complication of Rosemary, of course."

"Do you love her?" Savannah forced herself to ask.

"Yes," he replied. "At first I was just doing what Ferrante asked me to and hoping to get in good with him. But after a while, I grew to love her, and I hope that we can build a life together."

"Does she know about the FBI?" Dane asked.

Chad shook his head. "No. I'm afraid that when I tell her, it will make her think that I married her not for herself but for who her father was."

Savannah and Dane exchanged another quick look.

"Be honest with her," Savannah advised. "Tell her exactly what happened and that her relationship to Ferrante did matter at first, because it was your assignment, and later because you wanted to protect her from him."

Chad nodded. "I'm not looking forward to the conversation, but I know it has to happen."

"All you can do at this point is tell her how you feel," Savannah said. "Then it will be up to her to decide if she wants to continue the relationship."

"I hope it will work out, but like you said, it's up to her. And at least it wasn't my shot that killed her father. Not that she'll miss him," he was quick to add. "But I wouldn't want her to have to live with the fact that I was responsible for her father's death."

Savannah nodded. "I understand." She was equally grateful that neither Dane nor Doc nor Owl had fired the shot that killed Ferrante.

Dane pulled the Hummer over to the curb and angled his head toward the FBI headquarters building. "We'll drop you off here and head on to Fort Belvoir."

"I was hoping you'd come in," Chad said. "My superiors might have some questions for you, and I know my dad would like to talk to you."

"Sorry," Dane said, "but I have a meeting with my team at Fort Belvoir so we can wrap up this operation and move on to the next one. If we don't leave now, we're going to be late."

Chad accepted this without argument. He opened the door and stepped out onto the sidewalk.

"Thank you again for your help this afternoon," Savannah said, "and before when you helped me get out of the sanatorium."

Dane nodded. "You've assisted my wife twice now," he said. "I owe you."

Chad waved this aside. "You rescued my wife at Tulley Gate, even though you may not have wanted to."

Dane had the decency to look ashamed. "I was reluctant, but in the end I couldn't refuse to help her."

Savannah didn't object to Dane taking credit for her rescue of Rosemary on that rainy night. She was too busy reliving the moment when Dane had said "my wife."

"So I'd say we're even," Chad concluded.

Dane gave him a little wave and told Doc to pull the door closed. Then he eased the Hummer back into the DC traffic.

"Shouldn't we give the police a statement or something?" Savannah asked.

"No." Dane started the car and rapidly drove away.

"Why not?" Savannah asked once they were blended into the traffic. "Aren't we shirking our civic duty?"

Dane cut his eyes over at her briefly. "All of us were willing to kill Ferrante given the chance. It doesn't seem right to assess blame. And in the end, justice was done."

Savannah couldn't argue with that, so she sat back and watched as Dane maneuvered through the traffic.

Finally she said, "Even though I didn't kill Ferrante, I'm not sorry I tried."

He shook his head. "I've got to stop letting you participate in these operations. You're turning into a hard-hearted soldier."

She laughed softly. "I'd like to see you try to pry me loose from my position on the team."

"Yeah, I'd probably end up with a mutiny on my hands, since now my men love you more than me."

She was secretly pleased by this remark. "You know you'll always be first with them. They take care of me mostly out of respect for you."

"They are loyal," he acknowledged. "But they still love you more."

She settled back into the comfortable seat of the Hummer and smiled. "Why do we have to have a wrapup meeting tonight? Can't we just go straight to your cabin?"

"It's better to take care of things immediately after an operation ends, when the details are fresh on everybody's mind," he replied. As always his mind was on duty.

She tried not to be resentful of his commitment to the team and military procedure. "How long will it take?"

"I'll hurry, but realistically we probably won't make it to the cabin tonight."

Savannah was surprised and disappointed. But she only said, "Am I invited to the meeting?"

"Of course, but be warned that we'll be talking about Ferrante, and I know that's not something you'll enjoy."

"I didn't think it was something you enjoyed either," she countered.

"I hate discussing Ferrante," he assured her. "If I never hear his name again after today, I'll be happy."

Their eyes met briefly, and she couldn't hide her pain. "Every time you look at me, you'll think of him."

He shook his head. "You're wrong. I never see him when I look at you."

She wanted to believe him, so she didn't press the issue.

Dane got a phone call, and while he conferred with whoever was on the other end of the line, she stared out the window at the familiar landscape and tried to organize her thoughts. It was impossible to fathom that Mario Ferrante was really gone. He was no longer a threat to her or Caroline anymore. Her relief was immense and her guilt almost as much.

"What are you thinking about?" Dane asked as he put his phone back in his pocket.

"I'm wondering if it makes me a bad person that I'm glad that someone else is dead."

"Ferrante's death is a blessing to the entire country—not just you and Caroline. It's okay to feel relieved."

"I was getting used to the idea that he was going to be in prison for the rest of his life."

"Prisons are not permanent enough for someone like Ferrante," Dane said.

Savannah frowned. "What do you mean?"

"There was never a question that the only way to ensure your safety from Ferrante was for him to die."

"You were going to kill him?"

"I was prepared to kill him," Dane corrected. "All of us were."

"I'm glad you didn't have to kill him."

"Doc wasn't going to let me," Dane said. "As much as he hates guns—"

"He was going to do it for you," Savannah said. "And for me."

"Yes. But fortunately Giordano eliminated the need. He turned out to be a good ally."

"I'm glad I did something right."

He smiled. "You did a lot of things right."

"And now we know that the general and Agent Gray can be trusted."

"Yes," Dane agreed, "that is a relief."

They drove in silence for a few minutes. Then Savannah asked something that had been bothering her. "When we were at the federal courthouse and Ferrante said what he did about feeling my mother's anguish every time he got near me, do you think that's true?"

Dane kept his eyes firmly on the road in front of him. "I can't answer that."

She knew deep discussions were hard for him, but she couldn't just let it go. "I mean, do you think people who have died can feel anguish and happiness?"

When he spoke, his tone was cautious. "I do believe that we continue on in the next life—that we still exist. It makes sense that we would continue to love the ones we loved here."

"That makes sense to me too," she encouraged.

"I believe that relationships can be eternal," he added. "But I'm not sure how much communication is possible between this life and the next."

She considered this for a few seconds and asked, "So now that you've made your peace with God, are you going to teach me and Caroline how to be Mormons?"

"I'm not sure *I* remember how to be one," he said. "But my parents will be home from their mission next month. Maybe they can teach us all."

Her heart pounded. He was willing to include her in his family circle and discuss religion—two things she thought would never happen.

By the time they passed through Tulley Gate, the sun was beginning to set. Savannah was anxious to get the wrapup meeting over with and even more anxious to get something to eat. She thought longingly of the old candy bar Hack offered to share with her that morning. She should have taken him up on that offer. Soon she'd also be regretting her refusal of the ham salad sandwich from the hospital vending machine.

When Dane parked the Hummer in front of the commissary, she was surprised and not altogether displeased.

"Are we going to do a little grocery shopping before the meeting?" she asked.

Dane gave her half a smile. "Not exactly."

He climbed out of the vehicle and walked around to open her door like the gentleman he rarely was. When she stepped out onto the sidewalk, he took her hand and led her across the street where group of people were gathered on the grass in front of the old Fairfax Chapel. She put up a hand to shield her eyes and saw that Hack, Doc, and Owl were standing there watching them approach. General Steele was there too, along with Louise and Steamer. Then she saw Neely and Caroline.

"Welcome back, Mama!" Caroline cried with delight as she rushed forward to greet her mother. "We've been waiting for you."

Savannah grabbed her daughter and held her close. "I've missed you so much," she whispered as emotion threatened to choke her.

"I've missed you too." Caroline stroked her mother's hair. "But I've had fun with Aunt Neely. She said I could call her that."

Dane's sister walked over. "I hope you don't mind."

Savannah smiled. "I think it's very nice."

Caroline held out the skirt of the dress she was wearing. "Today Aunt Neely and Steamer took me shopping. Do you like my new dress? We got it at the same store where Aunt Neely used to buy clothes for her daughter when she was little."

Savannah studied the dress more closely. It was made of ecru eyelet, and the cut was simple yet elegant, which meant it probably cost a small fortune. "It's beautiful," she said.

Apparently Neely also had some of her brother's mind-reading abilities, because she sensed Savannah's hesitation. "I know it was a little extravagant, but this is a special occasion, and I wanted her to have just the right dress."

"Anytime Steamer is involved in a shopping trip, the word *extravagant* is appropriate," Hack contributed.

"If you think I'll consider that an insult, you're wrong!" Steamer called out.

Neely laughed. "I had fun. It's been a long time since I've bought little girl clothes."

"It was a lot of fun," Caroline agreed. "And we bought a lot of clothes. Steamer just kept finding more stuff."

Hack shook his head in disgust. "I told you."

Neely was laughing as she coaxed Caroline back into the small crowd that surrounded them. "Let's stand over here for a few minutes," she suggested. "Christopher has something to ask your mother."

Savannah turned back to Dane and was astonished to see him slowly, painfully drop to one knee. He took her good hand in his, and their eyes met. There was no hint of teasing or challenge in his expression. She saw only vulnerability, a little sadness, and the smallest glimmer of hope.

"Savannah," he began softly, "will you do the most foolish thing you've ever done in your life and agree to be my wife?"

She leaned down and whispered, "I've already said 'I do.'"

He smiled. "I want to be sure that you married me for the right reasons—not just to save my life."

She moved closer. "Maybe I should ask you what your reasons are for wanting to marry me?"

His lips trembled slightly as he said, "Because I love you, and I want to be with you forever."

Tears filled Savannah's eyes. "In that case, I accept."

"So what did she say?" someone called out.

Savannah straightened up and announced, "I said yes!"

The little crowd cheered as Dane stood. He pulled a small velvet box from his pocket. "I hope you won't be disappointed," he began, "but I haven't had time to shop for a ring." His eyes dropped to the cast on her left arm. "Which is probably just as well."

She took the box from his hands and opened the tiny latch. Nestled inside was her locket.

"I gave you my heart all those years ago," he reminded her. "And if you don't mind, I'd like for you to keep it."

She swiped at a persistent tear. "I haven't always taken the best care of it."

He helped her put the locket on. "Now it's back where it belongs."

"I've never seen a guy get so much mileage out of the same little necklace," Hack muttered.

"Yeah, when are you going to spring for a diamond?" Steamer wanted to know.

"Until she has a ring on her finger, other guys won't know she's taken," Owl contributed.

This got Dane's attention. "We'll take care of that the first chance we get," he promised.

"Are the two of you going to talk forever?" Hack asked.

Dane smiled with uncharacteristic good nature. "No, we're finished here."

"Then let's get on with the wedding," Steamer suggested.

"Wedding?" Savannah repeated.

He took her hand and waved toward the little church.

Savannah stared back at him blankly. "We're getting married again?" she asked. "Here?"

Dane nodded. "Yes, but keep the *again* part quiet. We don't want Caroline to know this is a rerun."

Savannah smiled down at her daughter, who was dancing happily beside her.

"When I planned this, I didn't know that Ferrante would, well, die today. If that's a problem for you, we can postpone the wedding."

She shook her head. "It's okay. He doesn't deserve any consideration from us. And in a way, it's fitting. Today I am free to leave him behind and go on with my life."

Dane smiled as they continued up the walkway toward the church. "This was built in the 1950s," he told her. "There are two fairly famous stained-glass windows in the chapel. One depicts George Washington at prayer in Valley Forge. You've probably seen a print of it."

She nodded.

"The other one shows soldiers at attention during a scene from Genesis where Abraham kneels to accept the blessing of King Melchizedek, the priest of the most high God."

"How do you know all this?"

"Because I always carefully research my options," Dane said. "This chapel is a place where soldiers and fairytales coexist. So figured it's the perfect place for us to get married." He leaned closer. "Again."

The guys joined them, and Hack said, "That whole marriage at sea thing seemed a little shady to me. I think it's wise to do it one more time—just for good measure."

"You know how Dane prides himself on being thorough," Steamer teased. "He's always got a backup plan."

Dane smiled down at her. "I'm definitely not taking any chances."

Louise elbowed her way through the team members and fell into step beside them. She studied Savannah's ring finger for a few seconds and finally turned to Dane. "I guess if you need to borrow my ring again, I can loan it to you."

Dane shook his head. "I had Steamer get us some wedding bands for the service. Then Savannah can pick out her own engagement ring later."

"I begged him to postpone this just a few more weeks so we could do it right," Steamer told her. "But Dane has no patience, so I've had to make do with the limited resources available on the post right after the holidays."

"That shouldn't be hard for a shopping genius like you," Hack teased.

"Actually, I did pretty well," Steamer commended himself. "But if you have a wedding here, Fort Belvoir requires you to go through the post-wedding coordinator, who is a power-crazed control freak."

"We appreciate all you've been through for us," Savannah said.

Steamer shrugged. "I was glad to do it. And the wedding planner is kind of cute. When our power struggle ends, I might even ask her out."

At that moment, a thin young woman walked through the door of an office to the left of the lobby and introduced herself as Jade Hamlett, the wedding coordinator.

"It's time for the bride to get dressed." She pointed at Savannah. "If you'll come with me, please. There's a small office here where you can change." She returned her attention to the others gathered in the foyer. "Major Dane, you and your groomsmen need to change as well. And all the guests, please take a seat in the chapel. We'll start the service promptly at six o'clock."

Steamer leaned close to Savannah and muttered, "I told you. Bossy."

Savannah didn't dare disobey Miss Hamlett. But as she walked into the office with the scuffed metal desk and a couple of mismatched vinyl covered chairs, she missed her mother with a longing she hadn't felt since Caroline was born. There were certain moments in a woman's life when she needed her mother. And her wedding day was one of them.

Miss Hamlett was about to close the door behind Savannah when Louise slipped into the room. "I'll help you get ready," she said, "if you don't mind."

Savannah smiled. "I'd be very glad to have you."

"We appreciate your offer," Miss Hamlett said, "but I can give the bride all the assistance she needs."

Louise planted her feet and put her hands on her hips. "I said I'm going to help the bride, and that's exactly what I'm going to do. Now you go and find someone else to boss around."

Miss Hamlett blushed crimson, but she knew when she had met her match. Turning to Savannah, she said, "I'll be right outside if you need me." Then with one final disapproving glance in Louise's direction, she left the room.

"Whew," Louise exclaimed. "That woman just got on my last nerve."

Savannah laughed. "Thank you for saving me!"

"Well, it wasn't the first time, and it probably won't be the last," Louise predicted. She reached behind the door and removed a dress bag from a metal hook. "Let's get your dress on before that annoying woman comes back."

"What's that?" Savannah asked, staring at the dress bag.

Louise unzipped the bag to reveal a dress that looked remarkably like the one Steamer had purchased to convince Raul Giordano that she and Dane were planning a wedding. The only things missing were a layer of sea salt and some boat sludge smudges.

Savannah walked over and fingered the soft fabric. "Is this my real dress?"

Louise rolled her eyes. "Of course it's your real dress. It's bad luck to have two wedding dresses."

"But I *did* have two wedding dresses," Savannah pointed out.

"And if you haven't had bad luck, I don't know who has." Louise pulled out the dress. "Now put this on."

Savannah pulled off the plum-colored suit she'd worn for her court appearance, to the hospital to visit her sister, and in the parking deck where Mario Ferrante had died. Then Louise slipped the wedding dress over her head. "I feel like a princess," Savannah said as the golden material drifted down and settled around her ankles.

Louise smiled. "You look like one too. Now let's see what we can do with that hair."

Louise combed through Savannah's hair and twisted it up into a loose French knot. Then she let Savannah repair her own makeup. She had just deemed Savannah adequate when there was a knock on the door. Savannah opened it, expecting Miss Hamlett. But she found General Steele instead.

"I've got a flower girl here who is dying to see you," he said.

Caroline poked her head into the room. "Oh, Mama, you look so pretty!"

Savannah did a little turn to give Caroline the full effect. "Thank you."

Caroline held up a basket full of rose petals. "I get to walk into the church and throw flowers right down on the floor," she told her mother. "Miss Hamlett said I could!"

Savannah laughed. "You don't get too many opportunities like that, so take advantage of it."

Miss Hamlett herself walked into the office at this point. She gave Louise a nervous look and then said, "It's almost time to start if you're ready."

Savannah nodded. "I've been waiting for this for a long time."

Louise used a tissue to dab her eyes. "I keep thinking about the two of you all those years ago—so young and crazy in love. Then Major Dane got hurt and Major McLaughlin died . . ."

"Louise," Savannah interrupted her. "This is supposed to be a happy day."

Louise smiled. "It is a happy day, and you're a beautiful bride."

Savannah gave the older woman a hug. "Thank you."

"And you're remarkably calm," Louise added.

"Maybe it's because I've had so much practice," Savannah suggested.

Louise laughed as organ music drifted in from the chapel. "It sounds like I'd better go find a seat before Miss Wedding Coordinator locks me out." She nudged Caroline into the small lobby and said, "You, little lady, are one of the stars of this show, so you'd better go line up there at the chapel doors."

"But don't go inside until I tell you to!" Miss Hamlett commanded.

Louise rolled her eyes, but Caroline obediently moved into place. She stood there clutching her basket of rose petals, waiting for further instructions.

General Steele walked up beside Savannah.

"You are a very lovely bride," the general said.

Savannah smiled. "Thank you. But don't you want to go and find a seat?"

He shook his head. "No, I won't be needing a seat. Miss Hamlett has assigned me to walk you down the aisle."

Tears sprang into Savannah's eyes, and the general looked uncertain.

"That is, if you don't object," he said.

Savannah hooked her good arm through his. "You're the closest thing to a father I've ever had, and I'd be honored to have you escort me."

The general led her through the foyer to the chapel doors. Miss Hamlett sent Caroline up the aisle with her basket of flower petals and then handed Savannah a bouquet of roses in various colors.

Miss Hamlett looked a little embarrassed as she said, "Mr. Steamer picked these out. I told him the colors didn't go together, but he wouldn't be swayed by conventional wedding wisdom."

Savannah smiled. "Major Dane's team make their own rules as they go along."

Miss Hamlett still looked unhappy as she passed a small note to Savannah. "Mr. Steamer said to give you this."

Savannah glanced at the words Steamer had written.

"At the florist they told me red stands for love, pink stands for elegance, yellow stands for friendship, white stands for innocence, orange stands for fervency, and lavender stands for beauty. So how could I leave any color out?"

Savannah bit her lips to keep them from trembling as she handed the note to General Steele. "Will you keep this for me? I think it's something that I'd like to save to help me remember this day."

He nodded and tucked the note into the pocket of his coat. Then Miss Hamlett opened the doors. Inside the chapel, rays of the setting sun were streaming through the stained-glass windows, creating a mosaic of colored light across the wooden benches filled with friends who had come to wish them well on this, their second wedding day. Like Dane had promised her, it was a fairy-tale church. A place where soldiers could find peace and maybe dreams really did come true.

With her heart pounding, Savannah looked down to the front of the chapel, where Dane and his team were waiting for her, all wearing their dress blues. Dane was always an inspiring sight in uniform, but she'd never seen the guys look so official, and the tears she'd been holding back all day spilled over onto her cheeks. With tear-blurred vision, she stared at them and remembered the first day she had come to Dane's cabin, seeking their help. Then it had seemed that she could never gain their trust, let alone their affection. Now they were the family she'd never had.

"It's hard to tell which one is the groom," the general teased.

"It's kind of a package deal," she acknowledged.

They watched as Caroline walked slowly down the aisle and distributed petals, careful to give each side its fair share. When she had completed her petal-throwing duties, she walked over and stood near Dane. He put his hand on her shoulder as the organist began playing the wedding march.

"Shall we join them?" the general asked.

Savannah nodded. "The guys can only stay on their best behavior for just so long."

The general smiled and patted her hand. "It's going to be fine."

They moved down the aisle together. The front of the chapel where Dane was waiting for her seemed impossibly far away. But after all they'd been through, after all they'd overcome, she knew she would eventually make it. Slowly but surely she closed the distance that separated them until she was standing by Dane's side. The general transferred her hand from his arm to Dane's and stepped back.

Dane looked a little pale, like he might faint at any moment. Savannah held on to that mental image, and it helped her make it through the short ceremony performed by an Army chaplain. Finally he pronounced them husband and wife and invited Dane to kiss his bride.

"Is this going to be our last wedding?" she murmured as their lips met.

He nodded. "I didn't want to leave any doubt."

She smiled at him through her happy tears.

The chaplain said, "Ladies and gentlemen, may I present Major and Mrs. Christopher Dane!"

The organist began playing again, and Dane led Savannah quickly back down the aisle and into the little foyer.

Savannah headed toward the minister's office, where she intended to change back into her plum-colored suit, but Miss Hamlett stopped her. "You need to go straight to the reception so you can get into a receiving line before your guests start arriving."

"Reception?" Savannah repeated as her eyes strayed back to Dane. "You planned a reception too?"

"The guys insisted," he said as the other team members joined them.

"It was mostly Hack," Steamer told her. "Ever since we planned your fake wedding, he's been craving wedding cake."

"Mostly me!" Hack objected. "You'd have thought Steamer was a florist the way he fussed over all those flowers."

Doc assumed his usual role as peacemaker. "We wanted it to be nice for you."

Savannah laughed. "I appreciate everything you've done. I'm sure it will be lovely."

"Are you ready, Major?" Miss Hamlett asked Dane.

"You go ahead and get our guests over to the Officer's Club," he told her. "I think we'll forgo the receiving line and just let everyone have a good time."

Miss Hamlett frowned as though this were a foreign concept. "That's most unusual."

Dane gave her one of his most intimidating looks.

"But if that's what you want . . ."

Dane offered a charming smile. "It's what we want."

Miss Hamlett blushed. "Okay everyone, you heard the Major. Please get into your vehicles, and we'll caravan to the Officer's Club. We have two MPs who will stop traffic for us so we can go in one long procession."

"Bossy," Steamer mouthed, and Savannah had to smile.

"Now this is the good part," Hack told them. "A big cake and lots of side items." Then he called to Neely. "You and Caroline wait up. You're riding with me!"

While the others were climbing into cars, Dane led Savannah back to the minister's office to collect her things. Once they had a little privacy, Dane took her in his arms and said, "You missed your chance. There's no backing out now."

She pressed a quick kiss to his lips and replied, "Yep. You're stuck with me."

Dane nuzzled her forehead and whispered, "I feel like the luckiest man in the world. Maybe God really has forgiven me for all the mistakes I've made."

She reached up and stroked his cheek. "Oh, Dane."

He caught her hand in his. "My family calls me Christopher. You should give it a try."

This was a startling idea. "I don't know if I can," she told him honestly. "You've always been Dane to me."

"But now I'm your husband."

"Christopher," she tried, and the name felt amazingly comfortable.

He kissed her again, and Savannah was a little breathless when he pulled away.

"Well, I guess we'd better go," he said with obvious reluctance.

She nodded. "The reception sounds very nice."

"I'm sure it will be nice, and I'm equally certain that it will go on just fine without us," he said.

She gave him an incredulous look. "We're not going to our own reception?"

He shrugged. "We've already fed each other cake. I figure we're entitled to all the good luck that brings."

She laughed. "So where are we going?"

"Well, for starters, to a romantic suite at the Borgata with a sunken tub surrounded by candles and a gorgeous view of the Atlantic Ocean."

Her mouth fell open in astonishment. "So you *did* notice!"

"Every detail," he assured her. "Even the mints on the pillows."

"We're driving back to Atlantic City tonight?" she clarified.

"Actually, I'm flying a small plane provided by the general."

"Why don't we just go to the cabin?" she suggested.

"Because I owe you a honeymoon at the Borgata," he said. "And besides, Neely and Caroline and all the guys will be at the cabin. We need some time alone to get used to being married."

Her heart was pounding, and it was a struggle to think clearly. "Then what?"

"Well, I planned that trip to Milan in case we needed to leave the country, and it seems like a shame to waste it."

She could barely breathe. "You're taking me to Italy?"

He nodded. "I figured a place like that might turn even a cynic like me into a romantic. We'll be there for a week by ourselves, and then the guys and Caroline will join us."

She was nearly speechless. "I don't know what to say."

He smiled. "Say you'll go with me."

"I'll go anywhere with you," she assured him. "But what about after our honeymoon? Will we live at your cabin?"

"When we get back from Italy, we'll make a stopover in Savannah, Georgia, so you can see your mother's high school and the house where she lived. We can even talk to a few folks who knew her and maybe find some of your relatives—ones who aren't related to Mario Ferrante."

Tears filled Savannah's eyes. "I'd like that."

"Then we'll go to New Orleans and hire a contractor to start work on our house in the French Quarter."

"Our house," Savannah whispered.

"I figure you've got equity in it," he teased. "After all the wallpaper you tore off the dining room walls."

She smiled. "So we'll live in New Orleans?"

"During the summer maybe. But the French Quarter is kind of a wild place to raise a child."

"What do you have in mind?"

"I was thinking that you could use some of that interest from Wes's millions to revive the CAC. The offices are still available, and if you sell Doug Forton's antique pool table you can make thousands to benefit the children of Washington. And then I can turn his game room into my office. That way I can keep an eye on you while I do the occasional odd job for the general. We can get post housing on Fort Belvoir, and Caroline can go to school this fall with the other Army brats."

"With a couple of Hack's men standing guard at her classroom door?"

He looked a little sheepish. "Just at first, until we all get used to this Ferrante-free world we're now living in."

Savannah smiled. "This really does sound like happily ever after."

"It won't be," he promised. "We'll have problems. But we'll be together."

"A family."

He nodded. "Yes."

Savannah took Dane by the hand and pulled him toward the door. "Let's go before you come to your senses."

He laughed. "I won't change my mind. We belong together—for better or worse."

"All for one and one for all."

He nodded. "Forever."

ABOUT THE AUTHOR

BETSY BRANNON GREEN currently lives in Bessemer, Alabama, which is a suburb of Birmingham. She has been married to her husband, Butch, for twenty-nine years, and they have eight children, one daughter-in-law, two sons-in-law, and three grandchildren. She loves to read—when she can find the time—and watch sporting events, if they involve her children. She is a Primary teacher and family history center volunteer in the Bessemer Ward. She also works in the office at the Birmingham Temple. Although born in Salt Lake City, Betsy has spent most of her life in the South. Her writing and her life have been strongly influenced by the town of Headland, Alabama, and the many generous and gracious people who live there. Her first book, *Hearts in Hiding,* was published in 2001, followed by *Never Look Back* (2002), *Until Proven Guilty* (2002), *Don't Close Your Eyes* (2003), *Above Suspicion* (2003), *Foul Play* (2004), *Silenced* (2004), *Copycat* (2005), *Poison* (2005), *Double Cross* (2006), *Christmas in Haggerty* (2006), *Backtrack* (2007), and *Hazardous Duty* (2007).

Find out more about Betsy Brannon Green and her books on her website: www.betsybrannongreen.net